W9-DIB-995

Mr. Stupid Goes to Washington

9-3-92

B+J - 16.95

Mr. Stupid Goes to Washington

by Jamie Malanowski

A Birch Lane Press Book
Published by Carol Publishing Group

Copyright © 1992 by Jamie Malanowski
All rights reserved. No part of this book may be reproduced in any
form, except by a newspaper or magazine reviewer who wishes to
quote brief passages in connection with a review.

A Birch Lane Press Book
Published by Carol Publishing Group
Birch Lane Press is a registered trademark of Carol
Communications, Inc.
Editorial Offices: 600 Madison Avenue, New York, N.Y. 10022
Sales & Distribution Offices: 120 Enterprise Avenue, Secaucus,
N.J. 07094
In Canada: Canadian Manda Group, P.O. Box 920, Station U,
Toronto, Ontario M8Z 5P9
Queries regarding rights and permissions should be addressed to
Carol Publishing Group, 500 Madison Avenue, New York, N.Y. 10022

Carol Publishing Group books are available at special discounts
for bulk purchases, for sales promotions, fund raising, or
educational purposes. Special editions can be created to specifications.
For details, contact: Special Sales Department, Carol Publishing
Group, 120 Enterprise Avenue, Secaucus, N.J. 07094

Manufactured in the United States of America
10 9 8 7 6 5 4 3 2 1

Library of Congress Cataloging-in-Publication Data

Malanowski, Jamie.
    Mr. Stupid goes to Washington / by Jamie Malanowski.
        p.   cm.
    "A Birch Lane Press book."
    ISBN 1–55972–132–4
    I. Title.   II. Title: Mister Stupid goes to Washington.
PS3563.A422M7   1992
813'.54—dc20   91–15474
                                                      CIP

To Ginny and Molly

Mr. Stupid Goes to Washington is a work
of imaginative fiction.
Any resemblance to persons living
or dead, or to
actual events, is
coincidental.
But if the shoe fits,
wear it.

Mr. Stupid Goes to Washington

One

It was at the moment his advisors were arguing their most strenuously about who should second his nomination the following evening—the stoop-shouldered, camelly-looking senator from Wyoming or the Cuban-American congresswoman from Florida, the one with the club foot—that Roger Ross's mind began to wander. The fifty-five-year-old, two-term governor of Connecticut had been campaigning hard for fourteen months, ever since that bright May day he had announced his candidacy from the top of the steps of the great, wide porch of the big white house that his grandfather had built in Washington's Ferry, the one in which Ross had lived for nearly his entire life, the one whose railing the TV people had broken off in order to improve their camera angles. Now, a year and a quarter later, after a ceaseless marathon of hotel rooms, rallies, speeches, TV appearances, commercial shoots, fundraisers, photo ops, radio call-in programs, briefings, debates, controversies, attacks, counterattacks, and victory upon glorious victory in primary upon primary, Ross was on the verge of becoming his party's nominee for the presidency. Fourteen months earlier, if the skies had opened and a vision had appeared that showed he had attained this moment of triumph and was favored by a wide margin to claim the presidency in November, his chest would have swelled with pride and happiness. But that was when he was brimming with ambition and confidence. That was when he was involved and inter-

1

ested. Now? Now—okay, okay—he was proud and happy, all right; but basically he was bored.

Bored. He had certainly never wanted to be bored. What he had always wanted, how he had always envisioned himself, *the man he had always been in Hartford,* was a fella who was interested—a guy on top of things, a man *in charge.* But here, in the midst of a national campaign, the details were innumerable, the minutiae overwhelming, the repetition, well, repetitious. And as Roger Ross peered down the long table before him, past the coffee cups and diet Coke cans and Chinese food containers and wads of crumpled paper; past the empty potato chip bags and corn chips bags and half-eaten Chee·tos; past the remnants of pastrami sandwiches and bits of pickle, the straws, the napkins, the sugar packets, the creamer cups, the computer projection printouts, pencil stubs, pen caps and dirty ash trays; past, finally, the tight, pensive faces of his most dedicated allies and closest advisors, all he could bring himself to think was *eighty-two more.* Eighty-two more days until the election; eighty-two more meetings of senior advisors in climate-controlled hotel rooms; eighty-two more ceaseless wastes of time spent delving into the esoterica of polling samples, into the employment prospects of the daughter of the chairman of the Alabama delegation, into Crane's latest insights about how better to attract the votes of some miserable, whiny, pathetic, no-necked, chicken-skinned segment of the electorate.

Now, of course, there would be meetings after election day, but they would be fine meetings and they would be held in the White House, and everybody would call him Mr. President, and they'd never discuss the problems of anybody from Alabama, and nobody would mess up the table. Not usually, anyway. There would, of course, be times when things would get messed up and that would be okay—say, if there was some big emergency, something like the Cuban missile crisis or the Persian Gulf war, something where there'd have to be a lot of people hanging around. Obviously under those circumstances we'd have food in, hang the mess. Maybe we'd order Chinese food, or pizza—pizza's a crowd-pleaser. Or both, okay, why not both? And we'd eat and watch CNN and hear reports from the field and issue statements, and we'd have fun, even if we were in the middle of a big emergency.

And, of course, Crane would be there; that grumbling about Crane's latest insights shouldn't be taken seriously. Why, Ross couldn't imagine being in public life without Crane. Crane had been with him back when Crane had had hair, twenty-five years ago, when Ross first ran for office. No, Ross thought, he and Crane were inseparable, and always would be. They'll get Crane to arrange my funeral, Ross thought, and after, he'll be one of my pallbearers, carrying my casket out of the Rotunda, where, as a beloved and venerated ex-president, I will have lain in state for three days and been viewed by millions who would have lined up for hours, even if it was cold or drizzling, to pay their final respects. *Wait,* even better, I'll go to *Crane's* funeral. Crane can die and I'll show up, probably snowy-maned by then, handsome, a little creaky, but still tall and dignified. And I'll shed a tear or two and everyone will be very impressed that I am caring and loyal enough to come out to this bleak little graveyard outside Wilmette or Joliet or wherever the hell Crane is from to see him off. Crane would like that, Ross thought. The visuals would be terrific.

The candidate heard Crane calling him. "I said, is that all right with you, Governor?"

"What?"

" 'I Gotta Be Me.' "

"What?"

"When you finish your acceptance speech, the band'll play 'I Gotta Be Me.' "

Ross rolled his eyes and waved his fingers in the way he did when he wanted to indicate that he had no interest in a subject and didn't want to be bothered with it, and Crane said "Okay" and wrote a note to himself, and moved on. Ross appreciated that about Crane, the way he proceeded methodically through these daily agendas in his determined, bearlike way; he liked the way Crane got things settled. No loose ends, Ross thought. A lot of answers, a lot of tidy little packages. No messes.

"Fine," Crane said. "Once Governor Ross concludes his acceptance speech, the band will play 'I Gotta Be Me' and the balloons will drop." He turned his eyes to Ross, and in a slightly softened version of his customarily gruff tone, said, "You, of course, will stand there and smile and wave and generally convey the impression that winning our party's presidential nomination is something that has brought you great happiness."

Ross nodded his consent. "So you think I ought to use one of the really big smiles?" he asked, cocking his head and curling his lips skyward.

"Mmmh," Crane responded, "maybe bigger."

"This one?" He widened the smile so that teeth were plentifully in evidence.

"That's pretty good."

"You know, I had planned to save that one for when I get elected in November," Ross said, pivoting his head to model the smile for his advisors.

"Well, I think you could use it again then."

"The news guys won't comment?"

"No," Crane said, "I think they'll just think you were happy twice."

Ross wasn't sure and revved up the big grin again, beaming it around the table. "Whaddya think, boys?"

"I like it, Governor, good, good, good." The advisors, an amiable group of former frat boys turned comfortably paunchy, baldish yes-men, murmured their approval.

"That's settled then," said Crane, jotting down a note. "We'll use the really big smile. Now, traditionally, at that point in the proceedings the nominee's wife would join him, but as you are a widower . . ." He looked at Ross. A pause bloomed.

"Well, maybe Mother will come out," the candidate finally offered.

"Have you asked her yet?"

"Yes. She's thinking about it. She'd have to come down tomorrow morning, so she'll miss her bridge club."

"She's aware that you're up for the presidency of the United States, isn't she?" the bullish aide asked dryly.

"Yes, Crane, she's aware. She's already promised that she'll come to the Inauguration. Let's pencil her in."

"Fine. Mother. That will be wonderful. So she will come out, then after her, your running mate will come out, and then the lovely Mrs. Running Mate will come out, then various party leaders, then the band will play a patriotic medley, then the convention will end, then we'll take two weeks off and watch the Democrats cannibalize one another."

Hearty laughter bubbled up from the advisors. Crane let it run its course, then pushed on. "That leaves us with just one matter to settle, Governor. Have you decided who your running mate will be?" Crane's voice took on a serious, fatherly tone. "You know, you have to formally announce your choice tomorrow morning. The delegates have to ratify your choice, and the convention ends tomorrow night. People are going to start checking out of their hotel rooms. No other nominee in history has ever waited this long. Now, no kidding around—who's it going to be?"

Nobody, Ross wished he could say. I've thought about it and thought about it, he could hear himself saying, and not to be unpleasant about it, I don't want to be associated with any of them. I don't need their help, I don't want their baggage, I don't want to pretend to like any of them. I don't want one of them to grab my hand and raise it above my head in victorious exultation. I don't want to see one of their smarmy smiling faces next to mine on a sea of campaign posters. And I don't want to have to lie to the press for years and years about what a fine job one of them is doing.

Ross could see Crane getting fidgety. Silence was mushrooming. Ross shrugged. "Let's go over the choices again."

The advisors groaned.

"If future President Ross wants to go over the choices again," Crane bellowed, banging his palm on the table like a gavel, "we will go over them again." The moaning ceased. "Forrester, give us the latest on the contenders."

The young, bespectacled Forrester, an Ivy League–educated public relations executive who had worked for Ross in Hartford, glided silently to a slide projector set on the middle of the table and aimed its lens at the blank wall opposite. "Lights, please," he said. And as the room went dark, he flicked on the first slide.

"Senator Greenstreet of Nevada," Forrester intoned. "A long-time supporter of Governor Ross, in accord on nearly every major issue. Unfortunately, he seems to have an unusually close relationship with Don Eugenio Nardo of the Gigliotti crime family of Reno."

"How close?" Ross asked, knowing full well the answer.

"It seems Don Nardo owns him lock, stock, and barrel."

"Next," said Ross.

A new picture. "Senator Bottomley of Michigan. Again, a loyal supporter. He would undoubtedly deliver his home state and would help us generally in the Midwest, where the Democrats have shown some signs of support. The downside is that he has admitted smoking marijuana as a teenager.

"We all know that, Forrester," said Crane. "So what if he smoked marijuana as a teenager? Don't you think the country is ready to accept that?"

"Unfortunately, sir, it's not quite what he's guilty of. We don't think he smoked marijuana as a teenager. We think he smokes marijuana *with* teenagers. As recently"—he rifled through some papers on his clipboard—"as Monday. Two of them. Girls. Naked. Over in the Sheraton."

"But," Crane said in a slow and measured way, "you say he could deliver Michigan."

"Probably. I should add that Mrs. Bottomley is having sexual relations with her minister—"

"Next," said Ross.

". . . and her psychiatrist."

"Next!"

Another picture. "Senator Ridley of Oregon. Governor Ross's closest rival for the nomination, winning nearly 35 percent of the vote in the primaries he entered and a total of seven primaries in his own right. Popular in the South. Shrewd. Cunning. An admired leader in the Senate. Telegenic. Handsome. Respected for—"

"What's the deal, Forrester?" Ross asked, his reedy voice tensing. "Are you supporting Ridley, or are you supporting me? I'll remind you, and I'll remind everyone at this table, that Senator Ridley is the man who went on 'The Larry King Show' in January of this year, just before the start of the Iowa caucuses, and called me a chihuahua. And when Larry asked him what he meant by that, Ridley said it was because I was like a tiny dog who yapped and yapped and yapped without ever saying anything. And I'll further remind you that for months after that, even after I took a commanding lead and my nomination became inevitable, even after I had thoroughly vanquished that miserable, stupid . . . *simian* in the California primary, I had to endure the yap, yap, yapping of fun-loving voters and pretend that I was a good sport if not actually amused. Now, if I understand you correctly, young man, you want me to put him on my ticket."

"No, sir," said Forrester. "Not deeply. Not tremendously. Not, as I consider the ramifications more thoroughly, at all. Shall we move on?" A new slide moved into place, and Forrester rattled on quickly. "Senator Dunn of Rhode Island. Smart. Able. Would go over very well in the Northeast. Has an impressive record as a legislator. On the downside, he has a reputation for being outspoken and blunt."

"Aw! Aw! Too bad! Too bad!" the advisors muttered. Crane shook his head. "What a damn shame!" he said. "Some guys just aren't vice-presidential material."

"I frankly don't know if this nation could endure a vice president who is outspoken and blunt," Ross said.

"He also once said that he thinks it's dumb for an elected official to waste his time meeting groups of visiting Boy Scouts and getting his picture taken wearing funny hats," Forrester discreetly piled on.

"Oh!" the advisors said, hooting. "That's rich!"

"Oh, well, funny hats and Boy Scouts, that's what the job is," said Ross. "How else would we use him? What's he going to do? Make policy? Make policy?!?! That's my job!" Ross could see his advisors were enjoying the good laugh. "My job!" he repeated. "Mine!"

Soon the noise subsided. "Okay," Crane said evenly, "let's decide. The mobster or the libertine?"

Ross was determined not to speak. Not to decide is to decide, he thought, remembering a phrase from his undergraduate days, though not recalling the context. Let one of these yes-men force the choice, he thought. *Newsweek* says Crane knows my mind better than I do. Let him figure it out.

Finally someone spoke. It was Forrester. All heads turned toward him. "Well," he said tentatively, anticipating the scorn and obloquy that would fall on him as punishment for having the guilelessness to speak first. "Well, there's Senator Bibby. Handsome, rich, from a powerful family of loyal party members. His father, Horace, the newspaper magnate, has been a major contributor. . . ."

"Bibby?" Crane bellowed. "Brent Bibby?"

"I-I-I-I was just—" Forrester stammered, but Crane steamrolled on. "Brent Bibby isn't a senator. Brent Bibby is a tennis pro. Yes, I know he won an election; yes, I know he's *called* a senator; yes, I know he has an office and some aides and franking privileges, and all that. But he's not a senator. A senator has to have a scintilla of intelligence. Even a bad senator. Brent Bibby doesn't. Brent Bibby is dumb. Dumb, dumb, dumb. If his father hadn't bought the damned election so the kid could have a job, he'd still be spending his days on a tennis court somewhere."

"As it is, he seldom leaves," Forrester, in retreat, acknowledged.

"There!" Crane crowed.

But Ross was not quite ready to let go of this not-yet-completely despised possibility. "Is he responsible for any legislation?" he asked.

"Ah—yes," said Forrester, consulting a file. "One bill. He was a major proponent of allowing business executives to deduct the cost of country-club dues from their taxes. He was quoted at the time as saying, 'According to my father, more business deals have been made after a few stiff belts at a country club than have ever been made in all the offices of New York.'"

"Mmmh-hmmh," Ross said, rubbing his chin. "Well, that doesn't sound so terrible to me. Our party has never opposed lavish tax breaks for rich business executives. I mean, those *are* our people, after all."

"Governor," Crane said, "we do have a responsibility here. The person you choose may one day govern this nation. We owe it to the country not to place the fate of the United States and of the world in the hands of the stupidest man in Washington."

"But I won't be placing our fate in his hands," Ross corrected. "*I'll* be the president."

"Yes, but you might di. . . . d. . . . get a better job offer."

The room erupted into chaos, with all the advisors weighing in at once, nattering on, settling nothing, and suddenly the whole thing seemed to be a nuisance too huge for Ross to bear, and he felt his will collapse. *Damn details!* "All right, everyone, enough," he said wearily, and rose to leave. "I'll just have to sleep on this and announce my decision tomorrow. Crane, go get into your tux. We've got to get to this dinner."

As the aides shuffled out, Ross saw the frustrated look on his loyal aide's face, and a tiny portion of pity bubbled up. "Don't worry, Crane, I know what I have to do. You'll have my decision before breakfast."

Two

With aching feet and a full bladder, Ross stood at the end of a receiving line in a small reception room above one of the large ballrooms in the Hilton, greeting party loyalists and thinking: Well, as large, formal, stultifyingly boring fund-raising dinners go—"Hey, nice to see ya"—this one wasn't half—"Hey, thanks again for your support"—bad. The fish wasn't—"You know, your help made all the difference"—awful, the speechmaking was blessedly brief, the crowd—"Thanks, buddy, you're too kind"—stayed awake, and best of all—"Ha ha, yap, yap, yourself, you old rascal"—somebody had had the wit to sit him next to Florence Bouvier, the seventy-five-year-old honorary chairwoman of the South Carolina state party, and they had spoken of nothing all dinner long except roses, about when to plant them and spray them and mulch them, and the dinner had just flown by. Lilith Ross used to tend to roses, and it made Ross happy to talk for an hour about flowers and dirt and things he had done when—"I mean it, Mr. Mayor, I couldn't have done it without you"—he had had a wife. And now the reception line was dwindling to a final few, and soon he would be able to go back to his room and go, blessedly, to sleep.

"Senator Greenstreet, nice to see you, Mrs. Greenstreet, you're looking well. How's the *family,* Senator?"

Behind him, bright television lights went on, and he could

hear ABC's top political reporter, Celestine van den Hurdle, filing a report that would later be used on "Nightline."

"To sum up, Ted: Governor Roger M. Ross, who will be formally nominated tomorrow night as his party's presidential candidate, tonight addressed a large audience of senators, congressmen, and major contributors—"

"Senator Bottomley, Mrs. Bottomley—" *You minx!*

"—spoke in general terms about economic matters—"

"Congratulations to you too, Senator Ridley, you waged an outstanding campaign—" *You piece of shit.*

"—making no comment about the increasingly tense situation in the tiny, strategically vital Latin American nation of San Rico de Humidor—"

"Senator Dunn, Mrs. Dunn—" *Mr. Big Shot.*

"—no word about his selection for vice president. This is Celestine van den Hurdle. Now back to—"

A tall, handsome man in his late thirties whom Ross couldn't quite place grasped his hand. Ross was about to make apologies when he saw a blob of Thousand Island dressing on the man's lapel, and the name came into focus. "Senator Bibby! How nice to see you."

"Thank you, Governor. I don't believe you've met my wife, Lucinda. Darling, I'd like to present Governor Ross M. Rogers. Or Roger M. Ross. Rrr . . . rrr . . ."

"Governor Ross," Lucinda Bibby said in a cool, throaty voice. "What an honor. I am one of your most ardent admirers." It was a simple line, but as Ross held her soft, warm hand, he thought it enchanting. Lucinda Bibby, with her dark eyes and dark hair and pale, pale skin, was simply the most beautiful woman he had ever seen.

"The pleasure is entirely mine, Mrs. Bibby. Now that I've met you, I have a much higher estimation of the senator. I suspect it would do him a world of good if he brought you out more often."

She smiled—a stunning smile, Ross thought—and lifted her

face close to his. "I think my husband believes that Bibbyville is the center of the universe, no matter how hard I try to convince him otherwise." He had been face to face with dozens of people during the course of the night, but hers was the first to make his heart quicken.

"Ah, Governor," Brent Bibby whispered, his nose suddenly looming inches away, "can I ask you a question? A lot of the guys at the newspaper my dad owns were guessing who your running mate might be. I think they'd really be impressed with me if I could give them some kind of inside scoop. It would mean a lot."

In a quarter century of political life, Ross reckoned, he had never heard a question put quite so maladroitly. It was endearing in its way, he thought—naive, stupid, insulting. "I'm sorry, Senator," he said with the patience he ordinarily reserved for children and fabulously wealthy contributors, "but I'm afraid your dad will have to wait just like everybody else. But I know he'll be impressed with our decision. Now you be sure to give him my regards when you see him. Mrs. Bibby, it was lovely meeting you."

Ross watched them leave. Rather, he watched Lucinda. The material of her dress shifted in response to the small movements of her hips. Ross felt as if he could stand there forever.

"That's it, Governor," Crane said.

"Thank God. I've really got to hit the head."

Crane directed him to a private washroom. "You fellas wait here," Ross said to his Secret Service agents. "There's just some things I'm not comfortable doing with an entourage."

Standing at the urinal, Ross all but decided to pick Senator Ridley. The others are useless or worse, Ross thought, but I will at least enjoy humiliating Ridley for four years. I can forget to tell Ridley about important meetings and leave him out of the loop. I can leak bad things about him to the media. I can ask him to fetch the coffee at National Security Council meetings. I can make him talk to me while I'm in the can. I was wrong, Ross thought as he was leaving the men's room. I was wrong, and I'm big enough to admit it. Ridley will make a very good vice president indeed. Yap, yap, you asshole, he smiled as he pushed open the door. He almost ran her over.

"Why, Mrs. Bibby!"

"Governor!" she said, as genuinely surprised as he. "I feel so silly. I thought I could beat the crunch at the taxi stand by taking a short cut, and instead I just got lost."

Poor little kitten, Ross thought. "Taxi stand? What happened to your husband?"

"Oh, he met some boring little Congressman Plotski from Scranton who started moaning about how lame his serve is. Brent offered to give him some pointers, and before you knew it the two of them took off in the limo to find an all-night tennis court."

"Well, Mrs. Bibby, all I can say is that I can't imagine abandoning you for Congressman Plotski, even if he is the Minority Leader of the House of Representatives."

"You flatter me, Governor."

"No," he said, watching her hair shimmer. "No, not in the least. Which way are you headed?"

"I think the taxis are this way," she said, pointing in the direction opposite the reception area where Crane and the others were waiting. Impulsively, he found himself asking if he could walk along. "Shouldn't we wait for your bodyguards?" she asked.

"I kind of like to slip off from time to time to surprise them," he said. He couldn't quite believe what he was doing, telling lies like a teenager. "I never go far, and it always makes them feel good when they find me." *Another whopper.*

They walked down the hall toward a pair of fire doors, talking of nothing special—hot weather, good food, nice speech—and yet he found himself nearly overwhelmed by everything she did, her laugh when she remembered the dumb joke he made at the start of his address, the way she casually reached over and pulled a stray hair from his lapel, an act of what seemed to him startling intimacy. They pushed through the doors, but instead of facing a taxi stand or lobby, they found themselves outside, under the stars, in a lush garden that was part of the hotel grounds. There was not another soul in sight.

"Well, this isn't it," she said, sounding a bit piqued.

"No, but this is lovely, isn't it?" Ross stretched his arms upward, and gazed at the sky. "My God," he said, "I can't remember the last time I stood under a moonlit sky without having a platoon of assistants and Secret Service agents around, all of them rushing me into a meeting or hurrying me into a car." Suddenly, fourteen months of frustration poured out. "Do you have any idea what it's like to run for president, Mrs. Bibby? How difficult? Spending more than a year on the road? Cameras in your face, getting challenged by hardware salesmen and accountants and beauticians who don't have a tenth of your experience, getting ridiculed by pipsqueak comedians on TV, begging one odious little millionaire after another for some piddling contribution. There's never any privacy, there's never a quiet moment, and there's seldom anyone around with whom you can just be yourself. It's bizarre—you run for the most powerful job in the world, and though you're constantly surrounded by people, you're really very alone." He saw her then, standing still and silent, her lips turned up in a warmly indulgent smile. All at once he realized he'd been rambling on, and he was embarrassed. "Seems dangerous, doesn't it?" he said shyly.

"I don't know," she said softly. "Perhaps. I don't think you're dangerous. Besides, don't you think it'll all be worth it when you win and you have all that power at your disposal?"

"When you put it like that," he said, "it seems more dangerous than ever."

She walked over and stood before him and, gazing into his eyes, took hold of his hands. "I don't think it would be dangerous to be in these hands," she said. "You're a strong man, Governor Ross. I can feel it."

He looked down at her, and, intoxicated by the moonlight, the perfume of the flowers, the softness of her voice, her tenderness, her beauty, his chest began to swell, and he felt he could kiss her. But instead he said, "You know, it's been a long time since I've had a talk like this with a woman," and pulled away. "I used to talk with my wife all the time," he said, looking back at the sky. "Since she died four years ago, there haven't been many women in my life."

"Come now, Governor, you don't expect me to believe that such a vigorous, attractive man as yourself has been . . . *alone* all these years."

He hesitated, afraid of what this woman would think no matter what he answered. Slowly he nodded. "Well, yes," he said, "for the most part, by and large, I—you know, you have things to do, speeches to give, meetings to preside over, budgets to . . . budget. And once you start running for president, your energies tend to get . . . focused . . . and certain . . . urges that might end up getting you . . . written up in the *National Enquirer* . . . tend to get—you know—handled in a discreet, *solitary* way consistent with the party platform"—there was that smile again, so affectionate—"and with one's image as a national leader and potential commander-in-chief . . . You know, you're very easy to talk to. I'd give anything to be able to do it more often."

They stood looking at one another for a long time. Finally, she spoke. "I think I'm going to have a terrible time finding a taxi," she said. "You wouldn't happen to be heading anywhere near the Marriott, would you?"

Three

There wasn't much conversation on the ride to her hotel. It was a short trip and, besides, there wasn't much to say. What could he say? I love the way the light washes over you, Mrs. Bibby? Do you know that your skirt has ridden a bit high on your leg, Mrs. Bibby? Did you intend that to happen or am I a fool? Is there a way I can stop being a presidential candidate? Is there a way you can stop being a wife? Is there a way we can get rid of Crane? Oh, Christ, Ross suddenly thought, I hated seeing that confused, stricken look on the poor bastard's face when I told him we were giving Mrs. Bibby a lift. Now he's sitting in the front seat, sullen, grumpy, angry that he can't figure out what the hell I'm up to. Well, why should he be any different from me?

"Is everything all right, Governor?" she asked. "You're very quiet."

"Oh, yes. Everything is just fine."

"Good," she smiled. "Well, here we are. Governor, thank you so much. I'll always remember the night a future president drove me home." She then emitted what Ross thought was the saddest sigh he had ever heard.

"What is it, Mrs. Bibby?"

"Oh, I feel so silly saying this, it's just embarrassing."

"Not at all. What's troubling you?"

"Well," she said, "I'm sure Brent isn't home yet, and I always

16

feel uncomfortable going into an empty hotel room by myself. I just hate the thought of finding a stranger in there. It scares me to death. I'm sorry for asking, but—would you see me to my room?"

"No!" Crane barked from the front seat.

"Now, Crane," Ross said, "let's try not to think only of ourselves. Mrs. Bibby, I would certainly like to help you, but surely you understand that there's a small problem with appearances. People might jump to conclusions if they were to see a presidential candidate accompanying the beautiful, enchanting, and if I may say, sexy, wife of a senator into her hotel room late in the evening. You understand. Would you like me to send Crane up with you?"

She seemed pained, her full red lips pursing, her brow falling into a tiny furrow. "Unfortunately, that wouldn't quite solve the problem. You see, you may know Mr. Crane, Governor, but he's still a stranger to me. And so I would still have the problem of a stranger in my hotel room. I'm afraid you're the only one who can help."

"Well, then, I suppose I must," he said firmly, climbing out of the back seat, ignoring Crane's mumbled epithets. Forrester, who had ridden over with some Secret Service agents, was waiting on the curb with Crane. "Boys," Ross said, "Mrs. Bibby has asked me to take her up to her room to make sure that there are no intruders in it. I've agreed. This is how we're going to do it." Ross ordered Forrester to accompany Lucinda to her room, but then to wait in the hall. "I will then come up and personally escort you into the room," he assured her. With that, the two departed. "We'll follow them upstairs in a moment," Ross told Crane. "You be ready to run interference. If you see anybody we know in the lobby, you intercept them, and I'll proceed upstairs to help Mrs. Bibby."

"What the hell should I tell 'em if they ask what you're doing?" Crane asked.

"How do I know?" Ross replied. "Caucuses, delegate counts,

strategy meetings . . . My God, Crane, you're a professional politician. Are you telling me you can't come up with some authoritative-sounding gibberish?"

Crane's head dropped in embarrassment. "What should I do with the Secret Service?" he asked.

"Oh, here's an idea," Ross suggested after a moment. "Why don't we say one of these people in the lobby threatened to kill me. That would keep the agents busy."

Crane mulled that over for a moment. "We could do that," he concluded, "but I think that would just attract more attention."

"Well, then, tell 'em . . . tell 'em the truth. Tell 'em to stay here, and tell 'em if they don't like it, they don't have to vote for me. And when I win, they can work for the Secret Service in Nome. Should we get going?"

Forrester escorted Mrs. Bibby down the long beige corridor. When they reached her suite, she unlocked the door. "Thank you, Mr. Forrester," she said. "You can go now."

"The governor wants me to stay," Forrester objected.

"I think we both know what the governor wants, Mr. Forrester. Good night."

Ross and Crane rode the elevator in silence until they reached Mrs. Bibby's floor. Ross smartly stepped out, then quickly leaned back through the door and pressed the down button. "Get some sleep, Crane," he said as the door started to close. "I'll call you early. By the way, I've made up my mind. I think you'll be surprised."

Ross turned around. Where was Forrester? he wondered. Cautiously he moved down the hallway until he reached her suite. He caught his breath when he found the door ajar. Gently, he pushed it open. The room was dark. "Mrs. Bibby?" he called. "Mrs. Bibby, are you here?" He found his way to the bedroom and pushed open the door. There he saw Mrs. Bibby standing in a negligee that hid nothing.

"Ah, Mrs. Bibby," he stammered, "I'm so glad to see that you've arrived safely. You appear ready to retire, so I'll just say . . ."

He didn't finish. She crossed the room and put her arms around his waist. "Shhh," she hushed him. "Hold me, please. I yearn to feel your arms wrapped around me." She embraced him. "Tighter, Governor! I want to feel your presidential sceptre!"

"Ah, Mrs., Mrs. Bibby," he stammered in his confusion, "you've been misinformed. There's a presidential seal, the one with the big eagle, but no presidential sceptre. Oh! Oh! Oh, I see! Yes, I see! Oh, Mrs. Bibby! Mrs. Bibby! Mrs. Bibby, Mrs. Bibby, *Mrs. Bibby!*"

Later—soon—Ross was floating on a buzz so pleasant that he dared not move, except to incline his head a few degrees to gaze at Lucinda, who lay propped up on one elbow next to him. "All I can say, Lucinda—may I call you Lucinda?—is that the last couple of hours have been the highlight of my entire year." She giggled, but he continued. "Don't laugh. I know what you're thinking—didn't winning the New Hampshire primary make you happier? Well, you know, winning the support of those frozen, flint-faced misanthropes did indeed make me happy. But these few moments have been glorious, Lucinda, just glorious." Her nipples peaked pinkly out above the bedclothes. "I never thought I'd be saying this," he murmured, "but I envy Brent Bibby."

She laughed again. "Brent would be astonished to hear you say that," she said. "Of course, Brent is nearly always astonished, particularly when someone bothers to speak to him about something other than tennis. He's so dumb people generally just ignore him."

"But you don't think he's dumb," Ross said.

"Sure I do. I thought he was dumb when I married him, but I thought maybe he was just timid, that his father had overshadowed him. I was wrong. Brent really isn't all that timid. He's just . . . stupid."

"But I'm sure he has his good points," Ross said.

"Of course he does. Brent's not as bad as he could be. He's not willfully dumb. He's not maliciously stupid. He doesn't try to hurt anybody. He's even likable, to a degree. He's like a child— a stupid, stupid child. He once asked Senator John Glenn if it smells bad when you fart in space. Now maybe on some level that's an interesting question, but you don't interrupt a debate on NASA appropriations and ask it on the floor of the Senate." She shook her head, and Ross reached over and gently stroked her shoulder. "The worst part is that I have to act like he's smart. Sometimes I think I spend half my life gazing up at him, pretending that I'm hanging on his every word, making believe that I'm in awe of him, knowing full well that everyone would be better off—him, me, his constituents, America—if old Horace Bibby had bankrolled a senate seat for his infinitely smarter daughter-in-law instead of the dimwit he sired. It's so galling."

Ross felt sorry for her. "Perhaps you ought to move to Washington," he suggested. "There'd be many more opportunities for you there, many more things to do. You would really shine. And—" he hesitated before saying this, but the warmth in her eyes encouraged him "—and it would give us the opportunity to see one another more."

"That would be fabulous," she said, "but it would take a miracle to happen. Brent swore during his campaign that as long as he was Senator, his family would remain in Bibbyville. Actually, his father swore that we would stay in Bibbyville, so that he could keep his eye on us. No, I'm afraid this will be our one and only rendezvous, unless, of course, you relocate our nation's capital to Bibbyville."

"Don't give up so easily, Lucinda," he said firmly. "We'll think of something. I don't know if I've fallen in love in these brief moments, my darling, but I know I want to see you again— and again, *and again*." Suddenly the passion welled up in him and he reached for her and pulled her close and buried his mouth between her breasts. Just then there was noise from the adjoining room, and then voices. He recognized one as belong-

ing to Minority Leader Plotski. He thought the other might be
that of Senator Brent Bibby, an assumption that was confirmed
when the woman under him cried "It's Brent!" and pushed him
over and leaped to her feet.

This isn't happening, Ross thought. Lucinda was scram-
bling—"Get dressed!" she hissed. "Where are my—oh, *fuck!* I
left my clothes out there." Ross rose, began scanning the room
for his pants. "So if you just take two or three hours out of your
day to work on that back hand," he heard Bibby saying to Plotski on the other side of the door, "your back court game will
improve one hundred percent." *Underpants at last,* Ross
thought.

The bedroom door opened a few inches, but Bibby paused to
talk to his guest. "Why don't you mix us up some martinis, Mr.
Minority Leader?" he was saying. "Usually I prefer a little
Gatorade after playing, but that doesn't mix well with gin, does
it? I can't tell you how much time I devoted to developing an
après-tennis Gatorade and gin cocktail, but it never amounted
to anything. I even had the name picked out. The Six-Love. The
name finally came to me during that awful tax debate we had
last year, remember? I imagined myself at the club, just after fin-
ishing a match, saying, "Boy, bring me a Six-Love." Wouldn't
that be something? Sure wouldn't mind having that on my
tombstone: "Senator Brent Bibby—Inventor of the Six-Love"
Let me see if my wife will join us. Lucinda!"

He barged in. Ross, to his relief, had by that point pulled up
his pants, and Lucinda had found a robe. They stood perfectly
still, deer caught in headlights.

"Governor Ross?" he said. "Oh my gosh, hiya. Did we have
an appointment I forgot about? You know, when I'm in Washington, my secretary pins a schedule inside my jacket so that I
know what I'm doing, but I'm all alone here. I apologize for
being—I wasn't supposed to have anything prepared, was I?
Nobody left me any instructions or anything. I'm so embarrassed."

Ross at that moment saw Bibby's expression change, saw his

eyes move from the unmade bed to his unmade wife to his party's unmade standard bearer. "Hey, we didn't have any appointment! What's going on here, as if I didn't have a darn good idea?"

"Darling," Lucinda blurted, "it's not what you think."

"What is it, then? This just shows how right Dad is. Two days out of Bibbyville, and this happens! What do you have to say for yourself, Governor?"

Ross looked at Bibby's hurt face, considered the woman, gauged how much trouble he might cause himself, wondered how many problems he could solve at one time, asked himself if he had the balls to throw the dice.

"Well?" Bibby demanded.

Go for it, Ross thought.

"Senator Bibby," Ross said steadily as he started to pull on his shirt, "things are not what they seem. I had come here tonight to ask you a question of the utmost gravity. The hour grew late and I grew weary. It's been an exhausting week for me, as you can imagine. Your lovely wife was kind enough to offer me your bed so that I could take a little nap until you returned, while she herself slept out in the other room. But just before you arrived, I apparently had a bad dream—I thought I was being chased by a pack of wolves, all of whom had Sam Donaldson's face—and I suppose I cried out and your good wife came in to comfort me."

Bibby, his face blank, looked at him for a moment. Then he rolled his eyes back and dipped his knees. "Well, what a relief!" he said. "You can imagine what *I* imagined! I mean, look what it looks like! Of course, that's a ridiculous thought. She's married, you're running for president, you couldn't possibly want to—you know—do it. I feel so silly." He paused, seemed to collect himself. "So what was the question?"

"The question?" Lucinda asked.

"The question of the utmost gravity that the governor came to ask me."

"Oh, yes," Ross said. Well, there was no going back. He

reknotted his tie, and looking hard into the eyes of Lucinda Bibby, Ross said, "Senator, would you be my running mate?"

The Bibbys, not unexpectedly, exploded. Together they shouted the word *What?* so loudly it might have been heard in Canada. "Yes," Ross said, slipping on his jacket. "Join me on the ticket. Run for vice president. As I consider what it will take to lead this nation in the years to come, I can think of nothing that would help me more than having you—and Lucinda—at my side."

"How wonderful!" Lucinda gushed.

"I—I'm speechless," Brent said. "I never dreamed . . ."

"No," Ross said, "I'll bet you didn't."

"Of course, we accept," Lucinda said, and moved to hug Ross just as Brent moved to shake Ross's hand, and the three of them ended up clutching one another in a clumsy embrace. Ross found Lucinda's eyes, and she smiled at him, Ross thought, wickedly. He pulled her closer, feeling the curve of her hip under the thin robe. "Ross–Bibby," Brent began to chant, and through her smile, Lucinda picked it up, repeating "Ross–Bibby!", louder and louder and louder, until they jumped up and down with glee.

"Hey, anybody for a martini?" said Minority Leader Plotski, blithely entering the room with a pitcher of martinis. "Oh, oh, my goodness, Governor Ross, what a surprise to see you here tonight. A-a-a-a drink?"

"Yes, Mr. Minority Leader, thank you, and with that drink, we can raise a toast to my running mate and the next vice president of the United States, Senator Brent Bibby."

The next sound was that of crashing glass, after the pitcher plummeted from the dumbstruck Plotski's hand.

Four

It had been fourteen hours now that the locomotive had been barreling about inside Crane's head, clattering constantly and sounding a steam whistle every time somebody thought to call his name, which happened to be every other damn second that particular day, starting the moment Ross had called him in the predawn hours and told him whom he'd selected. Told him in that little singsongy voice Ross used whenever he felt obliged to off-load some mess for Crane to tidy up. "Cra-ane," was what Crane had heard at 4:30 A.M. and right away he had known—he didn't have anything so weak as a hunch or a premonition, he had *known* that something awful was about to go down—and at that very second, the tiny engineer in his cerebral cortex had leaned on his throttle and—*woo-ooooo!*—Crane began kneading his temples. "Bibby!" he'd said. "Bibby? But Governor . . . Governor . . . Governor . . . *Bibby?*" And Ross had said something in that singsongy voice, and Crane had barged back in: "Can't you get out of it? Tell him you made a mistake. He'll understand that. He of *all* people will understand that. Tell him you mixed up your file cards and you meant to make him, I don't know, the fucking attorney general, I don't care, he'll be happy with it."

"Crane, the offer's been made. I had to do it."

"What do you mean, had to do it?"

"Let's just say he had me at a disadvantage."

24

He was going to say, "Let's just say what?" but then he'd remembered the woman, and where he had left Ross, and the air went out of him and the pounding increased, and Crane, the most realistic of men, had just said, "I see," and forced himself to open his eyes and face the rest of his day.

The media had been, of course, relentless. Ross handled the announcement smoothly enough, breaking out a sort of cat-that-swallowed-the-canary grin when he said Bibby's name, implying that he knew things no one else did. It took a fair amount of audacity, Crane thought, for Ross to describe Bibby as "a bold, exciting, dynamic choice, the best of a new generation, a fresh face for fresh Americans." The phrases made it seem as though Ross had been reading someone else's resume, but the press let him get away with it; at least nobody asked him right out why he'd want to put a stooge one heartbeat away from the presidency. The news accounts played it pretty straight— "startled the nation . . . young, little-known midwestern senator . . . former country-club tennis pro . . . son of Horace Bibby, the billionaire newspaper magnate, industrialist, and resort developer." For a moment Crane entertained the idea that maybe not everybody really knew that Bibby was stupid, that maybe just a handful of people knew, and because they were all in his circle, well, it just seemed like everybody. But then he watched CNN for a while and all the commentators were smirking, then ABC for a while and all the commentators were smirking, then he put on PBS and MacNeil and Lehrer were smirking, and with that Crane knew that nobody had bought Ross's fast one and that nobody was going to pretend very hard that they had.

Throughout the day, the networks ran instant biographies of Bibby that were painfully short, since he'd never done anything, and network news budgets were such that they could no longer afford to maintain vast libraries full of videotape showing nobodies doing nothing. NBC was the envy of its competition because it had actually come up with seven seconds of Bibby putting in a celebrity Pro-Am golf tournament that had taken place at the Bibbyville Country Club in 1987. The footage,

Crane would hear later, was a fluke; the cameraman was actually on hand to capture the appearance on the links of the heavy metal group Megadeth, and he just decided to use up his roll on this United States senator, who was mistakenly assumed to be important. Crane at least was a tiny bit happy knowing that although it irritated most people in the country to see their politicians at play, those few who didn't mind so much would see Bibby sinking a fourteen-footer, and not some damn gimme.

Without videotape, news producers filled the air with the commentary of experts. The Republicans, Crane thought, were about as agile as could be expected. On CBS, Senator Billups worked the "unique" angle—"Brent Bibby brings a unique perspective to the governmental process, a unique vision, a frame of reference not commonly found among our nation's leaders"—then adroitly changed the subject to Ross's qualifications. Senator Walls, galloping past the microphones outside the convention center about as nimbly as a portly octagenarian can gallop, paused to say, "I know that Governor Ross had a choice to make, and he has made that choice, and Senator Bibby is that choice, and I think history will come to regard it as such. I congratulate Senator Bibby, I am delighted for him, now on to victory in November." And former President Bush, speaking from Kennebunkport, was effusive, after a fashion: "This was an amazing choice, incredible, breathtaking, *one could never have predicted it,* and I think it just goes to show the kind of bold, unconventional leadership America can expect from Roger Ross." Still, Crane knew the ex-president was laughing up his sleeve, and he wondered if he didn't simply prefer the reaction of old Gaston Castleberry, the Democratic Party chairman, who danced a jig on the Capitol steps while three members of his staff sang "Happy Days Are Here Again" in the background.

Crane himself took his turn ritually abasing himself before the cameras, repeating with all the conviction he could summon, "We picked him because he was the one who would be most qualified to assume the office of the vice president." In fact, he found himself saying "We picked him because he was the one who would be most qualified to assume the office of the vice president" so frequently—over and over and over, in interview upon interview—that Crane was half-convinced there had actually been a meeting at which the question had actually been posed: "Seriously, fellas, who would be most qualified to assume the office of the vice president?" Whereupon somebody (Forrester?) had actually said: "Well, believe it or not, Brent Bibby is the man." No, it had never happened, but if the media ever pressed, he would say they met in a hotel room in Chicago, that they watched the White Sox game after on TV. None of them would have enough enterprise to check. *Woo-oooooo!*

At least Bibby seemed like a nice boy, Crane thought. His father, of course, Horace Bibby, was a miserable shitheel whom everyone hated, but the boy—*boy!* he was *forty-three!*—seemed likable enough. He said the strangest thing, Crane remembered. He said that when he told his father he'd been chosen, old Horace just plain didn't believe him. "He thought I'd been drinking," Bibby told Crane. "Told me to go sleep it off. I thought I could give him a scoop, but he just wouldn't print it. He thought somebody was playing a joke on me." It was all Crane could do not to say that he could sympathize with Horace's thinking.

Still, the boy—*sorry, the guy! the guy!*—was very nice. Crane had locked Forrester and three speechwriters in a room with orders to crank out the acceptance speech Bibby would have to deliver that night, and Bibby went out to McDonald's and bought them all lunch. The gesture didn't go unappreciated, Crane thought, but everybody was a little surprised he bought them Happy Meals. Ah, fuck it, Crane thought, fuck it, fuck it.

Fuck it. Get it through your head, Crane told himself, get your mind right. He's the one most qualified to assume the office of the vice president, and he's the one most qualified because he is the one who is going to be the vice president, and he's going to be vice president because you, Lionel Crane, are the toughest, meanest, ass-kickingest campaign manager in the world, and if you had to make America elect a woodchuck vice president you could do it, and make America like it.

"So did you get him a good speech written?" Ross asked him. They were in Ross's dressing room backstage at the convention center, less than an hour before he and Bibby would address the convention. Crane had dropped in, ready to take care of any last minute details, not really expecting to find any. Ross was quiet, composed, primed to follow Bibby and deliver an acceptance speech that would be read by the media and the public as one of the keys to his candidacy.

Crane nodded. "A good enough speech. It's clear, it's easy to read, it's not better than yours. If he manages to avoid stepping on his own dick on the way to the podium, I think we'll be all right."

"Good," Ross said. "Where will you watch the speeches?"

"Back of the hall."

"Good. I'll see ya after."

Then, by way of encouragement, Crane said, "This thing's in the bag."

"Really?" Ross said, perking up. "Do you really think so? Even with Bibby?" And Crane, thinking Ross needed confidence more than truth, said yes.

As he left, he passed Lucinda. "Is he in?" she asked brightly.

"If you mean your husband, ma'am, no, he's not."

"Oh Mr. Crane," she said smiling, "you're such a silly. Listen, we don't have to spend a lot of time fighting one another, do we? I mean, I'd be surprised to learn that I was duplicating any of the services you provide him. Haven't you ever heard of peaceful coexistence?"

The burly aide grunted and walked away.

Crane camped in the back of the hall between the Maryland and Guam delegations, arriving just after Minority Leader Plotski had taken the podium and begun introducing Bibby, both to the convention and to 23 million Americans watching on TV. God, you had to love Plotski, Crane thought, admiring what a good soldier the old man was, how he assumed his post at the microphone and began manfully serving up lauditory adjectives and plaudits in an effort to describe a person who could have been adequately summed up in two or three nondescript words. Crane hadn't been standing in the hall more than three minutes before, in the course of receiving the congratulations of the professional organizers and party veterans, he'd been forced to mutter "because-we-thought-he'd-be-most-qualified-to-assume-the-office-of-the-vice-president" five times. Never once was it to someone who particularly seemed to buy it.

"This fine young man," Plotski was saying, "this exceptional young man, this energetic young man, this very, very tall young man—"

It will be all right, Crane told himself. The old pros like Plotski will stand strong, we'll put some handlers on the kid to teach him some tricks and keep him out of trouble, the spin doctors will get out there and convince everybody that he can't be as bad as he looks, and everything will settle down. Come November, everything will come true, as predicted. The plan Crane had so cleverly hatched three years ago would be realized, the campaign he had so meticulously managed for the last year would be won, the man he had served for a quarter century would be elected president.

"Ladies and gentlemen," Plotski said, mounting to a crescendo, "I give you the next Vice President of the United States, Brent Bibby!"

"Are you ready, sir?" Brent Bibby heard Forrester ask him, and, as he peered out onto the floodlit stage and the roiling blue-shaded conventioneers beyond, he heard himself reply, "Well, yes, I guess I am." He walked out—*remember to smile, remember to wave, remember to smile*—thinking he'd never heard so much noise. The band, the applause, now here's the podium, this is just so exciting, so exciting. Okay, now. Ready, set, *speak:*

"Madame Chairwoman, Party Chairman Grich, Minority Leader Plotski, ladies and gentlemen, friends and neighbors, boys and girls, delegates and delegesses, you down there with the group from Hawaii—no, not you with the shirt, the lady with the Styrofoam hat and all the buttons—not you, but—oh, *golly* look how many people there are with Styrofoam hats and buttons! Everybody who's wearing a Styrofoam hat with a lot of buttons, put up your hands. Amazing . . .

"But then amazing is a word I've been hearing a lot these last twenty-four hours. Everyone seems amazed that Governor"—pause, get the name right, first the left cuff—"Roger"—now the right—"Ross picked me to be his vice president. I bet most of you were amazed. I know I was! I've been thinking, why would Governor"—left—"Roger"—right—"Ross select me? I haven't proposed a lot of bills, I don't sit on any key committees, and I don't have vast experience in foreign affairs. Why, I've never been out of the country, except for a junior tennis tournament I played in Acapulco. Well, wait, I played tennis in Cancun, too. And in the Bahamas, and in Jamaica—well, you see, that's my point. I think my selection is a testament to the ability of Governor"—left—"Roger"—right—"Ross to lead this country. I believe he has the vision to look into the heart and soul of this great land and see things that no one else has ever seen, the way he has looked into me and has seen talent and character that no one else has recognized. So I would disagree with the people who say that Governor"—left—"Roger"—right—"Ross's decision to pick an unknown and little-admired senator is a sign of political weakness. I say this is his political strength."

In the back of the hall, Crane was apoplectic. "Why isn't he reading the speech we wrote for him?" he raged. "Why isn't he reading the speech?" Crane stormed into the midst of the Maryland delegation, commandeered its phone and called Forrester backstage.

"I have no idea," Forrester yelled back. "What would you like me to do about it? Go out there in front of everybody and make him? Say, '*Here's your speech, numbskull*'?" Crane didn't really have an answer to that and wouldn't have been able to deliver it anyway, having slammed down the phone and shattered it in his anger.

Onstage, Bibby continued. "People say I'm not experienced.

Well, that's true. But friends, when I look into the future of America, I see decades and decades comprised of experiences that no one has experienced yet. *No one.* So what good is experience? I would say that for inexperienced times perhaps you need an inexperienced man, and I believe that I have that lack of experience, that I am perhaps the least experienced man available for the job.

"I would like to conclude, if I may, with my vision of America. When I look out upon this country, I see a happy land. Children play baseball on Little League teams, teens cavort in swimming pools, moms and dads prepare barbecues in their backyards. It is a pretty picture, but all is not rosy. Sometimes there are ruts on those Little League diamonds that can cause a bad hop. Sometimes those pools aren't properly heated, or the pool boy doesn't skim the gunk off the top as well as he might have. And sometimes the barbecue gets spoiled when Dad looks out and sees that his driveway's cracked and there's little weeds pushing up through the broken parts. Ladies and gentlemen, I have a dream of being the vice president of a United States of America that has no ruts, no pool gunk, and no weed problem, from sea to shining sea. Thank you, and God bless." Bibby stood at the podium, somewhat surprised that a tidal wave of applause was not at that moment lifting him to heights he had never known.

But that is what shock does to people, freezing them into utter stillness, leaving them unprepared to respond in ways they've been trained, striking them dumb. Only a strong personality— a Crane, say—can overcome it, which is why, after a moment, there could be heard in the otherwise silent hall some whistling and clapping and a lone voice chanting the candidate's name. "Bib-by!" Crane chanted. "Bib-by!" He grabbed a delegate. "Come on, old man," he growled, "get up and applaud! *Bib-by! Bib-by!* You, from Indiana, show a little spirit! *Bib-by!* You! Ed Varney! You still want to be a federal judge, Ed? You think a Democrat will appoint a reactionary bastard like you? Get off your ass! Start fucking clapping!"

Soon a full ovation developed, and the band began playing,

and Brent Bibby waved and waved. He left the podium beaming. The first face he saw was Forrester's. Bibby did not think Forrester looked very happy.

"Why didn't you read the speech?" Forrester agitatedly asked.

Bibby was confused. "What speech? *God!* Was that for tonight?"

In Ross's dressing room, Lucinda heard the ovation swell and fade. "Better get your clothes on, sugar," she said to Ross. "I think you're up next."

Five

The first campaign brain trust meeting since the convention was about to begin, and Forrester was feeling anxious. Forrester was feeling anxious, and it was Crane who was making him feel that way, grabbing him by the lapels in the men's room right before the start of the meeting and barking a bunch of last-minute instructions at him. Of course, Crane always made Forrester feel anxious a teensy bit with his gruff and intimidating ways, that was just normal. But in the five weeks since the convention, Crane was making Forrester feel anxious a lot. And in a different way, too. He was . . . scarier. Spookier. A little wild. His eyes seemed on the verge of bugging out of his head all the time, and the bags under them were bigger and purpler, and the few hairs Crane still had on the top of his head were all crinkled in funny ways and went off in different directions. And now, on top of all this bug-eyed, funny-crinkled-hair anxiety, for the always gruff-and-intimidating, but now spooky-scary Crane to grab hold of him in the men's room before the start of the big meeting—and just when Forrester was feeling pretty good, too, Governor Ross having greeted him with a sort of vague warmth—and to have barked this bunch of final instructions at him, well, it made him feel anxious, is all. Unsettled. A little bit. It wasn't that the instructions were so unusual—"When I call on you, just stick to the facts. No editorializing. Just look at Ross and stick to the facts. Ya got me?"—it was just that worried look on Crane's face when he gave them.

That was it. It was Crane's worried mug that was making Forrester so ill at ease. Because Crane never worried about problems. Crane usually just did whatever it took to fix them.

Forrester was beginning to take stock of just how anxious this realization was making him when Ross signaled Crane to call the meeting to order. Crane seemed his usual bearish self, Forrester thought. Which was comforting. A little.

"Gentlemen, we have not convened for five weeks," Crane began, addressing the twenty or so key operatives who had gathered from across the country. "Governor Ross has been hard on the campaign trail, and each of us has been working hard at raising money, filming commercials, manipulating the news media and generally doing the many things we've all done so well in campaign after campaign. Five weeks ago, I expected that this year would be no different. I expected that when we convened today, I would tell you that we were on course, and that if we just kept at it, we would once again kick some ass.

"Today, I stand here and tell you that I was wrong. Wrong, gentlemen, wrong, wrong, wrong, wrong, wrong. Instead, I am telling you that we are in the toilet, and those unfamiliar objects we see before our eyes are all the other turds that are joining us on our trip to the great sewage-treatment plant of history. *Do you morons get the picture?* Things aren't working out the way we had planned. *Forrester!* Read 'em the story."

Knees shaking, Forrester rose and unveiled an easel upon which he had placed some charts that he had prepared. "Gentlemen," he began. His voice squeeked a bit, but then he settled in. "Gentlemen, this chart, which I'm sure you will all remember, shows the result of a poll taken the day prior to the start of our convention. You will recall that Governor Ross then enjoyed a 79-to-7 edge over the then-likely and now-actual Democratic candidate, Senator Frank Femur, with 14 percent undecided. As you will see, we had strength across the nation, in all income, age, and ethnic groups. We projected that we would win forty-

nine states. The day after our convention ended—coinciden-
tally, the day after Senator Bibby was nominated—our lead fell
to 61-to-21, with 18 percent undecided. Two weeks later, by the
time the Democratic convention ended and Femur was nominated, we had a 55-to-39 lead, and Femur has continued to
make inroads. We now project that Femur will win six states,
which does not count New Jersey and Illinois, where we are running dead even. The softening, as you see, has occurred across
the board."

"Well, you know," Ross interrupted, "you had one Democrat
after another going *Baby Bibby, Baby Bibby* for four days. It was
bound to take its toll, but that'll wear off. And leaking his college
transcripts was a low blow, and I think as soon as the shock
wears off people will recognize that it was a low blow and that it
really doesn't matter how many times a guy has to take fresh-
man English before he passes, just so long as he eventually does
get that D and can move on. But it'll wear off. And most impor-
tantly, I don't think the Femur–La Beauf ticket has got a lot of
appeal."

"You don't?" Crane asked. "Well, let's stop worrying about
this, boys, and let's head out to Santa Anita. Governor Ross
doesn't think the Femur–La Beauf ticket has got a lot of appeal.
Governor, you may be right. But I don't think the voters are
finding us so damn appealing either. Let's not kid ourselves.
People like Frank Femur, even if they think he'd tax their nose
hairs if he got the chance. And they respect former Ambassador
La Beauf, even if he is nearly eighty years old. And Frank Femur
is cagy. He's not going to do us a big favor and self-destruct.
We're going to have to beat him head-on."

"Which means?" Ross asked, trying to pretend that he didn't
know what Crane was driving at.

"Which means we have to figure out what to do about Bibby.
Look at the polls," Crane said. "Everybody's worried about
Bibby. He's the dead weight. He's the millstone."

"Fine," Ross said abruptly. He was finding this meeting tire-
some and wanted Crane to stop being such a Cassandra and get

back to making things right. "Cut to the chase. What do you want to do with him?"

"Well, that's the point," Crane replied. "I don't think there's much more we can do *with* him. We've tried raising his stature. Gave him a speech to read on defense policy before the Veterans of Foreign Wars. Perfectly fine speech, perfectly friendly audience, all he had to do was read. What happened? He lost his way in the middle. Ended up leading them all in a rendition of 'When the Caissons Go Rolling Along.'"

"Then somebody in the audience asked him why he had voted in favor of funding the Wild Wombat attack plane," Forrester added. "First he asked the guy to repeat the name of the plane about four times—"

"Then he asked him to spell it," Crane interjected.

"He finally said, 'I don't know why, it just seemed like most of the other guys were supporting it.' Then he started talking about his own experiences in uniform."

"Well, what's wrong with that?" Ross demanded irritably. "I mention being in the navy all the time."

"Regrettably, Governor, though Senator Bibby has been in uniform, it wasn't the uniform of one of the armed services," Forrester noted. "He was talking about the time Horace Bibby forced him to get a job and he went to work at McDonald's for a week. Fortunately, the duties are similar and very few members of the audience seemed to notice."

Ross sighed, then shrugged. "Well, so, everyone has his limitations," Ross said. "If you can't make him look good, hide him."

"I would love to hide him," Crane said. "Unfortunately, he's become the great fucking road show. A dozen camera crews follow his every move. Nobody wants to miss out on the next big boner."

"It's been like that since he went to the flag factory," Forrester said.

Ross cringed at the memory. "I still don't know what he was thinking."

"What was he thinking?" Crane said indignantly. "He was thinking there's fifty-four states in the union. Why else would he ask a seamstress why she wasn't putting fifty-four stars on her flag?"

"But what does he think are . . . ?"

"The other states? Who the hell knows? I know he thinks Puerto Rico's a state and Guam's a state and Canada's a state. 'And what's the other one?' I asked him. He said to me, 'Wyoming.' That's when I gave up. My curiosity about the bizarre has its limits."

"He's probably just nervous," said Ross. "He's probably just overanxious."

"You think so?" Crane barked. "Tell me when it's going to get easier for him."

"You know, Governor, we tried sending him to appear at grade schools," said Forrester. "Little grade schools in little towns in faraway places, where we assumed the children would be dimmer. But he still acts like . . . himself. In one school there was a spelling bee. Before I could open my mouth, he asked if he could play."

"And . . . ?"

"He got one right. *Plate.* He spelled *plate* correctly. Then he missed his next one."

"Was it one of those tricky words?" Ross asked. "Something like *phlegm?*"

"No, sir," Forrester replied. "He misspelled *house.*"

"House?"

"He used a W, sir."

"He did?" Ross cleared his throat. "Well, you can sort of see that, can't you? H–O–W–S–E? At least it's phonetic."

"Unfortunately, sir, he placed the W at the beginning."

"Well, goddammit," Ross suddenly snapped, the frustration of having to apologize for his mistress's lousy choice in a husband suddenly boiling over. "What do you guys want? He's stupid, okay? You told me that. I didn't listen. You want me to call a press conference? I'll call a press conference, and I'll admit that

Bibby is stupid and that it's not my advisors' fault. Do you want that?"

Crane gave a little shrug and shook his head no.

"Spell it out, Crane," Ross pushed. "Should we drop him?"

"Maybe we could get him to resign of his own accord," Forrester suggested.

The idea was quickly picked up and tossed about by the operatives, nearly all of whom chimed in with their own sad stories about Bibby, and how the voters in their part of the country would feel better if Ross had chosen someone else, and how Ross would get a three- or four-point bounce in the polls just by replacing him, and how the campaign might engineer his removal. All the while, Crane stared at Ross, and Ross stared at Crane. "Well," Crane said portentously after a while, and the table hushed to listen, "well, maybe we could get him to quit. Hold a little press conference, dragoon Bottomley or one of those bozos onto the ticket."

"So," Ross pushed, "dump him?" God, he thought, what if Crane says yes?

Which is what Crane wanted to scream at the top of his lungs, but he just screwed up his face instead and breathed slowly and deeply until he could go through all the angles again. And when he had finished going through all the angles again, he came to the same conclusion that he had in the wee hours of every morning of every day during the last two weeks.

"Sure, we could dump him," Crane said slowly. "We could dump him and get killed. First, nobody on earth would believe we hadn't just thrown him overboard. And second, it would look like we don't have the first fucking idea about what we're doing. The columnists would jump on us, the commentators would jump on us, and we'd get ourselves a permanent fucking spot in the Leno monologue. We can't drop this asshole. We couldn't drop him if he was made of lead. We'll just have to keep doing what we have been doing. We'll hide him in out-of-the-way places, we'll have Forrester go with him night and day to prevent him from opening his mouth and saying anything except, 'How do you do?', and we'll try to get him ready for the debate. And we'll just hope he gets through that one without destroying himself and the rest of us, or we'll all get a taste of what life in the private sector is really like. Meanwhile, I'll try to think of a way to get the spotlight off of us and onto Femur."

"Like?" Ross asked. He didn't really care, he was so relieved.

"If I knew, Governor, I'd be doing it," said Crane. "Maybe we'll try mudslinging. See if we can't dump some muck on him."

"Now, there!" Ross exclaimed. "Do I have the smartest campaign manager in the history of politics, or what? Just when the chips are down, Lionel Crane once again comes through with the big idea!"

On that note, the meeting was closed. As Crane packed up his papers, Ross came and sat beside him. "Listen," he said, "I'd like you to have a word with the scheduler. I was campaigning throughout the South last week, and he had Mrs. Bibby in the New England states."

"Yeah, so?" Crane responded. "That's pretty standard. We're just trying to maximize press coverage."

"Well, I think there's a lot more to be gained by having us in the same general area."

"Why on earth would you think that?"

"Well, the campaign appearances would reinforce one another in the media, for one thing. There would be all that *synergy*. We'd really dominate the news."

"Where are you getting this 'synergy' stuff? I don't think it would make a bit of difference. You're the candidate. They'll cover you no matter what."

"Besides, I think things would go more smoothly if her handlers could interface more frequently with my handlers. If they were, like, in the same hotel more often. I mean, we're not talking every night here."

It finally dawned on Crane that this wasn't a tactical discussion. "Right," the most realistic of men sullenly agreed.

"Just four or five times a week."

"Right."

"So they could have those enormously useful—what's the word?—skull sessions."

"Maybe you mean tête-à-têtes."

"Yes, Crane, thank you," the candidate said dryly. "I'm so glad we understand one another."

The two men left the meeting room and stepped into the hall-way. Bibby was sitting on the floor, wearing his Walkman, lost in the music. He finally looked up. "Ready for me?" he asked, smiling.

Crane nodded wearily.

"Do you listen to rap music much, Mr. Crane?" he asked. "I'll lend you my Hammer tape if you want."

Six

"Ready, Senator Bibby?"

"Ready, Mr. Forrester."

Out the door of the suite, down the corridor, down another corridor, down the Waldorf's private elevator, down into the underground parking complex, over to the waiting Lincoln Towncar, into the back seat, no hitches. The Secret Service is really very good at this clearing-the-way thing, Forrester thought. Only one interruption, a desk clerk with an envelope for Forrester. An agent detained the little geek while another examined the documents before allowing Forrester to bring them into the car with the candidate.

Not until the car was out of the garage, picking up speed, the motorcycle sirens opening the way, Bibby safely staring out the window lost in his own little world, did Forrester allow himself to peek inside the tatters of the envelope. Ah, his tickets. At the mere sight of them, Forrester allowed his attention to wander for a moment, allowed himself to imagine the first weekend after the first Tuesday in November, when Forrester, his side victorious or defeated, would be lying in a deck chair on a secluded beach in St. Croix, gazing at the pristine white sand and the aquamarine sea, no one speaking to him and him saying nothing to nobody, no sound at all, really, except the gentle lap, lap, lap of the sea on the shoreline and Forrester's occasional calls to the cabana boy for a fresh drink, and the cabana boy's succinct "No problem, mon" reply.

Certainly he'd be saying nothing to Brent Bibby. Nothing about him, nothing to him, nothing on his behalf. For the last four weeks, the campaign had forbidden Bibby to speak. Instead, Forrester, sticking to the candidate like white on rice (another of those amusing expressions of Crane's), had done all of Bibby's talking. Bibby would visit some small town, and some reporter or some official—and sometimes just a citizen, an honest-to-goodness nobody!—would ask a question, and Bibby would nod yes or no, it hardly mattered which, and Forrester would leap in with an explanation. *Ah, regrettably the senator has so badly strained his vocal cords campaigning that his physicians have forbidden him to speak, lest he suffer permanent, irreversable damage to his throat. But our position on the question you have raised is this. . . .* And Bibby would nod solemnly, just as they had trained him to—whoever said he wasn't educable didn't know anything—and Forrester would go on with his explanation, elaborating policy proposals in a way, he tended to think, that probably enhanced his chances of being named President Ross's press secretary. If they won, that is. The gambit worked perfectly, or nearly so. The ruse broke down just once— an article in the *Chicago Tribune* mentioned that on the plane one evening, Senator Bibby could be heard exclaiming, "Hey, look, Nintendo! Hey, Super Mario Brothers!"—and the reporter who so injudiciously alluded to Senator Bibby's momentary vocal improvement was accidentally left at the airport in Fargo, North Dakota, the next night when the candidate's plane took off. It wasn't a very nice thing to do, Forrester admitted to himself, but it wasn't the meanest trick in the world, just a little bit of discipline that all the other reporters took note of and respected, just the sort of little enforcement action that would enhance Forrester's chances of being named President Ross's press secretary. If they won.

If they won. With ten days to go, the election was no longer the lock-solid proposition it used to be. No longer the lead-pipe cinch. No more "Book 'em, Dan-o." No, in fact, everyone in the campaign was sharply aware that Upset City was, well . . . possible. Not probable, Forrester thought. Not even close yet, really. Well, it was close, just not that close. Not *thatclose.* Still, the polls were clear, even if the pollsters tried to obfuscate the results with a lot of mumbo-jumbo qualifiers. Ross still held a slim lead, but Femur was sneaking up in the Electoral College predictions. Crane had pretty much written off New York and Pennsylvania, and would certainly have put Ross full-time into Ohio and Michigan if he hadn't already decided to put him full-time into California and Texas. Thank God the wealthy contributors Ross had toadied to all those years finally ponied up enough dough to let Ross cram the airwaves with commercials, Forrester thought. Everyone agreed: all that humiliating ass-kissing had been well worth it.

Of course, Forrester acknowledged, as the car headed west into Central Park, all the surveys were taken before tonight. And tonight, of course, everything could go right into the dumpster. Tonight, of course, the vice-presidential candidates were debating live on national TV.

Crane had worked hard to prevent Bibby from appearing. He'd bluffed, he'd threatened, he'd all but begged the Democrats to pass up a Bibby–La Beauf debate. No deal, Gaston Castleberry had said, loving every minute the spectacle of Crane squirming. The Democrats were eager for it, the League of Women Voters was insisting on it, and even the networks were intrigued by the idea. "Face it, Lionel," Gaston Castleberry had chuckled, "now that Bibby's in it, the entertainment value is unlimited." Amazingly true: Crane could not believe his ears when he'd flipped on "Monday Night Football" and heard Al Michaels say, "Tune in Friday night, when former Ambassador La Beauf and the always unpredictable Senator Bibby square off in a showdown of the vice-presidential candidates."

"Nervous, Senator?" Forrester asked, as the big Towncar swung around and headed uptown towards Columbia University, where the debate was going to be held.

"No," Bibby replied softly, and indeed, Forrester thought, he did not look nervous at all. "Hey, Forrester," Bibby called, "didja ever notice how, when it's raining and the windows of a limo get all streaky, you can kind of squint your eyes and the lights kind of all run together and make all these funny shapes and stuff?"

"It's something, isn't it, sir?" No, not nervous at all. Not nervous now, not nervous during any of his preparation sessions during the week. At first the thinking was to give him a crash course in everything that could possibly come up—"Let's just slop it all onto him, some of it's bound to stick," was the amusing way Crane had put it—but about ten minutes into the first briefing, just as some economist from Stanford began explaining the effect of the Fed's interest rate policies on the M1 and M2 money supplies, Bibby got that sweet, glassy expression on his face that Forrester had come to recognize as signaling Bibby's mental relocation to a tennis court at some sunny, distant country club, and Forrester knew he could tell the economist that he was free to go. Goodbye, Professor, thanks for coming. If we're ever elected we'll be sure to ask you what to do about things of this nature.

"Okay, Senator, let's make this simple," Crane said. "Just remember these four things. First, we're for the little guy. We oppose new spending and we're against raising taxes, and Frank Femur isn't."

"No?"

"No, he's not. Second, we favor peace through strength. We won the Cold War because we—"

"Because," Bibby interrupted, "we stayed in bed and drank plenty of liquids."

Crane looked at him blankly.

"It's a joke," Bibby said. "I do know how to make jokes sometimes."

"Bad Senator," Crane said sternly, wagging his finger at the candidate. "Never, ever, do that again. It just confuses me, and I hate being confused, okay? Now: Cold War, peace through strength, new world order, that sort of thing. Third, fair play abroad. Fourth, tough on crime. Now, pretty much anything they ask can be answered by referring to one of those four positions. And if the question doesn't relate, gently change the subject and talk about one of those positions. Okay, Senator?"

"Gee," Bibby said, a soft cloak of wonderment descending upon his visage, "I never thought being smart could be so easy."

"Gosh, chief," Forrester later said to Crane, "do you think telling him that was wise?"

"Wise?" Crane asked, his response blunt, furious, unassailable. "If I wanted to do something wise, I'd fuck porcupines for a living."

Bibby's first question, from ABC's Celestine van den Hurdle, was simple and entirely expected. "Senator, some economists are predicting that the economy will enter a slowdown sometime during the second quarter next year. They say that we may have a recession by year's end. What are your thoughts on averting this?"

Brrriiiiinnnngggg, Bibby thought. I can answer that question. "Celestine," Bibby said, speaking confidently, "our position is clear. We oppose increases in spending, and we oppose new taxes."

"And you think that will be sufficient to head off a recession?"

"Celestine, let me say this: We're for the little guy, and we've always been for the little guy. I don't think Frank Femur can say the same. Now, let me reiterate. Against spending, against taxes." He stopped and gave her, and then the audience, a great big smile.

"Is that all you want to say, Senator?" she said tentatively. "You have about four minutes of your allotted time left. Nothing you'd like to add?"

"I think it's all the American people need to know," he said. *Not too fucking shabby!*

Crane, camped with Forrester in the back row of the lighting booth of the amphitheater, listened for a moment as old Ambassador La Beauf began his long rebuttal, a drawn-out, windbaggy reply, featuring several instances, Crane was pleased to see, of La Beauf tripping leadenly over the many syllables of van den Hurdle's name. Not so bad, Crane thought. Bibby spoke authentic-sounding political gibberish. La Beauf answered like he had bats flying around in his skull. The exchange made for a really boring opening to the debate, Crane thought with a smile. He imagined hearing a thunderous clicking noise as all across the country viewers began changing the channel. Perhaps there is a God, he thought.

"Senator," Eldon Kurtzweil of the *Washington Post* soon asked, "what do you think we should do about the defense budget?"

Brriiiinnnggg! "Peace through strength," Bibby chirped. "Peace through strength." God, thought Crane, he's grinning like Vanna's going to come out at the end of this and hand one of them the keys to a Suzuki.

Kurtzweil politely waited for Bibby to continue, but soon realized that Bibby had no intention of elaborating. "Ah, Senator," Kurtzweil went on, "surely you must agree in light of the demise of the Soviet bloc, maintaining present levels of defense spending is unnecessary and a huge waste of tax dollars."

Brriinngg. "Well, as I said to Ms. van den Hurdle, we're against spending, and we're against taxes."

"What?" Uh-oh, Bibby thought, Kurtzweil seems annoyed. "I think we'd all like to hear you spell that out more," the columnist insisted.

Spell what out? Bibby licked his lips. "Mr. Kurtzweil, I don't think the American people need any long, drawn-out explanations for when we tell them what we know what's in our hearts and what's in their hearts that they want to hear. From us."

Okay, kid, Crane thought, not bad, full-blown gobbledygook, but stated sincerely. Then Crane realized: He's going to continue! No! Shut up!

"And of course, there's our strong support for fair trade abroad."

"I'm sorry, Senator, what do you mean?"

"By what? By fair play? I mean fair play. Fair play abroad. You know. Call your own fouls. And if your opponent's ball is in, you say so, let him have the point. But if it's out, it's out. And he'll believe you, because you support fair trade abroad."

The moderator, NBC's Vernon Adder, broke in. "Time, Senator. Ambassador La Beauf, do you have a rebuttal?"

The old man's creased face squinched up in disgust. "I can rebut a lot of things, sonny, but I can't rebut a marshmallow."

Ow, what a hit, Crane thought. Sound Bite City. Almost unconsciously, he began sliding Michigan into the Democratic column. Then, as La Beauf took a question of his own, Crane recalculated the electoral college totals. They seemed sickly.

"Senator Bibby, do you have a rebuttal to Ambassador La Beauf's response?"

Bibby looked at him blankly. "I'm sorry, I didn't hear the question."

The silver-haired anchorman cleared his throat. "My apologies, Senator. I said, do you have a rebuttal to the ambassador's response?"

"No," Bibby chuckled, "I didn't hear the question you asked Ambassador La Beauf."

"You didn't hear?" Adder asked incredulously.

"Well, it was probably more like I wasn't listening. I guess I don't always have my paying-attention ears on. What was it about?"

"Well, it concerned the situation in San Rico de Humidor."

"Oh," Bibby shook his head slowly, "I don't know anything about San Rico de Humidor. But you could ask the Governor or Mr. Crane or somebody. That's what I would do if I had a question about San Rico de Humidor. They're very smart. Big brains. And oh, oh, oh, oh, they're very anti-crime. Did I mention that? They hate criminals, hate those bad, disgusting crime guys. Bleh! Yuck!"

Adder stared at Bibby, eyes narrowed in skepticism, as though waiting for Allan Funt to pop out from behind the podium to tell him he was on "Candid Camera." Bibby, Crane realized, was grinning like he'd just beaten the house at blackjack. "Uhhhh, okay," Adder said finally. "Ms. van den Hurdle, do you have a question for Senator Bibby?"

"I suppose this would be as appropriate a time as any to bring this up," the reporter began. "Senator Bibby, throughout this campaign you've been dogged by accusations that you're stupid. Can you comment?"

Briing. Briing. Briing. Ah, no crime, no fair play, no tax, no peace, ahhh, okay, well, take a deep breath, *okay!* "Celestine, as one wise man put it, stupid is as stupid does. I don't think I'm particularly stupid. I think I'm an average American of average intelligence. I may not know things that my opponent does, like what certain big words mean or who America fought in World War II. But let's be candid. When you're vice president, you have people around who know those things for you, or who know how to look them up. And there's even more help when you become president. And as for my readiness to become president, well, I'll be fully briefed. Governor"—stop, check the cuffs, you're doing fine—"Roger Ross has assured me that we'll have lunch once a week, and he'll tell me anything I need to know. Look, I have the same preparation and qualifications that Vice President Dan Quayle had when he was elected a while ago, and look how well he turned out."

Bingo!

Adder could barely finish calling for La Beauf's response before the old man weighed in. "Senator," he began, "I knew Dan Quayle, I worked with Dan Quayle, Dan Quayle was a friend of mine, and I tell ya, Dan Quayle was a nincompoop, and Senator, you're no Dan Quayle! Hell, you're not fit to shine Dan Quayle's boots! Sonny, you wouldn't even make a wart on Dan Quayle's butt! Why am I up here with you? Who the hell are you? Why am I even speaking to you? You know, I once had to negotiate with Stalin. He wanted to invade China. I had to wrestle him in a blizzard to stop him. I solved the Cuban missile crisis by going to Havana. Met with Castro. Stopped the whole mess when I took him into the hallway and showed him that my pecker was bigger than his. What the hell have you done?"

"What's the best way to do it, Forrester?" Crane asked, extending a finger and cocking his thumb. "Right in the temple or up through the roof of your mouth? Aw, come on, Bibby," he groaned, "pick up your head! Don't be staring at your crotch the rest of the night now!"

Seven

In the days that had followed Roger Ross's embarkation upon his quest for the presidency so many months ago, the thought that he might fail would have made him nauseous. Actually *nauseous.* There would be a frigid night in Iowa or New Hampshire, a speech would go bad, the crowd would be surly, there'd be some stupid botched order in some greasy diner at eleven at night, and he'd be having to get up in three hours later to go stand in front of the media in some yokel's barn and yank on some cow's hind tit, in order to prove to the rest of the yokels that he knew something about farming (*which he did—placate the goddam farm bloc*), and he'd lose heart. And he'd think about getting beat, and the cramps would set in, and he'd curl up on his bed until he could get ahold of himself and harden his mind and get on with the task at hand. Which he always did. And then he pressed on and pressed everyone around him on, because he simply could not accept the thought of failure.

And yet, now that defeat was actually upon him, the feeling really wasn't all that bad. There was actually a kind of tranquillity that set in. No happiness, to be sure, no lightness, no pleasure. But at least he could stop fearing the possibility of defeat. It would happen. He would lose. He would have blown the biggest lead in American political history, and he would have to live with that thundering humiliation the rest of his life. And yet, somehow, that was all right, too. After falling so long, he thought, there was some comfort to be found in the splatter.

Of course, he could still win. That would be okay, too. More than okay, really, he'd *like* to win. And it was certainly still possible, if you could believe the *New York Times,* anyway. There, on the front page, Sunday edition, two days before the election, their final poll of the campaign: Femur, 48.8 percent; Ross, 48.7; Undecided, 2.5. Electoral votes leaning to Ross, 216; to Femur, 212; too close to call, 87.

"Should we do anything special?" Ross asked Crane the day before when the campaign's own pollster reported similar findings.

"Nah," said Crane. "Doesn't matter. Just keep on keepin' on. Do what you want. Don't do what you don't want. It all comes down to who shows up Tuesday."

Doesn't matter. The words were hurtful coming from Crane, but Ross knew what he meant. Knew what he felt, too. It almost didn't matter, Ross thought, almost not at all. Nothing would have made a difference. Well, something would have made a difference. He could have picked someone other than Bibby, but then there wouldn't have been a Lucinda, and Lucinda was the only thing that matters.

Ain't that a kick in the head? Ross thought. You start out running for the presidency, and you end up falling in love instead. Ross looked over at her next to him in bed—they had turned in early that night, there was nothing for them to do, it didn't matter—her dark hair falling loose and free across her shoulders, the little glasses she wore for reading perched on her perfectly shaped nose, her eyes—

"Look what that miserable prick Kurtzweil is saying about you in the *Post,*" she suddenly snarled. "I'd like to rip that ugly hairpiece off his head and cram it down his scrawny neck."

"Oh, what does it matter now?"

"What does it matter?" she repeated with alarm.

"Exactly. It doesn't. It doesn't matter. We're going to lose."

"How can you say that? You're still ahead in all the key states."

"Barely," he sighed. "I believe the tide has turned. The tide has turned, Lucinda, I can smell it on the wind. But, ah, listen, darling . . ." He paused, making sure she was listening, wondering if he should say what was in his heart. "Lucinda, if we lose, I was thinking: Would you leave Brent and marry me?"

"I would love to, sugar," she said, without quite looking up from her newspaper, "but, how would we live?"

Ahh, leave it to her to be the intelligent, practical one. "Well, I haven't practiced law in a long time," he began, "but I suppose I could get hired on as window dressing at a firm somewhere. That would pay a bit. What I think I'd really like would be to get a teaching position at some small college, away from the hue and cry. I think I'd like that."

She turned her head and looked across the top of her glasses at him. "A small school, eh? Like Bibbyville State?"

"Yes," said Ross, brightening. "Exactly. Bibbyville State."

"You know, college professors don't earn very good salaries."

"No," he agreed dismally. "But I have some investments, and a good pension, and I could write my memoirs. We'd live simply—I can see us canning peaches together on a rainy afternoon. We'd be poor, but happy."

"No doubt very happy, living on no money in some backwater, always having to kiss the commodious butts of the department chairman and the dean and the president and all their wives, attending all the wretched little faculty parties with all those patronizing associate professors, perpetually enduring the thinly veiled condescension they constantly direct toward a man who came within a whisker of the presidency *after blowing a tremendous lead.* Oh yes, great fun."

Ross shifted uncomfortably in the bed. "Well," he said hesitantly, "if you didn't want to go to the parties, sweetheart, I don't suppose we'd have to go."

Just then there was a sharp knock at the door. "Governor,"

Ross heard Crane calling, his voice urgent, "open up. There's been a major development."

Ross and Lucinda hurriedly rose and put on robes, and Ross let him in. "Governor, Mrs. Bibby," Crane nodded, breathing heavily, "Governor, there's big news. Frank Femur is dead."

The news was indeed a shock, and involuntarily Ross clutched his bathrobe about his throat. "Dead!" he repeated in disbelief. "My God, that's terrible! How'd it happen?

"He was campaigning in Manhattan, one of those walking tour–rally things. He was eating his way up Broadway, you know, egg roll, pizza, blintze, when he passed one of those yuppie nouvelle cuisine restaurants, and a waiter brought out a medallion of lamb with little vegetables. Frank inhaled a baby carrot and choked to death."

Ross's mind was racing. "How horrible! A baby carrot!"

"Down the windpipe!" cried Crane.

Ross couldn't help—"That's horrendous!"—starting to giggle. And neither—"You should see the footage on CNN!"—could Crane.

"I'll have to send his wife a note," Ross said, now laughing hard. "What was her name again?"

"Flor–har–har–har–ence!" said Crane, busting a gut.

"That's right, Frank and Florence Femur! Ha, ha, ha, ha, ha! Let's send her a note."

"Ha, ha, ha, ha, a whole flor–har–har–har–al arrangement!" Crane roared.

Then it really hit home, and Ross, controlling his laughter, put his arm around his longtime manager. "Crane, this is it, right? I can't lose now, can I?"

And Crane stopped laughing, too, and calmly said, "Not to a dead man. And it's too late for them to come up with a new candidate. You're in."

And for the first time since that hot August night when a badly smitten Roger Ross had first dared to think about selecting Brent Bibby, he knew he was going to become president. "I'm in!" he shouted, grabbing Lucinda. "I'm in!" And he and Lucinda and Crane jumped up and down, happy to be dancing on a grave that didn't hold their own dreams.

"Shouldn't we tell Bibby?" Crane later said.

"Good idea, Crane," said Ross. "You're really a very considerate person, you know that?"

"Where is he?" asked Lucinda.

"I sent him to Boise after the debate," Crane said.

"Very smart," said Ross.

Crane started dialing. "Should I tell him to come home?"

The next morning, Ross, his face a mask of sorrow, stood before the TV cameras and mourned the passing of his opponent. "Frank Femur was a good friend, a fine opponent, and a great American," he said. "I extend my sympathies to his wife and children, and I join the nation in mourning the departure of this great leader." Two mornings later, the day after election day, Ross was able to walk across the great, wide porch and down the steps of the big, white house his grandfather had built in Washington's Ferry and pick up a newspaper whose headline read:

ROSS TAKES 54% OF VOTE
FEMUR'S DEATH PROVES
INSURMOUNTABLE HANDICAP

Eight

"Ladies and gentlemen," boomed Wayne Newton into the microphone. "The President of the United States!"

He would have to get used to this, he thought as he strode into the great ballroom at the Willard Hotel, where the largest of the gala inaugural balls was being held. Not to being the center of attention; he had been the center of attention before. And not to parties. He would never get used to parties, he would always hate them. No, he was beginning to realize, what he had to get used to was his own sheer star power, his own amazing personal megawattage. Why, everything was bigger and keener and more colorful and more splendid than it had ever been in the whole fifty-five years that had preceded that instant some eight and half hours earlier when he'd repeated the oath of office after Chief Justice Loob. The aides around him moved more briskly, the Secret Service agents seemed more alert, the marine guards sharper, the flash bulbs flashier, and every tune the band played was just the *toe-tappingest*. Especially "Hail to the Chief," which they played every time he moved. God, he was beginning to like that song. (Make a note: Get somebody to find out if it had more words.) And everywhere he turned, he saw men in their tuxes, women shimmering in their gowns. And these weren't stupid county chairmen or pretty much bet-the-rent corrupt state legislators, along with their rotund wives, you understand, but bigshots, CEOs, movie stars, the giants of previous administrations who had navigated crises with an aplomb that Ross had admired from afar. Of course, Ross had been close enough to people like these for long enough now to realize just how pathetically human they were, really—how petty, how venal, how vain. And to realize as well, as of noon today he had surpassed them all. "Hey, how ya doin', Mr. Secretary? Thank you, thank you so much!"

Oh, the greetings had begun again. *Greetings to you, greetings to you, greetings, greetings, greetings, greetings, greetings to one and all.* Look at all those people! The whole day had been like a marathon broadcast of "This Is Your Political Life." Everyone who had ever helped him, endorsed him, given him money, shaken his hand, just *voted* for him—and even people he was sure hadn't voted for him, *Democrats!*—had thronged to this gala. Along with people he didn't know, he noticed. Who the hell were they? *Dates?* Too many for that. The media? In any event, freeloaders, he was sure.

I wonder how many of these people realize that the price of their ticket doesn't cover the cost of this shindig, that money has to be raised to make up the difference, the damn government doesn't do it, and you know who's got to do all the glad-handing to come up with the dough. Of course, Crane says the party apparatus is vast and most of those here have materially contributed to my success. I suppose he may be right, and I've just never seen them all in one place before. It's a little humbling, if Crane is right, seeing all these people who believe in me. Humbling, of course, in a kind of pride-enhancing way. "Hey, nice to see you! Thanks for your help. Did you get yourself something from the bar?"

But why would they come to a party? Ross hated parties, always had, from way back in college. Those frat house debauches—what was the point? You either went to watch a gang of rich yahoos get themselves plastered, or you jumped in and got plastered yourself. In which case you spent the next part of your immediate future vomiting and passing out and nursing a massive hangover. Ross could never vomit as copiously or pass out as dramatically as the other fellows, and so the next day, when everybody amused themselves by exchanging epic tales of each other's humiliating stupidities, no one ever paid much attention to his rather commonplace upchucks, and he always ended up unnoticed, back in the pack, and sick and smelly to boot. He hated that. And once he met Lilith, and realized that he could look at her and talk to her and touch her without embarrassment, then the whole point of parties as the tedious compulsories that preceded the evening's real entertainment, the opportunity to grope one of those debs from Albertus Magnus in the back of Kip Washburton's Ford, went by the boards. "Aw, thank you. Yes, glorious day. Yes, marvelous crowds."

Lilith. She would have liked this. She liked parties. She liked *people,* that was really it. She was warm and she laughed easily and she touched them, and he was always a little amazed at how gracefully she did it. Would he have gone so far without her? Would he have even taken the first step? Why, he remembered her asking him so long ago, when he first ran for office and was griping about all the false friendliness he had to suffer, why does a man who likes people so little want to get into politics? Years later, after he'd got better at dissembling and saying with sturdy conviction things he knew he didn't believe, he might have told her he liked people darn well. Might even have gone on to cite a thing or two people did—common people, that is, people he'd read about in a magazine—that he thought was perhaps likable, that might even be sorta fun. But he was younger when she'd asked that question, and Lilith was, well, Lilith, and even after he'd got good at lying, he'd never lied to her that well. And so he'd admitted it. "I guess I don't like people all that much," he'd said. And so she'd asked him why he did it. "Ambition?" she'd asked. "Hey, Mr. Mayor, how are you? You gonna invite to cut the ribbon on that new waterfront project? You better, I'm going to hold you to it."

Certainly not ambition. He didn't really understand ambition, thought it was for those sweaty ethnic types, the Jews and Italians, the ones who were so obvious about wanting to kick their way inside. Who, truth be told, he had never minded. If a man could kick his way in and overcome the obstacles of not having inherited wealth or good breeding, well, he thought, I can probably find a use for him. He hadn't responded to his wife, just shrugged and grunted, but he'd known the answer, and it wasn't ambition. Ross just thought he was born to lead. Why endure a government by inferiors? "Hey, yap, yap to you, too!"

At least they were yapping again. During the last month before the election, when the stench of death was emanating from his campaign, the yaps were few and far between. Now at least they all seemed to want to get on his good side again. The assholes.

Then—oh, there was Bibby, and *hey, there she was!* About ten feet ahead, Lucinda, her hair swept off her forehead, some kind of understated pearl thing holding it back, her sparkling eyes, a perfect dress, her shoulders, the whole look, so elegant, so, so, so, so . . .

Lush.

For ten weeks, ever since Roger Ross, bearing her husband on his back, had managed to stumble over a corpse into the White House (vindicating, she thought, everyone's charming faith in the common sense of the American electorate), Lucinda had been preparing for Inauguration Day. The politicians and policy wonks had their ways to prepare, and she had hers. If she was going to be an ornament to this administration, then she intended to become the standard of ornamentation for the world. It was not much of a goal, she realized, and it really wasn't worthy of her, but all things in time, she thought. Meanwhile, Brent got enough money from his family so she could afford to be whomever she liked.

Earlier, at the Inauguration itself, she portrayed the very model of modern midwestern American womanhood. She'd worn a good Republican cloth coat of American design and American production, adorned with a politically correct fake fur collar, a symbol of the message of prosperity without ostentation that this administration sought to deliver to the country at large. She'd worn a long-sleeved navy dress, silk, very nice, but not too dressy for the office. It was pretty, and it was smart. Yes, that was the word, smart. Not like the chunky matronly outfits that Barbara Bush wore, not offputting like Nancy Reagan's stiff, rigid suits, not as inescapably drab as the garments Marilyn Quayle occupied, but *smart*. And she'd topped it off with a small, wool hat that looked a little bit fun without calling too much attention to itself. Not the kind of thing that would upstage the oath of office. More the kind of thing that would catch people's attention during the president's address, when he'd gone on too long and people's minds were wandering. Women would think 'What a nice hat," and men would think, "Gee, she's pretty." Which she was, without the hat as well.

For the galas that evening, however, she had no interest in looking cute or smart or a model of midwestern anything. Long before the Electoral College convened in December to ratify the results of the election, Lucinda had flown to New York to spell out to the designer Christian Bois de Bolognese exactly what she wanted. "I want to look good, Monsieur Bois de Bolognese," she'd told him. "I want to look very good. I don't want to be a fashion victim. I don't want big poufs on my hips and shoulders. I don't want you and your designer buddies to have a good laugh at my expense over dinner one night. Read me? I want to look sexy, but I don't want to look like a tramp. I don't want guys getting boners just from glancing at me. And I don't want people staring at me all night to see if I manage to keep my tits in my dress, okay? I would like men to look at me and get weak. I would like to look across the ballroom floor and see little-man-puddles where guys had looked at me and melted away with desire. Got it?"

Evidently he had. From the looks she was getting, Lucinda reckoned that she was in the process of capturing the title of Most Fashionable Woman in Washington. From the number of times she was being photographed, she imagined that was about to begin a long and beneficial relationship with the Style section of the *Washington Post.*

Brent, who had been somberly accepting the congratulations of one and all—which confused him somewhat since many of those now praising him were people he'd seen for years on the Hill who'd never even been polite to him—beamed when he saw Ross. "Look, sugarplum," he exclaimed, "there's the president! Yo! Mr. President!"

"Brent!" she whispered urgently. "Don't say *yo* to the president! He'll come over when he's ready." Which, as it happened, he was.

"Hello, Mr. President," Brent said, grinning broadly and rocking up on his toes with excitement.

"Hello, ah . . ." Ross paused, knowing full well what to call the man, but being decidedly unwilling to respond in a way that made them sound like dopey schoolboy student council reps, goofing on each other's titles. Bibby saved him the trouble. "Mr. Vice President, eh?" he said, grinning like a fool. "How do you like that? It's still pretty unbelievable to me. Hey, how'd you like to say hello to Mrs. Second Lady?"

"Well, I would," Ross said. "Good evening, Mrs. Bibby. You look . . ." he paused for effect ". . . very attractive tonight." He could tell she was amused by his understatement. "I think it was worth running just to see you in that dress."

In it, my ass, she thought.

"Hey, I did want to ask you about that," Brent chimed back in. "Now, is Lucinda the second lady? Because, and you obviously know this, there is no first lady. So doesn't she just kind of move up?"

"Not unless she moves up in all other respects as well," Ross said, smiling thinly. "Is that what we should do? Should Lucinda become my wife?" Oh, why are you so wicked to this puppy? Ross asked himself as Bibby's face clouded over. Better call him off. "Forget about it, m'boy. All those first lady succession procedures are covered in the Constitution, but don't worry, the provisions are very seldom invoked. You'll be notified if any changes are required."

"Darling," Lucinda said to her husband, "Would you be good enough to get me some punch?"

"Certainly, sweetheart," Brent said and headed off, a retinue of aides and protectors following behind.

"I wonder how long it will take him to realize that he can ask one of those people to do that for him," Lucinda said in mild amazement as she watched the gang melt into the crowd.

"If nobody tells him?" Ross mused. "I'd bet forever. By the way, I was kidding before. You look very chic. And you looked very nice this morning, too."

"I was hoping you'd notice."

"Notice? It was all I could do to pay attention to the chief justice."

"Everyone thought it was very sweet that you let me hold the Bible for you after I held it for Brent," she said. "I saw some of the evening news as we were dressing. Vernon Adder said I seemed very daughterly."

"Mmmh," Ross said, bemused. "That's rich. I don't think I've ever thought of you as daughterly, my dear. Certainly not during the swearing-in ceremony."

"Do you know what I was thinking during the swearing-in?" She stepped up close and whispered in his ear. "I thought, I've had a senator, I've had a governor, but I've never had a president."

She stepped back and arched her eyebrows as she looked at him, pursing her lips slightly and then smiling in a way that let her little red tongue peek out from behind her teeth. Five months of proximity had not capped her ability to take him from zero to sixty on the distraction scale in an instant. "Um," he said, looking around the room, "let's, ah, try to take care of that. Look, ah, why don't we ask these people to leave?" She restrained herself, waiting for his common sense to kick in on its own. It seemed slow in coming. "Or maybe we should leave. We could get a room upstairs. Or find a supply closet. Or, you know, I have my own place here in town now."

"Darling, I think you're getting yourself worked up."

"No—*I have it!* We'll find the limo. It's got that smoked glass. No one would have any idea what we were doing if we were in there."

"Darling," she said, allowing a note of weariness to creep into her voice, though she was anything but weary of having the most powerful man in the world virtually begging for her favors. "Don't worry. We'll do it again soon. I'll come visit you this week. Clear some time at lunch one day." She leaned close again. "Make it a lo-o-ong lunch," she breathed. He rolled his eyes and inhaled.

I could tell him to order me a salad, she thought, and I bet he would faint.

The party continued for several hours. In one corner of the room, Forrester and a leggy, big-haired minor lobbyist from the Nuclear Power Association enveloped one another in smoldering stares until they slipped away together at the late hour—for Washington—of eleven. In another, Crane tossed back bourbons with Minority Leader Plotski, who told him there wasn't a political professional in America who didn't think saving the election for Ross wasn't the most brilliant bit of managing ever witnessed. "Thank you, Roman," Crane said, then grabbed the minority leader by the lapel. "Roman, you gotta promise you'll find more money for the Secret Service," he blubbered. "There's no way we can let Ross die." In a third corner, Lucinda finished charming the quintet from "The McLaughlin Group," then broke up a discussion between Brent and Wayne Newton, the gala's featured entertainer, about the pitfalls of maintaining a clay court in the Las Vegas area. She took him home and they made love—satisfactorily, they both felt—and fell asleep curled round one another, the way lovers sometimes do.

Meanwhile, in the fourth corner, President Roger Ross found

himself detained in long discussion with his newly appointed secretary of labor, who, he was pleased to see, came across exactly as his aides had predicted he would: dull-witted, but pleasant and capable of taking instructions. Ross then slowly departed, handshaking his way to the door, bidding one and all a good night as he slipped out through the kitchen and into his waiting limo.

Riding through the city, seeing the Capitol and the monuments and the mighty buildings of government illuminated, he felt a curious detachment, bordering on melancholy. This was his town now, really, his country; but it was as though he were watching a movie about somebody who looked like him and like whom he was expected to behave. The whole day had been built for him, he thought, by people who'd never thought to ask him whether he liked pomp and parades and parties. It was like one of those days you have when you're a kid, he thought, like your birthday or your graduation, when your parents invite all their friends and assume you'll like seeing a clown, when in fact clowns frighten you to death.

He got back to the White House and said good night to his guards and Secret Service agents and to his butler. He walked through what was now his bedroom and turned off what was now his light, and slid between cool sheets on what was now his bed, and waited for sleep to overwhelm him. As he slipped deep past drowsiness, there was something unfamiliar, a creak in a floorboard that was unexpected, a shadow across a window he did not know, and he bolted upright and called out. It hit him hard when he realized that what he'd said was *Lucinda,* and he turned fitfully for an hour or so before he drifted back into sleep.

Nine

It had become the favorite moment of his short and generally pleasant presidency, the opening minutes of his biweekly cabinet meetings. He would follow his secretary, Ms. Meara, down the corridor from the Oval Office to the Cabinet Room—light shining in, the bright young flunkies from Harvard and Yale who did all the scut work standing at attention as he passed, Ms. Meara's heels clack-clack-clacking across the floor, her hips swinging as efficiently as a metronome—him being unable not to notice, given that he noticed pretty much the first time they went to one of these things that Ms. Meara had herself a pretty nice little tush there—and then reaching the Cabinet Room and the doors swinging open; and then that delicious shuffling sound of chairs being disturbed, as all the cabinet officials, that great mix of solons, efficient administrators and, for the lesser department, not wholly incompetent party hacks, got up off their butts to pay him ritual homage.

God, it made him feel good, though he had to admit that in some ways it disturbed him feeling so much pleasure watching these nominally powerful and accomplished people, women and men who had been reverently profiled in national publications and who were listened to with great seriousness on the Sunday morning talk shows, suddenly lapse into obeisance in his presence. Sure, they'd get less slavish as they grew more relaxed, Ross realized; but now, four months into his administration, the level of suckbuttiness really hadn't fallen off any from the postelection period when he'd had all the contenders for cabinet jobs fly down to Hilton Head, where he and his transition team had headquartered, for interviews.

Oh, it had been lovely down there. The weather was perfect, Crane got some sun, Bibby got to play tennis ten hours a day, and Lucinda got a nice little bungalow overlooking the beach where he went every afternoon to indulge in his own particular brand of R and R. And every day for a couple hours, these big-shot foreign policy experts, economics experts, bank presidents, juiced-up Washington attorneys, governors and senators would parade in and talk to Ross, them uncomfortable in their big suits and stiff shoes, him in a sweater and Top-Siders, them kowtowing like crazy to get a job in the administration, him just soaking it all in. The best of them, the ones Ross could stomach, were the ones who just yessirred him to death, or maybe just went a little too far in offering him cigarettes and fixing coffee for him. The worst, the nervous ones who perspired and who, needless to say, didn't get the job, managed to bring out a subtly sadistic streak in the president-elect. One candidate, a portly economist from Harvard, was so obsequious that Ross found himself asking questions about the man's weight.

"Guess you don't get much exercise there at Harvard," Ross had prodded. "Guess there's a lot of stress eating." They'd spent the next fifteen minutes discussing the economist's failures maintaining the Ultra Slim-Fast program, and then it had been time to go. "You're so mean," Lucinda had said when he'd told her about it after lunch. "Somebody should smack your bottom. And I know who." Then they'd both enjoyed a good long giggle.

"Ladies and gentlemen, please be seated," Ross said to the cabinet, and just like that they were, leaving Ross a moment to look out with supreme pleasure across almost one hundred and sixty square feet of highly buffed, almost completely uncluttered oak conference table. Almost, because some of the cabinet officials liked to put their yellow legal pads or leather portfolios on the table in front of them, and Ross allowed that, even if it disturbed his edge-to-edge view. But that was all right, Ross thought, noticing with enormous satisfaction the utter absence of coffee creamers, pickles and Kentucky Fried Chicken bones. "Ms. Meara, please call on the departments for their reports."

One by one, each cabinet secretary rose to brief his counterparts about what he was doing. Ross hardly listened. If it was important, he'd heard it already from Crane. If it wasn't, well, he was only mildly curious at best. Well, he was more than mildly curious, really, being something of a government buff, but half the time none of them had anything to say except bad news. National reading scores, down. National employment figures, down. Farm foreclosures, up. What was he going to do about those things? Sure, sure, sure, sure, he'd give them all some more money, tell them to go fix things up and call him when they got better. Well, he couldn't say call him when things got better; he'd never hear from some of these bozos again. Call him when they had some new program to unveil.

Ross, Ross discovered, liked new programs. More precisely, he liked announcing new programs. Liked standing up with the TV cameras on; liked acknowledging Congress's help in some grandly generous way that both implicated them in case of failure and reaffirmed their supporting actor status; liked showing the public that he was concerned about their troubles. Which he was, even though he doubted he could do much about them. What could he do? What on earth could he do? Walk the streets at night and yell up to people to tell them to put on condoms, lock their doors, save their money, read to their kids more? Besides, he did a lot just by being presidential—looking concerned, looking optimistic, looking like he was in control.

And, after all, that was all he'd promised people he would do during the campaign, and anybody who forgot that could get a reminder just by remembering the campaign tag line that was on their commercials and bumper stickers and billboards: *Ross, Bibby, America.* That said it all, Ross thought, even better than the one he'd devised—even though *Ross, Bibby, More of the*

Same and Then Some would have been okay. It's just that *Ross, Bibby, America* said so much without getting bogged down in specifics. And wasn't that what the country really wanted, after all? To be happy, without all the complicated specifics? Of course it was. And that's why his poll numbers were so good.

"And that's why we need more aid for San Rico de Humidor, Mr. President," Secretary of State Friedman was saying.

"More aid?" Ross said, focusing quickly. "And you think that'll make the government happy?"

"I'm confident it will, yes, sir," the secretary said. "They tell me the guerrillas may be on the verge of nearing their last legs."

"Well, tell them fine, and we'll work out the specifics later this week." Okay, now he could tune back out.

The only thing that hadn't been all that wonderful about these first few months, he realized—apart from the nagging San Rico de Humidor business—was that he wasn't getting to spend enough time with Lucinda. It's not that he wasn't seeing her *any;* on the contrary, he was seeing her a lot, just never for very long. He had named her to head a committee to redecorate the White House, and in that capacity she frequently got to drop by a lot around lunchtime and pretend to show him paint chips and swatches of cloth, and they got to go off into different rooms by themselves, and everything was fine so long as he remembered to loudly harumph something about liking the striped one when they emerged. Still, as pleasant as these nooners were, he longed to spend more time in her company, and lately he'd been sending Bibby to make appearances on the West Coast so that he could spend a full night with his beloved.

"It is industry's position that the cost of retrofitting the plants with additional scrubbers will entail an additional expense of $11.73 per cubic ton of ore processed," Ross heard Interior Secretary Belknap droning, "an expense, however, which Congress has mandated." Ross started to try to figure out what ore the secretary might have been talking about when he heard the vice president cry "Aha!" from across the room.

"What have you got there, Mr. Vice President?" Ross called.

"My twenty-eighth in a row!" Bibby chirped cheerily. "It's a new personal best!"

Ross looked across the table and caught Crane's eye and offered him a salute. "That was an outstanding idea you had, Crane," Ross murmured. Ross remembered how bored Bibby used to get at cabinet meetings, and how he then would start to misbehave—talking out of turn, spilling his water, writing on the table—and how dubious Ross was when Crane brought in an electronic putting cup and a putter to occupy him during the meeting. "That's outstanding putting, Mr. Vice President!" Ross called. "I think that deserves a little applause. Ladies, gentlemen—" He stared down the table until the cabinet members joined him in a perfunctory round of applause. "Okay, thanks for that report," he said to Interior Secretary Belknap. "I'll review the rest of that material personally. Now, I have a final announcement before we adjourn. Several of us will be traveling this week. Mr. Secretary of State Friedman will be journeying to Saudi Arabia to discuss security arrangements, Mr. Defense Secretary Dupont will be in Vienna to discuss nuclear nonproliferation, and Madam Commerce Secretary Carrera will be leaving for Tokyo to discuss trade restrictions. I know that I speak for all of us when I say that the entire nation wishes you Godspeed."

Then he heard himself being called. "Mr. President!" he heard. "Oh, Mr. President!" It was Bibby. "Yes, Mr. Vice President?"

"I'm going to be on the road again myself," Bibby announced.

"Really?" Ross played along. "Where to?"

"I'm heading to Spokane—"

"Seattle," Ross heard Crane mutter.

"—to open a new tunnel—"

"Bridge," Crane said, rolling his eyes.

"They've asked me to be the first one to go over the side," Bibby grinned.

"To . . . go . . . from . . . side . . . to . . . side," Crane said, all but imploding.

"Well, Godspeed to you, too, Mr. Vice President. This meeting is adjourned." Now, fly, Roger Ross, fly to the arms of your darling!

"You know, sweetheart," Lucinda purred, stretching contentedly across his bed, her pink bottom upturned in such a perky way, "you're so smart, keeping Brent on the road the way you have. It's made him very happy."

"To hell with him," Ross said, "it's made me happy. It's made me *more* than happy—it's given me the only genuine pleasure I've had since I took this damn job. The economy is stalling, interest rates are about to go up, I've got nutty environmentalists coming out my ears, and, worst of all, the damn guerrillas in San Rico de Humidor don't seem to know when to quit. Friedman says I'm going to have to ask Congress for a lot more military aid."

"Troops, poopsie?"

"No," Ross shook his head. "No, God bless 'em, San Rico de Humidor might be the only trouble spot in the universe where the government thinks its own troops can do the fighting better than the American army. Which is admirable, of course, and a darn sight easier to sell to Congress. All they want is the usual equipment—guns, ammunition, medicine, vehicles, VCRs, televisions, that sort of thing."

"Televisions?" Lucinda asked. "Why do they need televisions?"

"Oh, I hate it when you can't figure something out and your little face gets all furrowed," Ross said, reaching over and pinching her cheek. "But it's not so hard to understand. I gather the troops from time to time need to unwind from the rigors of jungle fighting. So they go to their barracks, I guess, where they get cable. They watch their HBO and MTV and their Atlanta Braves baseball and movies on the VCRs and so forth. And then they feel renewed and no longer on the verge of succumbing to battle fatigue, and are ready to go out and fight the guerrillas. It seems a pretty reasonable amount of comfort for the risks they take. They're really on the front line of democracy's battle now. I admire them."

"And I admire you," Lucinda said.

"And I worship you," Ross replied.

"And I think you're cute," she rejoindered.

"And I think you're my little sex demon," he said, scrunching down next to her.

"And I think you're the presidential Engine of Love," she growled, stroking his chest.

"And you're Lucinda Bibby," he said.

"Lucinda Bibby?"

"But tight everywhere else," he sniggered, grabbing hold of her perky pink bottom, realizing as though for the first time that he liked the way she squealed.

A half hour later, he lay in bed, knowing he was keeping the National Security Council waiting, deciding he didn't care, choosing instead to stay and watch her dress. Watch her dress and listen to her talk. "You know," she said, leaning over, attaching a black silk stocking to her garter belt, her breasts still unfettered, "the only problem with the trips you send Brent on is that they're too short. Overnight to Topeka, overnight to Flagstaff—it's like Federal Express. He's never away long enough for us to relax and enjoy ourselves. Couldn't you send him someplace really far away?"

"Man, *I wish*," he said, shifting under the sheets. "You know it's hard to send him far away, because that means sending him out of the country, and that often means he has to go someplace important or sensitive, where he's likely to make a big fool of himself and embarrass the nation. And you know, I have to think of the good of the nation *some*times. I mean, it *is* my job to do that."

"I know," Lucinda said, with just the tiniest hint of a pout in her voice. "And you're doing it quite well. It's just—"

"Thank you very much," Ross said. "It's just what?"

"It's just that I want to be alone with you, darling. I never feel so alive as when we're together. I live for these moments, you know."

In all the years he and Lilith had been married, she'd never gotten quite so gushy, and even though it unnerved him a little, he now felt himself under the sway of the same irresistible power that he'd fallen under the night they'd met and she'd taken his hands and looked into his eyes and told him how strong he was. When she'd said that to him that night, he had felt that he could do anything—anything for her, anyway—and now, much to his surprise, he was feeling that way again. "I guess I could send him to Antarctica to look at the hole in the ozone," he suggested.

Lucinda puffed out her lower lip and furrowed her brow and thought for a moment. "I suppose," she eventually said, sighing deeply. "I don't think he'd really like that, though. The reason that he gets such pleasure from these trips is, first, he gets to play tennis in a new place, and second, he gets to meet people who think well of him. I don't think you can play tennis in Antarctica at this time of the year, and I don't think penguins would think of him one way or the other."

"Well, you know," Ross said, feeling a little exasperated, "we can't have everything our way. We are going to have to send somebody sort of important to go look at the ozone soon anyway." He was about to point out that it was just a teeny bit hypocritical to feel too badly for him, given that they were cuckolding him like crazy, but he thought better of it.

"How about this?" she said. "Send him to San Rico de Humidor."

Ross looked at her, waiting for her to crinkle up her face in that smile he had grown to love and to say "I'm teasing, silly." When she didn't seem to be doing that quickly enough, he felt obliged to nip that idea in the bud. "No-o-o-o," he said emphatically. "I'm afraid that's a maximum negatory."

But she was not easily dissuaded. "Why not?" she asked. "The Humiricans would be thrilled. President Alcozar would think it was an enormous compliment and an act of great friendship, no matter what Brent eventually said or did. Frankly, I think it would be a stroke of diplomatic genius."

Ross seemed a little unsure of his footing. He hadn't really had to argue about anything with anybody for years. "Yeah, but it's a dangerous place," he finally said uncomfortably, unhappy that he seemed to be yielding ground but not sure whether he shouldn't be overjoyed that she had hit on a solution.

"He'd be perfectly safe," she said, pulling on her blouse. "He'd be surrounded by troops from the moment he got there."

Ross felt confused, a feeling that generally left him cranky and depressed. He shook his head for a long time, wondering whether this woman meant what she said, or whether she was just testing him. And if she was testing him, wondering if it looked like he was going to pass. Finally, he just wagged his finger at her and chuckled. "Heh heh, you really had me going for a moment there," he said. "What a joker you are. Send Brent Bibby to San Rico de Humidor—heh, heh, heh, heh. Oh darling, I love you so. You make me laugh. Now, when will I see you again?"

"Tomorrow night, except I'll be dressed the whole time." She realized from his blank expression that he didn't know what she was talking about. "The state dinner for Prime Minister Tonga? Somehow the Bibbys got invited. Can I guess where I'll be sitting?"

"Wear something pretty," he smiled.

As though she needed his instruction on that subject. "Don't worry, you won't start thinking of me as daughterly any time soon."

"Good," he said. "Geez, it looks like I'll have a full day of Brent, then. We're having our regular Thursday lunch tomorrow, too."

She slipped on her jacket and bent over to give him a kiss. "Think about this San Rico idea," she said softly. Then she reached over and patted his crotch. "Just once I'd like to get as much as I'd like," she purred.

Ten

As the limo swung off West Executive Drive and onto the drive-way to the White House, Bibby leaned forward and looked over the front seat through the windshield. He shot a big thumbs-up to the marine guard who saluted as the massive gates swung open and the car pulled through, and then he watched the little blue flags with the vice-presidential seal on them flutter as the car whipped up the driveway to the West Wing, where he'd get out for his lunch with President Ross. These lunches were, in his opinion, the best moments of what had generally been a pretty damn outstanding, stupendous, magnificent vice presidency. If you asked him, anyway. Everything about it was great. He liked chairing the Senate, sitting up on the dais with the heavy wooden gavel, recognizing his former colleagues, even if it was pretty easy to recognize them since it was usually only him and the doorkeeper and a clerk and whichever senator wanted to get his mug on C-Span that day in the chamber. Sometimes, of course, it got busy and he had to bang the gavel and say "Order, order," and usually they listened, and he thought that was just the bitch-ingest thing. And he liked the traveling, and the speaking, and, well, just being part of the White House team. There'd been no team in the Senate when he was there. Sure, guys would say hi to you and the Minority Whip would come around a lot to tell you how to vote, but there was no sense that he was ever *on board*. Like, nobody ever recognized *him* when he was a senator.

In eight years, he'd never gotten to give a speech. Nobody'd ever called on him.

But now that he was vice president, the guys in the White House treated him a lot differently, like he was really one of the guys. The other week, the secretary of transportation was talking about highway reconstruction, and Bibby brought up that he'd been on a stretch of I-80 outside of Denver a few days previously and there were a lot of potholes. The president told everybody to make a note of what the vice president had said, and he saw that a lot of them wrote it down. Bibby assumed they wanted to make sure they'd have it later to use for hearings and reports and speeches and stuff.

But what really impressed him, of course, was just hearing the president say "Make a note of that." And that's why these Thursday lunches were so great, because it was just him and the president, one on one, guy to guy, just munching on their tuna sandwiches, talking about the state of the world. That was the downside, of course. Bibby didn't really care for tuna fish all that much, certainly not enough to have it week after week. But that was what the president ate—*apparently every day,* he'd heard— and even though the president said Bibby could have whatever kind of sandwich he wanted, or even a burger, Bibby didn't want to give anybody grounds to think he wasn't loyal to the president in every way and cause rumors to start flying that he was some kind of loose-cannon malcontent. Besides, the tuna had its advantages, sort of. He could be out visiting places, making a speech or just stopping off somewhere at some diner en route to some event, and he would tell people he was sitting with, or his waitress, how much their president liked his tuna; and he saw that it made a kind of difference, that people felt a stronger bond to their president, knowing that he ate something they ate. Bibby, of course, liked a BLT with a slice of Muenster and a pickle, but when he was at the White House, he kept that to himself. When he was on the road he sometimes mentioned it, though, just in case anybody wanted to bond with him.

All of which was what was going to make it tough for him to bring up what was bothering him. But he sort of had to, probably.

"Good afternoon, Señor Vice President."

"Good afternoon, Manolito," Bibby said to the president's butler. "How's the tuna today?"

"Muy bien," Manolito replied with a smile. "Chicken of the Sea. I'll have it out in just a minute. I think the president is just about ready."

Which he was. In a moment the president appeared and in short order greeted Bibby, sat down, spread out his napkin, and began getting a grip on the sandwich Manolito had just briskly whipped into the room.

"So, Brent, how are things?" Ross asked, already chewing.

"They're just great, Mr. President, thank you for asking. Just great. So great, I mean, I don't know if I've made it clear to you just how happy and thankful I am that you selected me. I mean, I love everything about it. I mean, I know I shouldn't really say this, but it makes me think it was the job I was born to have. I mean, you're great to work with, the guys are great to work with, I love the traveling. I had just the greatest trip on Friday, got to go out to Butte—did you know that's how you said that? That it's not like 'But-ty'? I found that interesting. Where was I? Oh, in Butte, at the opening of this great new mall. Twenty-three stores, including a Kmart, and I was the main attraction. Well, me and this big heifer. Big brown eyes. I think she weighed thirteen hundred pounds. But I got this warm reception. I think it was one of the highlights of my life. And Lucinda"—and here the president stopped chewing like a machine and listened—"Lucinda just loves it here. She's so happy you appointed her to that redecoration committee. And so humble about it, too. She told me she's not even sure why you picked her. I told her that you probably realized she was smart and that you wanted her to feel comfortable here."

"So true, my boy," Ross said, nodding. "I will tell you frankly that one of my deepest regrets is that the rigors of my job keep me from getting to know your wife better than I have. She strikes me as someone who seems to have a lot of good qualities."

"*Exactly!* God, you're a marvel. You're just so tuned in to people."

"Well, thank you, Brent," Ross said, swallowing the last of his sandwich. "Don't like the tuna today? You've hardly touched it. Well, take your time. Manolito! I'm just going to have a little cup of coffee and then I'm going to have to get back to work." He shrugged elaborately. "Those Balkans! But what can you do?"

You'd better say something, Brent, Bibby told himself. If you don't say something, you're going to regret it all week, and then you'll just get yourself all nerved up thinking about doing it next week. Better to just get it over with. Just take a deep breath.

"Um—Mr. President," he blurted, "I hate to bring this up. You know, I love going on these trips, and—*God!* I'd hate it if you didn't let me go anymore, so maybe I shouldn't say anything."

"Manolito! Where's that coffee? Now, now, come on, Mr. Vice President, spit it out."

"Well, I don't want to make too big a deal about this—"

"Spit it out!"

"Sometimes when I'm on these trips people ask me questions that I don't know the answers to, and it's a little embarrassing."

My God, Ross thought, he really is troubled by this. Oh, take some pity, what could it hurt. "Now, now, don't get down on yourself, son. Everybody can't know everything. What are these, some sort of science questions or something?"

"No," Bibby said, his face screwed up in a confused little scowl, "they're always about policy." He hung his head. "Stuff I probably should know."

"Well, you know, Brent, we let you come to all the Cabinet meetings, and we send you a copy of all the reports. And I made sure that Crane bought you your own subscription to the *Post*. And we gave you Forrester's home phone number so that he can explain things to you."

"I know, but it's all so technical. Treasury Secretary Banks gets up at those meetings and starts in with this balance-of-payments stuff, and trade deficits, and I don't know what else, and then he sits back down and never once just flat out says, 'Things are fine' or 'Things stink,' or anything that a guy could understand."

It was all Ross could do to stifle a laugh. "No, I don't think *stink* is part of Banks's vocabulary. So what would like me to do?"

"Well, I don't want to impose. I know you're busy. But maybe I could just ask you some questions, and you could answer them in a way I'd understand, and then I'd have something to say if somebody asked me a question."

"Oh," Ross said, looking at his watch. "What the hell, I suppose I could try. For a few minutes. But then I have to go."

"The Balkans, right?"

"Right," the president said, smiling.

"Okay, I'll try to hurry. Here's the first one: How's the economy?"

Ross nodded soberly, mulling over where to start and how much information the lad could hold. "Well," he began, "given that the budget deficit continues and that the recession has yet to run its course . . ." He looked up, and saw that Brent's face was already contorted in distress. Oh, why beat your head against a wall, he thought. "The economy is fine," he said confidently. "Just fine. That isn't to say some sectors won't have some rough sailing, but that's always the case. Basically, things are fine."

"Really?" Bibby said. "That's great. I'm so glad to hear that. Okay, next, I get a lot of questions about the environment. So tell me: How's the environment?"

This time, Ross wasted no time. "It's fine," he said.

"Really? That's great. But didn't I hear on the radio—no, I remember, I saw it on the MTV news—there's some bill you're thinking about vetoing?"

"Yes, the Clean Seas Act," Ross said. "But do you know why?

Because it's a bad bill, Brent, a bad, bad bill. But we're working on the problem, and we'll come up with a solution that everybody can live with, and everything will be fine."

"Really?" Ross thought Bibby was about to burst. "That's just so great, Mr. President. Now, last but not least, I keep hearing you guys talking at the cabinet meetings about San Rico de Humidor. So tell me: How are things in San Rico de Humidor?"

"In fact, Brent, they're fine."

"Really? So the rebels are about to be defeated?"

"No," Ross said, shaking his head.

"No?"

"No. Look, Brent, I think we can speak man to man here, leader to leader. We're never going to defeat the rebels."

"We're not?" Bibby asked, shocked. "But you say we say we are."

"I know I do, but we're not. Come on, we have to be a little grown up about this," Ross said, doubting even as the words left his lips that this suggestion was at all possible. "We tell the Congress that and we tell the people that because, well, because they're just not as sophisticated as you and I. But this is going to be a long struggle. As Ambassador Oakley has informed us, the rebels are intransigent and unyielding. As long as they continue to receive weapons from terrorists abroad, we will probably be unable to defeat them without a sizable commitment of troops. And I don't think anybody wants that. Do they?"

"No-o-o," Bibby shook his head.

"But although we may never defeat them, we've succeeded in confining them to the hills—except for occasional bloody forays into the capital—which means that most of the time, most of the good, freedom-loving Humirican people can go about their business in peace. So—"

"So?" Bibby interrupted.

"So things are fine."

"Fine," Bibby repeated in a soft and distant voice. Then, to Ross's complete astonishment, tears began forming in the vice president's eyes. "I'm sorry, Mr. President, I can't help myself,"

Bibby said, accepting Ross's proffered handkerchief. "I'm just overwhelmed to be in the presence of such a great leader. And to be associated with you so closely! How lucky can a guy get? I bet there's never been a moment in American history when things have been as . . . *fine* . . . as they are today. You are undoubtedly our finest president ever."

Bibby wept openly for a while longer. Ross was patient for a few minutes, but then couldn't put up with it anymore. "Manolito!" he called. "Would you clear the dishes, please? Want some ice cream, Mr. Vice President?"

Eleven

"Good night!" Ross was calling to his departing guests. "Good night!" Not a bad little evening, he thought. Chef got the chateaubriand right for a change, the wine was tasty, Prime Minister Tomba held up his end of the conversation—was he trying to get Celestine van den Hurdle's number? He had to remember to ask Lucinda about that. And did she give it to him? Maybe; they seemed to be making a lot of eye contact while Garth Brooks was singing. And he was pretty good, wasn't he? In fact, all the entertainers were: Garth Brooks, Yo Yo Ma, Whitney Houston, Bob Goulet. Well, Whitney Houston really wasn't his taste, but the youngsters probably went for her, and besides, you couldn't go around having the Whippenpoofs at every state dinner. Or so Lucinda said. And Lucinda! That was the best part. Got to sit next to her for three whole hours, look into her eyes, make small talk, watch the dainty way she cut up her meat. Didn't get to get up close and personal with her, though. Yet.

"Good night, Lloyd!" Ross called to the last of them. "Drive safely! Whoops! Ha, ha! Maybe you should let Verlene do the driving. No, let Verlene have the keys. I'm serious. Let Verlene—that's better. Ha ha—and don't go tyin' up my Appropriations Bill there in committee, you old cowpuncher! Ha ha ha!"

Ross signaled to Manolito to shut the door on the south portico, then turned around and was happy to see that everyone was gone except the always welcome Lucinda, along with her not entirely welcome husband. Still, after facing a roomful of dignitaries and VIPs and wealthy contributors for an entire evening, it was fairly painless for Ross to see at least one person he did not have to strive excessively to impress. "Geez, I thought he would never leave," he felt free to gripe. "Reagan this and Reagan that. Even after I told him about having some bunch of Tadzhikistanians coming in early and wanting to be at my best. Anybody for a nightcap? Boy, did you see Prime Minister Tomba putting it away? Guy must have a hollow leg."

"I'm sorry, Mr. President," Lucinda said, turning first to Ross, then to Bibby, "Brent, I don't know I really feel all that much like a nightcap this evening. But there is one thing: Last week I did manage to buy the most unique antique bureau with two terribly interesting handles, and I know the president has been interested in an item like this for his bedroom, and he was such a well-behaved man tonight that I thought I would take him upstairs and show him the knobs on my chest. Will you be all right while we do that, darling? It won't take a minute and I know these things just bore you."

"No," Bibby said, "Go ahead, I'll be fine. Maybe I'll go down to the Press Room and see what's on TV." As he headed down the hall, he heard the two of them giggling upstairs, and he was glad that they seemed so happy.

He found a basketball game on ESPN and had just settled back and was starting to get into it when he was startled to hear that he wasn't alone. "Good evening, Mr. Vice President," Celestine van den Hurdle said politely.

"Ms. van den Hurdle. What a surprise. I mean—hello. What are you doing here? I mean, I know you work here and all, but I thought I saw you at dinner. And I guess I did. Your dress is very nice." Why don't you shut up? he asked himself. He knew why. He was nervous around important people; he was nervous around the media; he was nervous around women. Therefore: Big Chief Flapping Gums. So: Just slow down. "I'm sorry I didn't get a chance to say hello."

"So say hello now," she said, plopping herself down on the arm of his chair. "Let's talk for a bit. I have a few questions I've been dying to ask you for *weeks.*"

"Now, you know my policy is to have Mr. Forrester handle all my questions," Brent said firmly.

"Yes," the veteran reporter replied, "but he's not here now. What are you worried about? Don't worry, I won't quote you. I swear to you that this is strictly deep background. Tell me: How's the economy?"

Don't tell her, Brent thought, don't tell her, don't tell her, don't tell her. You'll just get in trouble.

"Mr. Vice President?"

But you know the answer, Brent. You *know* the answer. Hey, bud, this interview business probably isn't as hard when you know what to say. So just slow down and tell her. *Go ahead.* "Well, Ms. van den Hurdle, the economy's fine."

"It is?" she said with decided skepticism. Brent nodded with as much confidence as he could muster. "Deficit?" she prodded. "Balance of payments?"

Don't panic, bud, just stick to the program.

"They're fine," he said.

"So—no capital gains tax increase this year?"

"We-e-ell," Brent said slowly, not only not knowing the answer to the question, but also not knowing exactly what the capital gains tax was. *Careful.* "You know, Celestine"—try to be confident—"I'm not saying every sector will have smooth sailing . . ."

"But the GNP?" she offered.

"Fine."

"Well, that's a scoop," she said. "Now about the environment . . ."

"That's easy," Brent said. "Things are fine."

"Now wait a minute," she shot back. "What about the hole in the ozone?"

"Well, you can believe what you want, but I'm telling you, it's fine." Hey, this is okay!

"You guys must have some secret plans to fix things."

"Is that what your sources are telling you, Ms. van den Hurdle?" he said, feeling himself on sort of a hot streak. "Well, let's just say that it wouldn't surprise me a bit if there were things going on that I didn't know anything about."

She laughed that snorty little laugh that viewers of her pre–Oscarcast specials so loved. "That's a good one, Mr. Vice President. I didn't know you were such a wit. Now tell me: Is the president really going to veto the Clean Seas Act?"

"It's a bad bill," he said solemnly.

"But you have an alternative?"

"I have no doubt that we have our own way of thinking about that problem, and I have to believe that things will be . . . fine."

"Interesting. Okay—San Rico de Humidor."

"Things are fine," he said quickly.

"Will we see a breakthrough soon?"

"All I can say is that things are fine."

"Will we send troops?"

Geez, this is getting a little close. "All I can say is that things are fine."

"Will the guerrillas surrender?"

Let's try to get this over. "Celestine," he said, offering her his best smile, "I said things were fine. You'll notice I didn't say, fine and dandy."

Van den Hurdle nodded sagely. "I get it," she said with a small smile.

"And I especially didn't say finer than Carolina in the morning."

"No," she said, smiling broadly. "No, I see that you didn't. Mr. Vice President, this certainly has been enlightening. I hope we can do it again soon."

A moment later, she departed. Brent wondered if Lucinda's furniture show had ended. He flicked off the TV and wandered back to the living quarters, whistling cheerfully as he went.

In their comfy bedroom in their official residence at what was the old Naval Observatory Building, the Bibbys adhered to their morning ritual: She had some sliced fruit and coffee and read the *Post;* he trudged along on his Stairmaster and drank his Gatorade. On the television in the corner of the room, all but unobserved, "Good Morning, America" played. In the living room of his small apartment in Anacostia, Forrester jumped rope while at the center of his modular wall unit, on a big, twenty-five-inch Panasonic screen "Good Morning, America" played. In the dining area of his efficiency apartment in Dupont Circle, Crane sat at his Formica dinette set with the *Times* and the *Post* and the *Journal* and a bucket of doughnut holes and a big Washington Redskins mug of black coffee, while on a Sony portable perched on the corner of the table "Good Morning, America" played. And at the White House, the president sat with the Executive News Summary some young Ph.D. from the Kennedy School of Government had had to wake up and prepare for him at 6:00 A.M., plus a foreign news summary some overcredentialed future under secretary of state in Foggy Bottom had had to similarly collate and staple together, and ate his bowl of All Bran and his banana and drank his cup of black decaf while across the room, on a state-of-the-art monitor encased in the built-in bookshelves, "Good Morning, America" played. None of these people was particularly watching the program, at least not until it was time for the political commentary segment.

"And now," the host said, "here's our chief political correspondent, Celestine van den Hurdle." And all across Washington, if nowhere else, viewers elevated their attention. They started half-watching.

"Thanks, Joan," said van den Hurdle. "Well, it doesn't happen often that a government in Washington—particularly one facing challenges as enormous as this one does—is so shortsighted as to overlook one of its principal assets. And yet, that is precisely the case with the current administration of President Roger Ross."

"Ah, nerts to you," Ross said, not bothering to look up.

"Though few people realize it," van den Hurdle continued, "the Ross administration has within it one of the more able young leaders in Washington, a man who could be one of the most effective defenders of the president's policies, and yet who has, strangely, been kept out of the public eye."

"Yeah, who?" Ross said to the TV.

"I'm speaking, of course, of Vice President Brent Bibby," said van den Hurdle, who, safely ensconced in her studio, naturally could not hear the clatter of feet slipping on Stairmasters, or the crash of tumbling coffee cups, or the dull thud of doughnut holes bouncing on linoleum, or any of the other noises caused by the many mishaps occurring all over Washington. "As we all know, Bibby received ample abuse when he was selected by candidate Ross to be his running mate. Unknown, inexperienced, untutored, naive—all of these seemed appropriate adjectives for the fresh-faced senator from Bibbyville. Yet, after he and I held a wide-ranging discussion recently, I'm convinced that, like many of you, I underestimated the vice president."

"She is speaking about Señor Vice President Bibby?" said Manolito, peering over Ross's shoulder, fearing that his English had suffered a setback.

"Crafty, subtle, a man of few words, Brent Bibby managed to illuminate the current state of affairs with insight and discretion," van den Hurdle emoted. "Indeed, Bibby virtually encapsulated events with one word: *fine.* Indeed, as the term New Deal became synonymous with FDR, The New Frontier with JFK, and The Great Society with LBJ, the ambitions of the Ross administration might just be summed up in one phrase: The Fine Society."

At the former Naval Observatory Building, Lucinda set aside her sliced fruit, and rose to console her husband, who sat on the bottom step of his Stairmaster with his head in his hands. "They're going to yell at me," he moaned as she patted his shoulder. "I had no idea that this was going to happen, and now they're going to be mad."

And Ross was mad, though just in a general way, mad at van den Hurdle for being so cunning, mad at Bibby for being such a cluck. But he was less consumed by anger than determination.

He had a plan. He picked up the phone and punched in seven familiar digits. "Did ya see it?" he asked.

"Boy, did I!" Crane replied. "I'm just flabbergasted. Do you think Horace Bibby paid her to say that?"

"I kind of doubt it," Ross said. "She's paid about two and a half mil by the network and still gets to pontificate about her journalistic integrity. Why blow that by taking a dumb bribe? I was wondering if she was back on the sauce."

"She didn't touch a drop last night. It's more likely she was having an acid flashback from some love-in in Golden Gate Park. She hasn't goofed like this since she picked Dukakis."

"What an embarrassment. Hey, listen, Crane," Ross said, a serious tone suddenly in his voice, "I'm wondering—isn't there some way we can use this rave review of Bibby?"

"Sure—comic relief. We'll probably get a good chuckle out of it for many years to come."

"I'm not kidding, Crane. If Bibby can fool van den Hurdle, maybe he's gotten good enough to fool some other people as well."

"You think everybody is as prone to misjudgment as Celestine? I think you're looking for miracles."

"Oh, Crane," Ross said, mustering great sadness in his voice. "Crane, Crane, Crane, Crane, Crane. We must be in deep trouble if I have more imagination than you. You know what I'm thinking? Let's send him to San Rico de Humidor. It's really perfect. The Humiricans will like him 'cause he's handsome and has a good title, and we can blame anything he says wrong on the interpreter, and I'm sure whatever happens they'll view the visit as a further sign of our commitment to the spirit of democracy within that tiny, courageous nation."

"I think it's a nutty idea," Crane said. "What about the guerrillas?"

"Fine," Ross said abruptly. "You keep thinking the glass is half empty when I think it's half full. Maybe old Brent can surprise us."

Recognizing that the snippity tone in Ross's voice meant discussion had gone on long enough, Crane caved in. Half the things the president thought of never got done anyway, he reminded himself. "Mr. President," Crane said, making sure there was a modicum of pique in his voice as well, "apparently your mind is made up. I'll see to the arrangements." They hung up and Crane absentmindedly picked a doughnut hole off the kitchen floor and began nibbling on it. Maybe old Brent can surprise us, he mused. Right. And maybe God didn't make no little green apples, and maybe it don't rain in Indianapolis in the summertime.

The call from Ms. Meara summoning Brent to a special meeting at the White House was not unexpected, but the timing was. It took only twenty minutes after Celestine van den Hurdle's sign-off for Ms. Meara to phone him, Bibby recalled, as the heavy gates outside the White House swung open and the car pulled through. As he watched the little blue flags with the vice-presidential seal flutter while the car whipped up the driveway, he concluded that this was undoubtedly the worst moment of a vice presidency that seemed on the verge of turning to shit.

"Good morning, Mr. Vice President," Ms. Meara said pleasantly. "Please go right in. President Ross is expecting you."

Bibby, worried sick, slipped into the Oval Office.

"Good morning, Mr. President," he murmured, half-hoping Ross wouldn't hear.

"Well, go-o-od morning to you!" Bibby was startled by Ross's effusiveness. "Here, m'boy, have a seat. That was some mention Celestine van den Hurdle gave you this morning."

There, out of the bag. "Honest, Mr. President, I didn't know she was going to do that," he babbled. "I always try to do what Mr. Crane tells me, so I never, ever speak to the press. But she sort of sneaked up on me, and I just . . . just . . . ."

"Now, now, now, don't be upset," Ross said, coming around the desk to pat Bibby on the shoulder. "I'm sure she gave you no choice. It's what we keep telling you: Keep in mind that reporters are treacherous, bloodthirsty, merciless vermin. The ones that aren't stupid and lazy, anyway. But the thing is, I think just maybe Ms. van den Hurdle had a point."

"You do?" Brent asked.

"I do indeed," Ross said, nodding, a mysterious, pleased-with-himself expression on his face.

"A point about what?" Brent asked.

"Why, about *you,* sir. Maybe we have been underestimating you."

Brent could not quite believe what Ross was saying.

"No-o-o," he said, more out of politeness than anything else. "Well, maybe just a little bit. I thought volunteering me to work at the St. Anthony of Padua parish carnival in Baltimore was a little . . . you know . . . below my capabilities."

"Oh, perhaps," Ross quickly agreed. "But you met a lot of nice people, didn't you?"

"Yes," Brent nodded.

"And we made sure you weren't stuck just anywhere, didn't we? You got to work the stand with the goldfish bowls and Ping-Pong balls, if memory serves me correctly."

"Right," Brent nodded.

"And you liked the fish, didn't you?"

"Yes."

"Got to keep one, right?"

"Yes. I named him Tony. Like after the saint?"

"Very cute. You see, son? We try to look out for you."

"I know you do."

"Good. Which is why we've lined up something very special for you for your next assignment. We think this will make you very happy."

"Another bridge opening?" Brent asked, bobbing up and down in his chair. "I liked that."

"No, even better. Much more special. We're going to send you on a state mission to San Rico de Humidor. You'll meet with President Alcozar and his cabinet, discuss aid, and generally show our support for their struggle for freedom and democracy."

Ross expected Bibby to literally jump for joy, but instead he saw the vice president's face collapse into anxiety. "What's the matter, son?" Ross asked, trying to project an air of serenity.

"It sounds hard."

"It's not hard."

"Suppose I screw up?"

"Don't worry, you won't screw up. Everything will be arranged for you. Negotiators will work out the details of any agreements, a speechwriter will prepare everything you have to say, we'll make sure you have a lot of free time—"

"Do I have to make my own flight arrangements?" Bibby asked.

"No," Ross said, "not this time, and probably never again. Aren't going to have our vice president getting lost in the Denver airport anymore, okay? Nosiree, Bob. We'll take care of everything. And—how's about this?"

"What?"

"How's about we give you something to give to them? We'll make the presentation of your gift the centerpiece of the trip."

Bibby pondered this for a moment. "What will we give them?"

Oh, for heaven's sakes, Ross thought. "I don't know," he said a little testily. "Secretary Friedman already gave them some rocket launchers when he went down. Why don't we just give them a check this time, and let them buy something they really want for themselves?" He was dismayed to see Bibby making a face that looked like a bad odor had entered the room. "What's the matter with that idea?"

"Well," Brent said, "isn't a check kind of impersonal?"

Oh, why argue? Why bother to explain? What difference did it make? "You know, Mr. Vice President, you're right. Let's give them a jet fighter."

"Yeah!" Bibby said, his eyes lighting up.

"Okay," Ross said, "that's what we'll do. I'll make a note." He went back around behind his desk. "Give VP Bibby an F-111 Tomcat for San Rico de Humidor," he said to himself as he scribbled on a Post-It note. "Wonderful. Now go home and start packing," he said, starting to usher Bibby out. "Leave all the arrangements to us. You'll fly out tomorrow, and you'll be gone for a week. Go see Crane and see if you need any inoculations or anything. Any other questions, ask him. Thanks for coming by and have a good trip."

He shut the door behind Bibby and leaned against it, allowing a big sigh to escape. An instant later, he perked up and, nearly prancing, bobbed back behind his desk and picked up the phone. "Darling," he said, "it's me. Good news. I've arranged for us to have a whole week together. And pretty much just the way you suggested."

Twelve

As Air Force Two began it's descent, Bibby gazed out the window. The plane grew closer and closer to the ground, and the scenery seemed to zoom past with amazing speed, to the point where it seemed to consist of nothing but a mass of jungle, densely packed about fifty yards beyond the landing strip, stretching out for miles in front of the purple Santa Euphoria Mountains, lying serenely under a bright, crystal-blue sky. Then there was the bump on the tarmac and the whine of the engines decelerating and the pull of the brakes taking hold. And then the pilot, an air force colonel, came on the intercom. "Mr. Vice President, ladies and gentlemen, we have arrived in San Rico de Humidor. Please remain in your seats until I taxi this baby up to the reviewing stand so that the media can get your picture as you get off. On behalf of the people of the United States, the crew and myself wish you success in all your endeavors."

"Excited, Mr. Vice President?" Forrester asked.

"Well, you know, Forrester, I think I am," Bibby replied. "I thought about it all night, didn't really get that much sleep. This is my first trip out of the country as vice president, and I'd really like everyone to be proud of me." He turned his head away for a moment, wondering if he would end up being embarrassed by what he was thinking. *Ah, the hell with it.* "The thing is, Forrester, I don't think the president really expects things to improve down here so noticeably. And I sort of think that's a shame. I guess what I'm trying to say is that one day there's going to be peace here, and I guess I'd like folks to say I helped."

"Well, I hope they will, sir," Forrester said. "That's a very admirable sentiment. Now, do you need any help with your seat belt this time, sir?"

"No, I think I figured it out, thanks." The navigator had come back and opened the door to the bulkhead. Outside, Bibby could see attendants wheeling steps into place.

"Time to go, sir," Forrester said.

Emerging from the airplane and surveying the welcoming party below: the flags, the band, the podium, the soldiers, the—well, they looked like beauty queens—and all the other dignitaries, Bibby felt another wave of excitement. But he couldn't help thinking the whole display looked a little smaller than these things seemed on television. Still, it was a nice welcome, he thought, as he descended the stairs, and the bitchingest, most unbelievable part was that it was all for *him.*

"Sir, let me present to you our man in San Rico de Humidor," Forrester said, "Ambassador Charles Oakley."

A tall, ruddy man with frizzy orange hair stretched over a mostly bald pate stepped forward and shook Bibby's hand. "How do you do, sir?" he said. "Welcome to San Rico de Humidor. I hope you had a pleasant journey. Please allow me to introduce His Excellency, El Presidente de San Rico de Humidor, Julio Alcozar."

Bibby had seen Alcozar often enough on television, but in life the president seemed shorter and plumper than he did on the news. He must be about my age, Bibby thought. Maybe just a little older, a little wrinklier, baggier under the eyes, probably should shave that stupid bushy mustache. "How do you do, Mr. Vice President," Alcozar said, pumping Bibby's hand. "We are pleased and honored that you have come to our land. Please, I will now offer my official greeting and welcome." He stepped to the podium, tapped his finger on the microphone—"testing, testing"—turned to the two news cameramen stationed to the left of the speaker's area—"You guys ready? Yeah?"—and began his formal remarks.

"Mr. Vice President Bibby," he said, "welcome to our country. Your visit is being celebrated as a glorious moment in the history of our nation. Today, we have given our poor, barefoot, nearly illiterate children the day off from school in order to celebrate the arrival of The Lion of Democracy, as you are commonly known here. Additionally, as you will soon see, many of the impoverished, chronically unemployed workers of San Rico de Humidor have been roused from their festering idleness in order to line the route of your motorcade. And tonight, most of our people will huddle around a small candle stub in their huts—poor, dilapidated huts that have neither electricity nor running water—and will compose songs expressing their joy over the momentous visit of the vice president who is helping them to rescue themselves from life under totalitarian repression. We thank you for coming, we welcome you here, we know we can count on your friendship. Viva Los Estados Unidos!" he said. "Viva Bibby!"

The gathered dignitaries and officials broke into applause, and the photographers dashed forward to snap more pictures of Bibby and Alcozar shaking hands, and everyone seemed quite pleased. Then it was Brent's turn.

He stepped to the podium and removed his notes from the breast pocket of his suit jacket. A small breeze picked up and tousled his hair, but it felt good; and in the sun, with the band there and all the shiny brass on the officers' uniforms, and him surprising everyone, including himself, by suddenly enjoying everyone's confidence that he could make a difference in international relations, he just felt terrific.

"Your Excellency," he said, "I am overwhelmed by your greeting. After such a welcome, I am certain that the eagle of the United States and the giant poisonous lizard of San Rico de Humidor will always be friends."

He turned to smile at Alcozar, and he felt the wind pick up

again, and he heard the light *flap, flap, flap* of something being caught in the breeze; and when he turned back, he saw nothing on the podium; and out of the corner of his eye he saw some Secret Service agents and a few Humirican soldiers madly chasing his notes down the runway.

"Do you need them, Mr. Vice President?" Alcozar murmured under his breath. And Bibby was about to say "Could we break?" when Alcozar, not pausing for a breath, asked, "Or do you remember what you wrote?" And not wishing, on his first trip out of the country as vice president, to insult his host by revealing that he himself had not even glanced over the material, let alone written it, he just smiled and said, "Of course," and winged it.

"Yes, the United States and San Rico de Humidor will, in fact, always be friends. We'll be friends through thick. And we'll be friends through thin. And you may ask me, why? Mr. Vice President, why will the United States and San Rico de Humidor always be friends? And my answer to you, friends—and I mean that, I think of you all as my friends—is that friendship . . . friendship . . . is the perfect endship. And when other friendships have been forgot, ours will still be hot."

Can I stop now? Brent wondered, sneaking a glance over his shoulder at the dignitaries. Alcozar just smiled at him. Forrester was staring at his goddamned shoes. All right, then, *more . . .*

"And so I say to you, Your Excellency, I say: Ain't it good to know that you've got a friend when terroristic guerrillas can be so cold? They'll hurt you, and desert you, and take your soul if you let them. Ah, but don't you let them."

Bibby could not quite believe it when those assembled broke into what certainly seemed like genuine applause. Well, let's try . . . *more!*

"No, Your Excellency, don't you let them. For we in the United States have come to understand that we must think of our fellow man, lend him a helping hand and put a little love in our hearts. And the world will be a better place for you and me. Just wait and see. For we are the world. We are the children. It's true we make a brighter day, just me and you. Thank you very much."

Huge cheering erupted, and like the bowling ball he resembled, the short, dumpy Alcozar rushed to the podium and embraced his visitor. "Gracias, Mr. Vice President," he said, hugging Bibby around the shoulders. "The poor, beleaguered people of my land will be more than happy to receive a commitment like that."

Well, Bibby thought, that went well.

Thirteen

"Now remember, sir," Forrester was saying with some urgency as they headed from the sleeping quarters they had been assigned in the presidential palace down to the conference area below, "this is just our first meeting this visit, just a feeling-out process, you don't really have to say anything, the under secretary for Latin American affairs is handling the real negotiations. But you can say stuff, it would be okay, we'd just have to be ready to clarify anything you happened to say that wasn't altogether in sync."

"In sync with what?"

"With anything. You know, previously stated positions, long-standing policies, treaties that may be in effect, international law—anything. The point is, just relax and be yourself. Up to a point, that is. Be careful. Ultimately, just try to be pleasant."

"So we're here just to be . . . ?"

"That's right, sir, just to be pals, just to show we care, just to make sure that they think we understand them. By the way, sir, you were brilliant this morning." Yeah, Forrester thought, put him on "Name That Tune."

Bibby took his seat at the big, long conference table across from President Alcozar. He had Forrester on his right, which made him feel comfortable, and he had Ambassador Oakley on his left, which made him feel nervous, since he didn't know Oakley and since in the car after the welcoming ceremony Oakley revealed that he had sort of an unusual background. "Gee, I'm embarrassed to say this, Ambassador Oakley, but I can't remember the occasion when we met," Brent said pleasantly enough. "Which is strange, because I thought I got to meet most of the big donors to the Ross–Bibby ticket at the Inauguration." And Oakley said he hadn't been a big donor, nor had he been a defeated officeholder, nor a state party official, nor was he a relation of the president. In short, he possessed none of the usual credentials which Ross used to select ambassadors. Then Forrester said, "The Company, perhaps?" and Oakley said, "Bingo."

"Ah-hah," Bibby said. "What company?" And he must say he felt a little spooky when Forrester discreetly whispered, "CIA."

And now the guy was sitting right at his side. No telling what kind of private information he was secretly absorbing with whatever kind of unbelievable detection devices he knew how to use.

"How do you find your room, Mr. Vice President," Alcozar began. "Are your accommodations appropriate to your needs?"

"Yes, very nice. Beautiful view. Thank you for the lovely fruit basket. And thanks for the rental car coupon. We have our own cars, but that ten percent off is a pretty good discount."

"Well, just remember, it's not only good for you, it's for anybody in your party. Okay, then, Mr. Vice President, let's get down to work. We talked to Ambassador Oakley, and we thought that maybe the best way to proceed would be for us to conduct a little business first. Then we'll have something to eat, and then after that we'll introduce you to some of the deeply needy peasants who reside in our strife-torn land. How's that sound?"

"Just great. I'm just happy to be here." *Here's a chance.* "Just happy to show you that we want to be your pal."

"Well, thank you, Mr. Vice President, that's very nice," Alcozar said. "Now, if you'll open the folder we have provided for you, you'll see that on the first sheet we have prepared a list of the materials we will need in order to continue to wage our struggle against the so-called Hondanista guerrillas. Naturally, these are the minimum amounts we require, and we would obviously encourage you to be as generous as you can."

"Okay, let's see what we got here," Brent said, examining the list. "Computers, copiers, lamps, carpets, microwave ovens, washers, dryers, dishwashers—what's this word?"

Alcozar peeked over the edge of his glasses.

"Barcoloungers," he replied.

"Okay, then, barcoloungers, big screen TVs, camcorders, VCRs, CD players, tape decks, perfume, cologne—perfume and cologne?" he asked in surprise.

"From the tone of your voice I am assuming that you did not expect to find perfume and cologne on the list of materials we require," Alcozar said. "Please, Mr. Vice President, let's not be naive. In the evenings, when the valiant fighting men and women of the Humirican Defense Forces have finished pursuing the ruthless Hondanista guerrillas through the steaming jungle and over the dusty foothills, they do not have much time or opportunity to shower before becoming overwhelmed with passion. And when you are a soldier in the field and you realize that your life could be snuffed out the next instant, deferred gratification is not widely practiced. The perfume and cologne are vital for morale."

"I see," Bibby said, "and I want you to know, Your Excellency, that I certainly meant no disrespect. But—and maybe I'm confused here, which wouldn't surprise me, I bet that could happen a lot—but don't you want any weapons?"

"Well, Mr. Vice President, I see you are as shrewd as you are eloquent. Mr. Vice President, my friend, make no mistake. We are grateful for the weapons you've given us, and for the weapons you'll give us in the future. But we've got lots of weapons. We haven't quite finished using up all the weapons Ronald Reagan gave us, and we still have all the weapons George Bush gave us. But we could really use some of these other items."

Mmmh. Forrester hadn't briefed him about this possibility. "See, Your Excellency, I think the problem—and Mr. Forrester can correct me if I'm wrong, or any of you guys, just jump in when you feel like it—is that we have the weapons, but if we're going to give you the rest of this stuff, from what I understand from the newspapers, we'd have to buy most of it from the Japanese. Now although I'm sure our economy is just *fine,* I'm just not sure if we can afford to buy anything like that." He glanced over at Forrester, who seemed to wink at him and flash him a thumbs-up sign, which made Brent happy until he realized that maybe Forrester was just twitching.

Meanwhile, Alcozar's face had taken on a sad little look, with his eyebrows tilted and his lower lip puffed out, and Bibby began to get worried that perhaps he had somehow insulted his host. He was on the verge of apologizing for something—for what, he wasn't exactly sure, but he often had to apologize when he wasn't sure what he had done wrong; it wasn't all that big a deal for him anymore, and he was pretty good at it. But then Alcozar began to speak. "It's too bad that you are having trouble affording the money to help your friends," he said. "But you may rest assured that we understand, and that you can count on us to help. I have read in the *New Republic* all about your country's decline, and as one who comes from a poor nation, I certainly sympathize with your concerns. And now that you are becoming a poor nation, we in San Rico de Humidor will be able to return all the kindness you Americans have shown us over the years. Our people have vast experience in living in poverty while you, of course, have had little, so we will be happy to share our survival secrets with you. My own mother, for example, knows one hundred twenty-eight ways to cook dirt. And she's a fairly well off lady. Poor women have even more recipes. Ah, but let's discuss Humirican aid to America later on, shall we? You look hungry. I think it's time we broke for dinner."

Seeing the look on Bibby's face, Alcozar chuckled. "Don't worry, Mr. Vice President, we're just having dirt as a side dish tonight."

Fourteen

Dinner, Brent thought, had gone exceedingly well. Though this was not one of the three formal banquets planned for this visit, just a get-better-acquainted dinner for Bibby and Alcozar and their teams of advisors, everyone still sat at a large banquet table, in roughly the same positions that they had occupied at the conference table earlier. Bibby tried to follow all the rules for graceful dining his mother had taught him: Try a little bit of everything, compliment the cook, avoid seconds, eat slowly, chew carefully; if you don't feel well, stay home and don't vomit on your host; don't talk with your mouth full, and, in your particular case, don't talk all that much with your mouth empty. Bibby found neither of those last injunctions too tough to follow, as Alcozar comfortably dominated the discussion.

God, the man seemed to love the sound of his own voice. Bibby heard Alcozar on the break-up of the Soviet Union, Alcozar on Castro's flatulence problems, Alcozar on his country's disastrously expensive experiment in developing a coffee industry, Alcozar on why Latins make the best baseball players, Alcozar on how the Academy of Motion Picture Arts and Sciences discriminates against Barbra Streisand, Alcozar on everything. All Bibby had to do most of the evening was nod.

Finally, over dessert, Bibby got a word in edgewise. "Dinner was exceptionally tasty, Your Excellency," he said. "I don't think I've ever had that dish. What was it?"

"Parrot," Alcozar responded, signaling the waiter. "More coffee, Mr. Vice President?"

"Really?" said Brent. "I never would have imagined."

"Most people are surprised," Alcozar said, nodding.

"But it went so well with the corn!" Bibby said, trying to sound enthusiastic. "The two were just perfect together."

"What corn?" Alcozar asked.

"Th-that," Brent stammered, pointing to some remnants of the material on his plate. "The vegetable."

"That wasn't a vegetable," Alcozar said dryly. "That was gravel."

"No!" said Brent, deeply shocked. "Was it really? But it was so tender."

"The secret is to soak it long enough," Alcozar confided in the same hushed tone he had used earlier in the evening when disclosing that a very famous salsa singer Bibby had never heard of was actually a transsexual. "The thing most people overlook is the soaking part. That particular batch of gravel has been soaking since 1952. I remember the day my grandmother put it into a big barrel—and it was hard then, like *rock*—and she told me, 'Julio, let this soak for several decades. Then you can serve it to a very, very important friend.' And so you see—her hopes for this gravel have been realized."

"Gosh, what a charming story," Brent said.

"It is, isn't it?" said Alcozar, wiping a napkin across his face. "Now, Mr. Vice President, not to change the subject, the hour is growing quite late. Why don't we resume our discussions in the morning?"

"Good idea," Brent said. He started to say his good nights, but Alcozar interrupted.

"Not to detain you, Mr. Vice President, but before you retire, we thought that perhaps you would like to unwind a bit. Being far away from home always creates certain tensions. Perhaps you would like a massage. Colonel Caliente," he said, gesturing to the chief of the Humirican Internal Intelligence Agency.

The blade-sharp, vaguely sinister colonel opened the door. Six beautiful, voluptuous women, all wearing skin-clinging party dresses, entered the room.

"We told you you'd have an opportunity to meet some of the hard-working peasants of San Rico de Humidor. These six happen to be among the most accomplished in their field."

Well, Brent thought, he really wasn't in the mood for a massage, and frankly, none of these women looked like they could match the treatment old Sven Nordqvist gave him at the senate gym. Still, he couldn't be rude. "I'm always delighted to meet people when I travel," he said to Alcozar, and got up and crossed the room. "Hi, Brent Bibby, United States of America," he said, shaking the hand of the first, a dark-haired beauty whose cleavage would seem to promise many enjoyable hours of exploration. "What's your name? How's the weather been?" Then he moved on to the next. "Hi, Brent Bibby, the United States of America. Hi, Brent Bibby, from the United States. Hi, Brent Bibby, American." He finished and dropped his hands to his side, waiting for the high sign that he could retire.

"Well, which one do you like?" Alcozar asked.

Bibby wondered why Alcozar expected him to be able to come to that kind of judgment on the basis of such a brief acquaintance. "Well, they all seem nice," he said. "I guess I like them all."

"*All?*" Alcozar said in astonishment. "Two, three even I could see, but ay! Señor! Don't you want to save one for tomorrow?"

"Save?" Brent asked. "I don't"—my God, these women are here for me to have sex with!—"Oh, Your Excellency"—now, above all, don't be rude—"Your Excellency, that was very considerate of you, but no, no thanks, I'm not like that."

"You're not?" Alcozar said in astonishment. Slowly he turned his head and looked down his row of aides. They all hung their heads and fidgeted. Then Alcozar's eyes brightened, and he turned back to Bibby and said evenly, but with a hint of lightness, "Would you prefer one of the waiters?"

"The waiters?" Brent was confused, but then it hit him. "No," he said quickly. "No-o-o. Heh heh heh heh heh. But thanks, anyway. I'm married."

"Well, we're all married," Alcozar said. "We're not trying to find you a wife."

"Well, thanks again," said Bibby. "I guess I'm just real married. But about what you said before there, if you want to help me unwind, nothing does it like a good game of tennis. I could really go for that. What do you say, Your Excellency? Any chance of us volleying a few around?"

Alcozar's brow furrowed, and he seemed hesitant. "Well, I don't know," he said. "We're such a poor country, we don't have the luxury of playing games. You know, we seldom have any fun here. What do you think, Colonel? Is it possible?"

"Yes, Your Excellency," Caliente nodded confidently. "In fact, I know just the place. There is a public tennis court just behind the old Cathedral of Our Lady of the Junta. The monks used to play there. They have lights."

"Yes, I know the place," Ambassador Oakley said from the end of the table. "I think it will be just fine."

"Bueno," Alcozar said. "This will be fun, Mr. Vice President. I'm glad you thought of it. Let's all go change and meet back here in fifteen minutes. We can all go in my car. Velasquez," he said to an aide, "send the girls away. Well, send a few of the girls away. Have a couple wait." He then pulled Forrester over to the side. "My apologies, Mr. Forrester. I hate to leave you out, but why don't you stay? My car's not that big, and you'd probably have to ride in back of us in the armored personnel carrier with the troops and Secret Service agents, and it will be very uncomfortable." He gestured over his shoulder toward the women. "I believe you'd be able to make yourself more comfortable here, eh, Señor?" He was pleased to see Forrester nod so avidly.

In a few minutes, most everyone was heading out to the courts. Forrester chose a pretty girl with copper-colored hair. Then he chose the dark-haired lady with the cleavage. As they climbed the stairway to the suite where the Americans were quartered, they had to pause on a landing to let past Colonel Caliente and some soldiers, maybe twenty in all, dressed in camouflaged fatigues and black berets. Forrester noticed that they were running in double time, but given the way his new best friends were squeezing up to him to make room for the troopers, he noticed little else.

Fifteen

Damn, Brent thought, jogging onto the court, this is fun. He stretched out a bit, shook out his shoulders, did a few air overhand serves, and was ready. Wasn't going to be much of a game anyway, he thought. Didn't mean to be cocky, didn't mean to be rude, just wanted to face the facts. Julio McEnroe there hadn't even bothered to put on tennis clothes, just took off his suit jacket and put on sneakers. Really wasn't going to be much of a challenge, but it would be fun to be outside and running around a bit. Pleasant night, too, not a bit muggy—and who knows? Maybe it would even be good, bilateral relations–wise. You know: Bibby beats Alcozar, U.S. achieves a new-found level of respect, that sort of thing. "Ready when you are, Your Excellency," he called.

"Please, Mr. Vice President. You serve."

Okay, Brent agreed. He wound up and sent a smashing serve toward Alcozar, who swung at it lamely well after it had blown past him on the court. "Good for you, Mr. Vice President," Alcozar called, trotting after the ball. "Go again," he said, tossing the ball back across the net.

Bibby wound up and sent a drive nearly identical to the first. Again the ball whizzed past the tubby Alcozar before he could get his racket around. "Excellent, Mr. Vice President!" Alcozar called as he once again lumbered back for the ball. "You really got me. Go again."

Again Bibby served, though this time he let up a bit. With the ball traveling ever so much more slowly, Alcozar managed to get the edge of his racket on it, redirecting it at about a ninety-degree angle toward the left side of the court. "Outstanding!" Alcozar called. "You have an amazing serve!"

"That's nice of you to say so, Your Excellency," Brent said. "Tell me, do you get to play much?"

"Oh, never," he replied, puffing back with the ball. "It's probably been twenty years since I last picked up a racket." Alcozar was about to toss the ball back across the net when Bibby realized that the game was never going to get off the ground. He doubted he was going to help the Humiricans realize the Americans were their pals if he used their president as his ball boy all night. "Naw, you keep it, Your Excellency," he called. "Now it's your turn. You serve a few."

"All right," Alcozar said, with what Bibby took to be a grateful smile. He went back to the line, positioned himself awkwardly, and swung, somehow managing to get under the ball in a way that made it go high in the air and over Bibby's head into the bushes behind him. "That's okay," Bibby said in an encouragingly peppy way. "I'll fetch it later. Go ahead and serve another one."

"I'm sorry, Mr. Vice President," he heard Alcozar say. "We are such a poor country. That's the only ball we have."

Only ball they have, Bibby thought to himself, turning around to retrieve the ball. Fix that tomorrow. Take care of that personally. Get these people some balls. Hey, got ourselves some really thick underbrush here. Is that—? no, a turtle. What's—?

There was a man in front of his, a man with a mustache and a beret. The man put his finger to his lips and said sshh. Then there was a thump, and Bibby went out.

On the court, Alcozar waited. And waited. Finally he glanced at his watch. "Mr. Vice President?" he called. "Oh, Mr. Vice President? Do you see the ball?" He looked over to the sidelines where Colonel Caliente and Ambassador Oakley were sitting and shrugged. "Colonel, the Vice President seems to be having some trouble. Why don't you send some men in to help?"

Caliente ordered two soldiers into the brush, then sauntered over to Alcozar. The two of them lit up cigarettes and stood silently, smoking and waiting, smoking and waiting. Before long, Oakley joined them. Finally the soldiers charged out of the bushes. "He's gone, Colonel! No sign of him!"

"Is there anything there?" Caliente called.

"Nothing, sir!"

"Morons," Caliente muttered under his breath. Then, calming himself, he patiently asked, "Are you sure there's nothing there? Isn't there . . . a note?"

The soldiers charged back into the bushes. In a moment they returned. "Colonel!" they called, running toward him. "We found a note!"

"Good work, men," he said as he took the letter. He read it and passed it to Alcozar, who, after reading it, turned to face Oakley. "I'm sorry, Mr. Ambassador, but I'm afraid you will need to inform your superiors in Washington that Vice President Bibby has been kidnaped by the Hondanista guerrillas and is being held for ransom."

Sixteen

Dark.

Dark and smelly.

Can't see. Can't move, head hurts. Cramped. Stretch out—ow!—can't. Try up. Ouch, goddammit! Something hard, right in front of my face.

I'm dead. That's it, *I'm dead.* I'm dead, and I'm in a coffin. But if I'm dead, why am I in pain? And why aren't I in heaven? Maybe I'm not dead. Maybe—*my God, I've been buried alive!* He-e-e-lp! Help me out of here!

But if I'm buried alive, why am I moving? Sliding a little here, sliding a little there, swaying . . . Wait! I'm not in a box, *I'm in a car.* I'm in the trunk of a car. That accounts for the engine sound and the gas smell *and for the moving!* That's it, we're moving! Swerve, turn, ruts in the road—ow, dammit. Geez, slow down. This is like sneaking into a drive-in. But why? Why wasn't I just asked to go to the drive-in? And if we're going to a drive-in, why are my hands tied? And who tied my hands? How does anyone expect me to eat popcorn if my hands are tied? And another thing: If I'm in the trunk, why can't I remember drawing straws or flipping a coin or anything that would have decided that I had to be the one to get into the trunk?

We're stopping. Listen . . . *footsteps!* A man humming, and—what's that? Water? Water running, like out of a hose? And what's he saying? Sounds like something . . . foreign. Spanish.

Spanish? Oh, that's right, I'm in San Rico. Footsteps moving away. Car door slam. We're going again.

Man, what is going on? Who has . . . ? Where am . . . ? What if I've seen what's play—? Is this somebody's idea of a joke?

Is somebody going to kill . . . ?

Now don't panic. Calm down. Figure it out when you get there. Until then, just relax. Nothing's going to happen to the vice president of the United States. Calm down, relax, think peaceful thoughts. Think Borg-McEnroe, Wimbledon, 1980. Set one, game one. Here's the serve.

Bonk. Bonk. *Borg comes to the net!* Bonk . . .

Light.

Faces. Big, wavy-haired guy with a toothy smile. "Ayyy, Vice President Bibby, is that you?"

Bibby, squinting, nodded. Who are you? he wanted to say, but his mouth was dry and tight, and he couldn't quite get it out before the big guy was off and running. "Ayyy, all right!" he said, gesturing grandly. "Congratulations, muchachos! You have done well." Bibby raised himself up on his elbow, wincing at the stiffness he felt all over. He could see that the big, wavy-haired guy seemed happy to have him here. Wherever here was. "Any trouble, Raul?" he asked a lanky soldier with a large, automatic weapon.

"Ninguna," Raul sneered. "We knocked him out and hauled him away without so much as a cry for help. It was like plucking a ripe papaya from a tree. Even easier. Not even a monkey chattered an objection."

"Bien!" the big one said. "Muy muy bien. So tell me then: Why did you tie his hands?"

"Why did I tie his hands?" Raul scratched his head. Bibby thought Raul didn't have the answer. *Oh boy, now who's in trouble? Well, don't hit me on the head and then expect sympathy out of me.* "Well," Raul suggested, "to make sure he didn't escape, I guess."

"He was unconscious and locked in the trunk of a car, Raul.

How was he going to escape? Were you afraid he was going to claw his way through the back seat and attack you?"

"Aw, man," Raul whined, "is it really that big a deal? He's here now, he's okay. What's the problem?"

"It's the principle of the thing, Raul," said the big one, the one so obviously the boss. He turned to Bibby. "Mr. Vice President, my apologies for picking you up in such an unceremonious manner and for tying your hands." He whipped out a switch-blade and snapped it open. Before Bibby could finish sharply sucking in his breath, his bonds were cut. "Ordinarily, we would have sent you an invitation, but then we would have had to include directions, and I'm afraid Colonel Caliente and his murderous henchmen would have insisted on seeing them. That would have been unfortunate. Heh heh heh. You see, Mr. Vice President, I am Carlos Amaro, the head of the Hondanista Freedom Fighters, and you have been brought to our secret hideout."

The guerrillas! Brent thought. Led by Carlos the Puma! By God, I have been captured by the most cold-blooded demons in the western hemisphere. Now it's all obvious—a clearing in the jungle, thatched houses under banyan trees, the unshaven men, their berets, their fatigues, the machine pistols and the automatic weapons with the banana cartridges. *I am being held at guerrilla headquarters!* "Wh—" his voice squeaked. Try again. "What do you want with me?"

The big one—Carlos—laughed. In a pretty unnecessarily sarcastic way, Bibby thought. "Mr. Vice President," Carlos said, "You have been tried in absentia for crimes against humanity committed by the repressive gangster regime of which you are one of the principal conspirators."

So a mistake *was* made, Bibby thought. "Sorry," he responded, "but I have to clarify something. I'm really not one of your conspirators. Ross, yes. Friedman, yes. I'm—ah, I'm—ah, I'm more the bridge-opening guy in the administration. I think you really want one of the San Rico de Humidor guys."

Carlos laughed. "If you are not one of the San Rico de Humidor guys," he asked, "then what are you doing here?" Bibby hemmed and hawed, couldn't even find a word. "Are you opening a bridge, Mr. Vice President? Oh, gee, apparently not. You must be here to help implement your colonialist foreign policy. So sorry. You leave us little choice but to find you guilty and sentence you to death."

Carlos let that sink in for a moment, then continued. "Just so we're clear on this matter: Your miserable, privileged, pampered existence means nothing to me. If you were being held by any one of the world's other fine freedom-fighter organizations, you would be dead by now and your bullet-hole-ridden carcass would be lying in the jungle being picked at by jaguars. Would you like that?"

"No-o-o," Bibby said soberly, though he thought if he ever saw jaguars eating a carcass, like on one of those PBS nature shows, he was pretty sure he'd find it interesting. "I don't think having my corpse eaten by jaguars is in anybody's plans. My family has a mausoleum in Bibbyville. I think I'm supposed to go there."

"Well, we wouldn't want your daddy to waste his money," laughed Carlos. "As it happens, you are most lucky. We Hondanistas are a humane group, and so we have decided to offer you an alternative: We will commute your sentence and simply levy a fine, payable by your government to us. Once we've got the money, you will be released."

Well, that certainly sounded reasonable, Bibby thought, and felt a little of the tension in his shoulders give way. Still, things weren't totally settled. "What if they don't pay?"

"Oh, they'd better pay," Carlos said evenly. "Otherwise, I hope you like thatch. It's all you will see for the rest of your life. Raul, get the Polaroid." Suddenly Carlos had closed in cheek to cheek with his arm around Bibby's shoulder. "Smile, baby." Raul pressed the button and the camera, with its expected *brrr-ch-ching,* expelled a picture. "Better take another."

"Does my hair look okay?" Bibby asked.

"Yes, fine."

"It feels like something's sticking up."

"Dios mio, Bibby, it's a ransom picture. It's not like we're entering you for Cosmo Bachelor of the Month. Can you believe this guy, Raul? He's been lying in the back of a '67 Bonneville for nine hours, he's got oil stains all over his clothes, I bet he's hungry, I bet his bladder's going to burst, and *he's* worried about his hair."

The camera *brrr-ch-ching*ed again. Well, it is pretty funny, Bibby thought to himself. And I do have to pee. Still, he wanted to look his best. Oh, and one more thing: "How much do you want?" he asked Carlos.

"Take another, Raul, and that will be enough," Carlos said. "Okay, Mr. Vice President, big smile now. Smile like me." Bibby, looking out of the corner of his eye, thought Carlos had plastered on a seriously wide grin. "Give your people a one-hun-dred-million-dollar smile. Make them believe you're worth that much." *Brr-ch-ching!* "Bueno. Okay, Raul, get those out over the AP wire. Make sure it's clear that they've got twenty-four hours to pay the fine or he's toast."

Which is how Bibby came to appear the next day, with a dumbfounded expression on his face and his hair sticking up, on the front page of every paper in America.

Seventeen

"Time to go now, Mr. President," said Ms. Meara. "They're all ready for you."

Okay, then, here we go. Down the corridor, down another corridor, not to the Cabinet Room but to the Situation Room— the Sit Room, he liked to call it, or sometimes just the *Sit*— walking, walking, aides running around, jackets off, ties askew, all of them looking a little frantic, Ms. Meara ahead of him, heels clack-clacking with more determination than usual—I'll thank you to keep your ass to yourself today, Ms. Meara—into the Sit, everybody gets up. Different everybody than usual, of course. Don't have a lot of your cabinet guys here for something like this. No Interior, no HHC, no Labor—*thank God!* Instead, you got your State guys and your National Security Council guys and your Pentagon guys and Connolly from the FBI, and— there they are, you could have predicted it—the pastries, the bagels, about six boxes from Dunkin' Donuts, everybody with big cups of coffee, creamers all over, sugar packets, stirrers. "Coffee, Mr. President?" Ms. Meara asked. Already a ton of cigarette butts in the ash trays.

"Yes, Ms. Meara, thank you," he said. Why the fuck not?

"Gentlemen," Ross said, "as I think most of you have already been informed, the vice president of the United States, Brent Bibby, was kidnapped at about 10:48 P.M. last night in San Rico City. No one from the Humirican government saw anything,

113

nor did anyone from the Humirican defense forces, nor did our Secret Service agents. Claiming credit, however, are the Hondanista guerrillas. There was a note left that said he was taken by them"—NCS aides circled the table, smartly distributing copies of the note—"and about an hour ago, I am informed, the CNN bureau in San Rico City received this photograph of the vice president and a man who claims to be Carlos the Puma"—now the copies of the photo went around—"and who has been positively identified by the CIA as actually being Carlos the Puma." Ross paused for a moment. "Questions, so far?"

"What's with his hair?" Secretary of State Friedman asked.

"We have no information on that. Kipper?"

"What are their terms?" the National Security Advisor asked.

"They are holding him, and they say they will execute him if we don't pay them one hundred million dollars." Everyone around the table said Whew! "Yes, can you believe that?" Ross continued. "A hundred million dollars. A hundred million dollars. That's one hundred times a million dollars, more even than professional athletes make. More than even that guy who runs Coca-Cola makes! What do they think I am, *made of money?* I mean, what are they thinking? They see we got a trillion dollar deficit, and just think, 'Oh, well, what's a hundred million on top of that?' Like it didn't fucking matter? And another thing, why'd they have to tell the media right away? No, I know, they had to tell the media 'cause they wanted to, 'cause it just wouldn't be a big, official kidnapping if the media wasn't all over it, but I ask you: Isn't it just my fucking luck? Fucking Bibby could go sit on the crapper for four months and nobody would ever notice he was gone. But now the world knows, and we have to come up with a response. Right?"

The Sit Group sat silent, more than a little stunned by Ross's outburst. "Right?" he repeated more forcefully. "Yes, yes, yes, yes, yes," they all hastened to say.

A phone rang. Joint Chiefs Chairman Wooten answered it. "It's President Alcozar, sir," he said.

Ross, rolling his eyes, reached for the receiver. "By the way,

Crane," he said, covering the mouthpiece, "was Forrester kidnapped also?"

"No, sir. He wasn't with the vice president last night."

"Wasn't with him?"

"No, sir. He was ill. Galloping Aztec Two-Step, I believe was the diagnosis, sir."

"Well, that's too bad. Look, as soon as he gets better, fire him. Hello, Julio?"

"Mr. President? This is President Julio Alcozar de Portega y Gasset of San Rico de Humidor."

"Yes, I know that." Every conversation, on the phone or in person, he starts the same way, as if Ross couldn't remember anything. Or didn't have a staff to tell him.

"Mr. President, I'm calling to tell you that Vice President Bibby has been kidnapped."

"Yes, I know that, Julio."

"Oh. Well then, how are you?"

"I'm okay, I've been better." Ross made exaggerated faces into the phone, making his advisors giggle. "How are you?"

"I've been better, too," Alcozar said. "This whole thing has caused my ulcer to act up."

"That's a shame," Ross said. "Maybe you ought to swear off the spicy food for a bit."

"What do you mean by that?"

"I didn't mean anything by it."

"No, tell me. Did you mean that all of us in Central America were just a bunch of spicy-food eaters you could lump together and dismiss because we like a few peppers?"

"No! No, Julio, I didn't mean anything like that. I was just making a comment, a little joke."

"Well, I hardly think this is a time for levity. These Hondanistas are ruthless totalitarian ideologues, and I think Vice President Bibby's life is very much in jeopardy."

"Yes, I'm sorry, Julio, you're right, please forgive me." God, he hated apologizing to leaders from the underdeveloped Third World. "So, anything new on the case?"

"No, nothing. But our investigators are working very hard to develop clues. They worked throughout the night making plaster casts of the footprints in the bushes in order to identify the perpetrators. So we will have those casts later."

"Julio, I mean no disrespect here when I say this, but don't we have a darn good idea who the perpetrators are already?"

There was a pause. "Who?" Alcozar asked.

"Well, *think,* Julio. Who sent us the ransom note? Didn't the Hondanistas send us the ransom note?"

"Right. And it was Carlos the Puma in the picture with Bibby!"

"Yes! Exactly! So we know it was the Hondanistas."

"Did you think that was a good picture of the vice president?"

Ross couldn't quite believe he was having this conversation. "Ah, no, I didn't think it was a good picture of Vice President Bibby. I thought his hair looked funny."

"Me, too!" Alcozar excitedly agreed. "What about Carlos?"

"I don't know," Ross said peevishly, "I never met Carlos. Is it a good likeness?"

"Quite good. He's pretty handsome, isn't he?"

"Ah, yes, I guess he's handsome."

"I bet he has to beat them off with a stick."

"Maybe. Probably." *What do I know?* "Look, Julio, tell me, are your men out combing the countryside for the vice president?"

"Not yet. They will be when the rain stops."

"Uh-huh. Have you been able to use the reconnaissance planes we sent you last year?"

"No," Alcozar said dispiritedly. "Unfortunately, we used up all the film last year taking aerial pictures of my birthday party. Didn't I send you one?"

"Ah, I don't—oh, I'm sure you did. I'm sure you sent one, and I'm sure when I got it I thought, Gee, I'd like to have a party just like that some day."

"When is your birthday, Mr. President?"

"Well, it's in January."

"Well, you should have a party. Will you invite me?"

"Will I—? Sure, why not? Look, would you like some more film for the cameras? I'm sure we can get some down to you today. Then you could do a little reconnaissance."

"That would be very helpful."

"Okay, Julio, count on it. Now, is Ambassador Oakley there? Could you put him on for just a teensy second?"

"I will. And even though this is a toll call, I won't charge your embassy for your portion of the call."

"Thank you, Julio."

"Before I go, I just want you to know what a pleasure it was to speak to you, mi compadre."

"Thank you, Julio. It was a pleasure speaking to you, too, old friend."

"May God give you strength during this hour of crisis."

"And you, too, Julio. May he give you strength too. Is Amba—"

"And may he shower your people with blessings."

"Thank you. And your people as well, Julio. Bye, now. Bye. *Bye!*" There was a brief pause while Ambassador Oakley got on the line. "Oakley, what the hell is going on there?" he demanded.

"You have to understand, Mr. President, the Humiricans have their own way of doing things."

"Obviously," Ross said, as dryly as a highly anxious man can. "They have their own way of doing things, and they have their own way of not doing things. Now listen to me, Ambassador: Tell Alcozar that we want some action or we're going to step in."

There was a pause. "I'm sorry, sir," Oakley asked. "But what does that mean, exactly?"

"Exactly? I'm not sure what that means, exactly, but I've got several hundred thousand soldiers and marines working for me who don't have a lot to do. Maybe I can ask them to devote all their energies to solving this problem."

"I see. Have you ruled out paying the ransom, Mr. President?"

"No, we haven't ruled anything out, we haven't ruled anything in. Believe me," Ross snarled, "when we get to the point
of ruling on things, you'll be the first to know." He slammed
down the phone.

Why does this always happen to me, he wondered. Almost
involuntarily, his head sagged, and he began to rub his eyes with
his hands. Gradually he came to realize that even though he
couldn't see his advisors anymore, they were all looking at him,
and he wondered what they were thinking. Did he look upset?
Weak? Overwrought? Or did he look like he was bearing up courageously under the burdens of leadership? Better not lose sight
of how you look, he told himself. Some of these goofballs would
be writing memoirs one day.

He wondered if he would write memoirs one day. Probably.
There was too much money in it not to. What would he put in?
Not why Brent was in San Rico de Humidor. Well, not *really*
why. And not that Lucinda and he had just finished making love
the moment before Crane furiously banged on the door of the
Lincoln Bedroom to tell him of Brent's capture; and that it had
been sweet, and satisfying, and that they were lying heavily in
the bliss that is the reward of the truly passionate. Or at least
that's the way Ross liked to think of it. And then Crane had
come in and pulverized the mood, and now he had to be here in
the Sit, talking to a moron like Alcozar, the president of this fly-
speck San Rico de Who-Gives-a-Shit, discussing the fate of one
of the great nonentities of the universe, and worrying about what
his yes-men were going to write in their memoirs. Sometimes life
was just so unfair.

"Mr. President?" he heard Crane softly ask. He was talking in
the voice he always used when Ross had fallen asleep in an airplane or a meeting or somewhere and Crane had to wake him
up. "Mr. President?"

"I'm here, Crane," he growled. "I'm here. I'm awake, and if
any of you happens to be wondering what I might have had on
my mind during this hour of tremendous crisis, well, here it is: I
was just saying a private prayer to my Creator to give me the

strength I need to bear up courageously under the burdens of leadership. Did everybody make a note of that? A private moment between me and the Almighty." He sighed and sat up straight. "Gentlemen, there hasn't been any progress. I think we ought to be prepared for it to come down to this. We have a deadline in twenty-four hours. We have to decide whether or not to pay. If we pay, we break a longstanding policy against dealing with terrorists and leave ourselves vulnerable to widespread ridicule, not to mention further acts of terrorism. If we don't, we may never see Vice President Bibby again. So: Do we pay or not?"

"Mr. President," Treasury Secretary Banks began, pausing virtually not a moment to think, "let me say that as treasury secretary, I can tell you that it would be inadvisable just to tack a hundred million dollars onto the federal budget. It may seem like a drop in the bucket, but we're in a period of austerity, and I don't think we can toss out a hundred million dollars whenever we've convinced ourselves we have a worthwhile cause. First, it would be saving Vice President Bibby. Then we'd want to fund some environmental program, then a space program, then a program to feed poor pregnant women, and there would just be no end to it."

"Okay," Ross said, jotting down a note, "the Treasury Department votes for Bibby to die."

"Well, not necessarily. Excuse me, General," Banks said to Joint Chiefs Chairman Wooten, pointing at the Dunkin' Donuts box, "is that the last chocolate covered?"

"Looks like," Wooten said, checking the box. "Do you want to split it?"

"Well, if I have to, yes. But haven't you had three already?"

"Oh, here, take the damn thing if you're going to be such a baby about it."

"Thank you, General," Banks smiled coldly. "Now, where was I? Oh, I know—my idea. Suppose you agree to pay the ransom. We'll print up some special money for the occasion. Let's say we print a hundred-million-dollar bill. We could put your

picture on it, Mr. President. And we'll use that to pay the ransom. It would be legal tender. They'd have to accept it, but
they'd never be able to use it. If they brought it to a bank, we
could arrest 'em. And there's not a store in the world that could
make change for a bill that large. Can you imagine them going
into a grocery store? 'Yeah, give me a quart of milk and a Snick-
ers. Ya got change for a hundred-million-dollar bill?'"

Some of the Sit Group chuckled, but not as many as giggled
to themselves after Ross said, "Thanks, Barney. You keep thinking, and if you come up with anything that isn't completely asi-
nine, you let me know. Anybody else?"

"We could bomb 'em, Mr. President," General Wooten said.
"Get some idea where those rebels are hiding, send in the flyboys
with those smart bombs, and just level the place."

My God, if these are the most intelligent people in America,
Ross thought, then for the sake of our children I'd better devote
more energy to sucking up to the Japanese. "General Wooten,
I'm afraid I have to remind you that San Rico de Humidor is a
friendly nation," he said with what he thought was great fore-
bearance. "An ally, in fact. We don't bomb allies. Moreover,
since we don't know where the guerrillas are hiding, we really
wouldn't know where to bomb. Now, under those circumstances, doesn't your plan risk causing a lot of random destruction? And couldn't the vice president get hurt, or even killed?"

Wooten licked his lips and looked around the table. "Maybe,"
he said sulkily.

Ross covered his face with his hands again, and sighed as he
thought about Lucinda.

Four thousand miles away, in San Rico de Humidor, the vice
president of the United States sat shivering in his hut. It
wouldn't be so uncomfortable, Brent thought, if he was wearing
something more substantial than tennis whites. And when were
they going to feed him again? Those beans after that long car ride
had been darn tasty, but that was a long time ago. What, didn't
you get three squares when you become a guerrilla? Outside, he

heard his captors talking around a camp fire and smelled something that sure smelled a lot like meat sitting on the spit. Bibby stuck his head out of his hut. "Excuse me, Raul?" he called to his guard. "I'm sorry, I don't mean to be a bother, but it's a teensy bit chilly in my hut. Do you think your friends would mind if I went out and sat with them by the camp fire?"

Raul grunted in what Bibby took to be disdain, but toddled off to speak to Carlos. He returned a moment later. "Carlos says, 'Why not?'"

Bibby found a seat next to Carlos at the camp fire. "Thanks so much," Brent said, trying to remember everything his mother had told him about being a good house guest. He figured it probably applied to camps as well. "It's turned surprisingly chilly," he said. "I always figured San Rico would be hot everywhere."

"Yes," Carlos said, "everybody thinks that, but it's not really true. And up here in the hills—hey, pretty tricky, trying to get me to reveal our location."

"I was what?" Brent said, flabbergasted. "No, honest, I was just trying to make conversation," he said. But the way Carlos was scowling, Brent didn't think Carlos believed him. I'm just going to sit here by the fire and mind my own business and not say a word. "Say," he nonetheless started up again, "that stuff on the spit smells pretty good."

"It does smell good, doesn't it?" Carlos said. "Would you like some?"

"Boy, would I!" Bibby said. After Carlos sliced off a piece with a ferocious-looking machete and it had cooled a bit, Bibby dug in. "Mighty tasty," Bibby enthused. "What is it?"

"Iguana," Carlos said. "Is this your first time with it?"

"Yes," Bibby said, "and let me tell you, I'll look for a chance to order it again. Frankly, this is much better than what we had at the presidential palace the other night."

"Oh, really?" Carlos asked. "What did they serve?"

"Parrot," he said, trying to sound knowing. "Parrot, with dirt and gravel on the side."

All the guerrillas laughed very hard. "You certainly received, ah, unique treatment," Carlos said. "Parrot is not often served in this country. Not like iguana," he added, rather wearily.

"It has the flavor of chicken, doesn't it?" Brent asked.

"Yes," Carlos said proudly, striking Brent as someone who hadn't had anyone new to talk to in a while. "Yes, very tasty, and it's quite plentiful here in the hill—hey, you were trying to trick me again."

"Please," Brent said sharply, "why would I try to trick you? I know where we are. And I'm sure my government knows where we are. These are the Santa Euphoria Mountains. Every story written about you says you strike and then you fade into the Santa Euphoria Mountains. And where else could you go? It's not that big a country. You either run here or run to the ocean, and my feet aren't wet. Besides"—he was on quite a roll now and surprising himself—"why wouldn't you come here? It's very beautiful. Of course, it's lovely on the coast, too. I told President Alcozar that I was surprised there aren't any resorts here. You have the climate and the location for a profitable tourist industry."

"Yes," Carlos said, "but you need somebody to put up the money."

"That's funny," Bibby said. "That's exactly what Alcozar said when I talked about tourism with him."

Carlos stared Bibby in the eye. He had a little grin on his face. Bibby didn't know why Carlos was staring at him that way, but he stared back and tried to grin in much the same way. "You know, Mister Vice President," Carlos finally said, "you're not so dumb as everyone says you are."

"No?" Bibby said, trying to sound cool, even though no one had ever complimented him quite that way.

"No, I don't think so. You still look cold, though. Raul, get the vice president something to wear." Almost like magic, one of the olive drab fatigue jackets was produced.

"Thank you," Bibby said. Then, noticing the label, he added, "U.S. Government issue, eh?"

Carlos grinned. "When you can get the best, why wear the rest?"

The doughnuts, with the exception of a jelly thing that somebody had taken one bite out of and abandoned, were gone. The six-foot-long submarine they'd gotten from Donatelli's Deli on K Street was also nearly gone, though there were still a couple of pickles left and a little mound of prosciutto and an entire jar of Italian peppers that looked almost untouched. Ms. Meara, her hair now starting to tumble out of its bun—making her look quite fetching, Ross noticed, at once realizing why Turnbridge of the NSC had appeared to be looking at him with this come-hither expression at various times during the meeting; actually, and now it made sense, he had been looking past Ross to make goo-goo eyes at Ms. Meara—was now passing around copies of the Joy Luck Restaurant take-out menu. All day long the Sit Group sat, and nobody could come up with a compelling reason to save Brent Bibby. And now they couldn't even figure out whether to get three orders of moo shu pork, or more. Finally, Crane had had enough.

"Mr. President," he said, and when that didn't settle everyone and grab their attention, he said it again; and then said it again, and then again, each time his bearish drone growing louder. Ross, of course, had heard him the first time—he'd been waiting for Crane to weigh in—but he sat quietly and allowed Crane to command the room. Once that happened, Ross figured, as long as Crane hadn't taken complete leave of his senses, they would do whatever he said.

"Mr. President," Crane said when everyone had hushed, "I think we have to pay the ransom. I think we should pay it, get Bibby back, and then devote the full measure of our resources to apprehending his abductors and bringing them to trial. As much as I hate to see us deal with terrorists, Vice President Bibby is a highly placed official of our government who has been privy to secret meetings and private conversations wherein matters of great sensitivity have been discussed. If he is subjected to torture and discloses any of these secrets, the consequences could be devastating. We must protect our secrets. We must bring Brent Bibby home."

Ross let that sink in for a moment, then rose to his feet. "Thank you, everyone. I think this meeting is over. Mr. Crane has once again proven himself to be one of the clearest thinkers in political life. Ms. Meara, let anybody who wants to stick around to order what they want. Me, I'd like two portions of lemon chicken and some sesame noodles brought up to my room. And some of that diet beer, too. I'm going to think about what Mr. Crane said, and I'll announce my decision in the morning. Thanks again, everyone, and be sure to clean up this mess."

"So you're telling me old Senator Stiles is gay?" Carlos asked incredulously.

"Hey, if I'm lyin', I'm dyin'," Bibby said. Sitting around the camp fire, having a couple of brews with some jovial companions, discussing important lawmakers and such—man, this was the most fun Bibby had had for months. "I mean, that was the rumor for a long time, and then one Saturday afternoon, I was playing handball in the senate gym. I went back to the locker room and found Stiles and Senator Chute diddling one another in the shower."

"No!"

"Yes. Not that it makes any difference to me."

"No," Carlos said, "of course not. But right there in the shower room? Tack-ee! Senator Chute doesn't surprise me, frankly, but I always thought Senator Stiles was so distinguished. I would see him on the Foreign Relations Committee, arguing that your country shouldn't be propping up the corrupt Alcozar regime, and I thought 'What a great American.'"

"Well, he is a great American," Bibby said. "He should just learn to go back to his office."

"You got any more?" Carlos asked.

"Well, this one's pretty good, but remember: You didn't hear it from me, okay?"

"Scout's honor," Carlos promised.

"Okay. There was a state dinner for Prime Minister Voegler of Austria, and after dinner, President Ross, you know, he wants to play the big host, he says, 'Any of you guys want to see the Lincoln Bedroom? If you want to go up, I've got a Polaroid up there, I'll take your picture on the bed.' So some of the guests say sure, and Ross took a group of them upstairs. I think it was Voegler, the archbishop of Canterbury, Ambassador Nazish of Pakistan, Monica Seles, I think Tom Selleck went—"

"Tom Selleck!"

"Yeah. Nice guy. So a bunch of us go up, and Ross opens the door, and what does he discover but the wife of the national security advisor doing a little shake-and-bake with Secretary of State Friedman there on the rug."

"No!" said Carlos, roaring with laughter.

"Yes!"

"No!"

"What am I going to do? Lie to my abductor? You don't even know the best part."

"Wh-wh-what's the best part?" Carlos managed to say between spasms of laughter.

"The president sees them and closes the door. Then he opens it up again and says, 'Pardon me, Marv, but how long are you going to be?'"

"How long are you going to be?" Carlos roared with laughter. "How long are you going to be? Oh you got to stop it, man, you're killing me. You're too much!"

"At least he didn't ask if he could take their picture."

Carlos did not cease laughing for a quarter hour.

In Washington, in Ross's bedroom, Ross and Lucinda, like a great many typical Americans, sat in bed, he in his underwear, she in her slip, eating Chinese food out of the cardboard container, watching the coverage of the abduction. Mostly they focused on the ABC special "Bibby Held Hostage," mostly because while they had been having sex earlier the channel changer had gotten lost, and now Ross was too beat to get up and change the channel the old-fashioned way. Besides, Ross liked ABC: More often than the other networks, they seemed to know less than he did without pretending to know more. This always made Ross happy. He never liked it when reporters were smarter than he was.

"Look, darling, there we are," Lucinda said, and indeed, on the screen, there was tape of a grim-faced Ross and a somber Lucinda, solemnly entering the White House. "Meanwhile," Celestine van den Hurdle was reading, "President Ross invited the vice president's wife, Lucinda, to take up temporary residence in the White House for the duration of the crisis, in order to forestall any kidnap attempts against her. Turning now to how little the Bibby kidnapping seems to have affected Wall Street . . ."

"Well, that part went well, at least," Ross said. "Everyone accepts it that you're here. The instant polls seem to show that people think I'm acting like Brent's good buddy and protector by doing this. Nobody suspects the truth."

"Well, you are my protector, darling. I know I feel safer here. And besides, we don't know if some kidnap ring would have tried to grab me. It's possible."

"Yeah, I know. It's just that I'm so damn . . . *frustrated.* Here we were, looking forward to having this week together, we got you actually living here, and now the damn Hondanistas butt in, and suddenly I have to go to meetings and briefings and so on and"—Ross emitted a humongous sigh—"to be frank, I guess I just don't feel that damn romantic right now."

He glanced at her out of the corner of his eye, hoping that she had the warm, understanding, indulgent expression on her face that always brought him such comfort. He was greatly relieved to see that she did. "That's all right, darling, I understand," she said. "In fact, I probably admire you for your lack of ardor today."

"You do?" Ross said.

"Yes. A woman always appreciates a man who knows his priorities, even if she isn't one of them." She smiled at him. He didn't get it, she thought, mostly in amazement.

"Well, it's hard, but I guess it's all just part of the job," he said in a whiny sort of way that made her think of Barney Fife. "A president can't be a sex machine all the time. He has to handle the pressures, make the big decisions."

"Oh, how I know that," she said, moving close so that he could put his head in her lap. "Speaking of which, what have you decided? Are you going to pay the ransom?"

"I think we will," he said. "Crane made a good point. Brent knows too much secret data to leave him out on a limb like that."

"Darling," she said, stroking his head, "what sort of data?"

"Well, I can't say. It's secret."

"Oh, I don't want to know the particulars, silly. Just what in general?"

"Well," Ross said, groping for an answer, "you know—secrets."

"Does he know anything about troops?" she gently asked.

"No," Ross shook his head.

"Our nuclear capability?"

"No," Ross said firmly, "certainly not."

"Codes?"

"Don't make me laugh," he snorted.

"Does he know any state secrets at all?" she pressed.

"No, by God, I guess he doesn't."

"Then what's the risk?" she asked. "What *is* the risk? He can't talk under torture—he doesn't know anything to talk about!"

"You have a point," he conceded, suddenly intrigued.

"Think about it," she said. "Isn't it far riskier to set a precedent that says the United States will wheel and deal to rescue one of its officials? I think that would just invite further kidnappings, no doubt involving officials who really are important to the workings of the government."

"Yes," Ross said, "I suppose it would." He jumped out of bed and started pacing. She watched him go back in forth in his underwear and socks, his white, veiny legs scissoring around the room.

"You know that whatever you decide I'll be here for you," she said. "but you really should think it over."

Of all the many moments when he had thought she was the most incredible woman on earth, and there had been many, this was the one—the one when she had showed herself to be wiser and more insightful than his mainstay Crane, when she had unleashed in him torrents of love and gratitude and desire and awe, when, talking bottom line now, she had proved herself indispensible to his presidency—this was the one that left him overwhelmed. "I will," Ross promised. "By God, Lucinda, I surely will."

Eighteen

He awoke to a soft, warm breeze gently blowing in through the window of his hut and the smell of coffee brewing on the fire. Outside he could hear toucan calls and the chatterings of bush monkeys flowing in and out of the happy morning conversation of the rebels. Ah, what a great time we had last night, Bibby thought, smiling, recalling the way they had laughed and told stories and joked with one another, and *about* one another, and—and they had joked a lot about President Ross, Bibby remembered with a guilty little smile. But he's a good sport, he'd have enjoyed it. Probably. Except for that crack from Carlos about how he needed a woman. That was rich. Like President Ross couldn't get a date if he really wanted one! But so the guerrillas were a little mischievous. They were really a great bunch of guys, and Bibby resolved that once he got out of captivity, he'd set Ross and Alcozar and everybody straight on that matter. The thing he couldn't understand though, was, if everybody was such a good guy, why couldn't they get along?

He rose and put on the freshly pressed fatigues Raul had placed in his tent the night before. Good fit, he thought, though not exactly a military look with the tennis shoes. Funkier, though. More home boy. Perhaps he could wear something like this if he was ever instructed to make an appearance in a black neighborhood. "Good morning, Raul," he called to his guard as he stepped out of his hut. "Good morning, Esteban. Buenos

129

días, Pepe! How's the head today? I'll bet. You certainly had your share. Good morning, Che. What's for breakfast?"

"Eggs and beans, flatbread, mangoes if somebody will go pick them."

"Well, I'm not doing anything," Brent said. "Raul, why don't we go pick some mangoes?"

Raul looked at him coldly. "Do you take me for a fool? You'll get me out there alone, you'll try to steal my gun and escape. Only two things can happen then, both bad: you kill me and escape, or I kill you."

Bibby smiled and shook his head. "Raul, old buddy, I think you're reading this situation a lot differently than I am. First, I'm not worried about being in Hondanista custody. The accommodations are comfortable, the company is delightful, and as for the food—I just love this man's cooking! Why would I leave? And second, I just think everything's going to work out. Have you ever met President Ross? No, I didn't think so. Well, he's a very decent, aboveboard kind of guy. And President Alcozar is a wonderful fellow as well. Even Colonel Caliente, I think, if you got to know him, you'd start to recognize his good points. So I see a lot of room for agreement here. And I think we ought to start by getting some mangoes."

"What's going on here?" asked Carlos. "I try to sleep in one morning and what do I hear but all this yapping about mangoes."

"He wants to go pick mangoes for breakfast," Raul said. "I told him I thought he may try to escape."

"Well, so he may," Carlos said. "That's when you kill him. Meanwhile, put him to work. Why should he sit around all day like a fat old dog while we wait on him?" Carlos smiled at Bibby. "See what you got yourself into?"

"Are you kidding?" he replied, heading off to the jungle, Raul traipsing behind, unlocking the safety on his AK-47. "This is fun!"

And it was fun. Fun to have breakfast with the guys, fun to hike through the jungle, fun to be named the honorary calisthenics instructor, fun to march over to El Rio del Bundegas and catch fish for dinner, fun to play badminton with Carlos in the late afternoon. Badminton? Brent had asked him. How come badminton? We have a very full life here, Carlos told him; it's not all training and raiding and indoctrination. But inevitably everyone had to get back to business. As captive and captor enjoyed a postbadminton papaya, they saw Raul charge out of Carlos's big hut and sprint across the compound toward them. "Excuse me, sir," he gasped, "but there has been an important development."

"Yes?"

"CNN is reporting that Washington has refused to pay the ransom, er, fine, for Bibby's criminal activities."

"Damn!" Carlos said angrily. "Shit! What a bunch of damn skinflints! What the hell's wrong with them? What kind of friends do you have there? Don't they understand that we are ruthless killers, possessing virtually no regard for human life? Don't they see that your tenuous hold to your puny existence grows dimmer with each passing moment?"

"You have CNN here?" Brent asked. "You have TV?"

"Sure we have TV," Carlos said. "We have a satellite dish. We keep it covered up so it can't be spotted from the air very easily. You look shocked. You think just because we're guerrillas we can't take advantage of modern technology? Of course we do!" he said, clapping Bibby on the back so hard that Brent lurched forward. "We're rebels, not savages. You want to watch something tonight? We get a lot out of Miami—Dolphins, Hurricanes, the Heat—plus most of the premium services: CNN, ESPN, HBO, TBS, Playboy Channel. Come on, let's go to the hut, I want to hear the report for myself."

They entered the hut. Esteban and a few others were watching. "Here, it's a replay of Ross's press conference. It just started."

"And so," Ross was saying, "as painful as this choice may be, we have concluded that our long-standing refusal to negotiate with terrorists must be honored. We will, of course, continue to pray for the vice president's release, and also for the success of the defense forces of San Rico de Humidor, who are out combing the countryside in search of the vice president and his abductors."

"The Humirican Defense Forces, eh?" Carlos wisecracked. "Hear that, boys? The defense forces are on our trail. Oooooooooooooh, I'm so afraid. Bibby, let me tell you, man, if that's what they're banking on, you're going to be living here for a lo-o-ong time."

On the television, Celestine van den Hurdle was questioning the president. "What if the Hondanistas torture him?"

"I don't think they will," Ross said curtly.

"But what if they do?" she pressed.

"They won't," he said, and then shot her the kind of little smile and wink that Bibby knew he liked to use when he wanted to reassure some skeptic that he was in full control.

"They might."

Geez, who put the chili powder in Celestine van den Hurdle's coffee today? "Well, I think they might not," the president said.

"They might even kill him," she said.

"No-o-o."

"Maybe."

That made the president angry. "Look," he barked, "if the news media is going to raise a lot of speculation and irresponsibly conjure up a lot of scenarios and egg the rebels on and generally act in a not very patriotic way when a man's life is at stake, well, then there's no telling what the guerrillas might do. But let me just say that if the vice president is injured, then the rebels will have to face the full brunt of American power, and I think they're a little too cowardly for that."

A pretty good answer up to that very last part, Bibby thought. Right up to those very last few words.

"Cowardly!" Carlos boomed. "That pampered old douche bag says we're cowardly? Well, I've got news for Mr. President Ross—the Hondanistas are no cowards. I think we ought to send him a little message to show him that we do not faint at the sight of blood."

"Want me to wax him, sir?" Raul asked.

"Wax him?" Carlos asked. "Like how? Like with car wax?"

"No, you know, wax him. Like, have him whacked."

Carlos, still puzzled, shook his head.

"Take him out?" Raul tried.

"Do you mean kill him?" Carlos asked. Raul nodded eagerly.

"Well, that's a dumb idea. What do we get by killing him? Take a seat, Mr. Vice President," he ordered, and Bibby, who had been momentarily frightened but who was now quite relieved, complied. "You see, it makes no sense to kill him. Not now. We'll do a lot better if we just cut off his little finger."

"Pardon me?" Bibby said. "I don't think I got that exactly."

"Cut off your little finger," Carlos said gently. "Don't worry, you'll hardly miss it. You can get along just fine. Raul here, his father is a coffee picker. He's only got seven fingers."

"Six, actually. He lost another last week. But he's still picking and eating, and still making the ladies happy, if you know what I mean."

"There you go," Carlos said.

"Doesn't play the guitar as well, though."

"Enough, Raul, *thank you*. Bibby doesn't strike me as being much of a guitarist anyway. Am I wrong, Bibby? Mmmh? Not talking to me? Okay, boys, hold him down."

Bibby felt Raul and Esteban and some of the others grab him while Che spread out his fingers on the table. Bibby looked up to see Carlos unsheathe an enormous machete and raise it above his head.

"Ahem," Bibby brought himself to say.

"Yes?" Carlos said, the machete poised above his head.

"Pardon me, but can we discuss this for a moment?" Bibby asked. "I don't know very much about being a guerrilla, and you've obviously been a very successful one. And maybe this finger thing is a major component of that success. But let me ask you: Do you really have to take a finger?"

"Well," Carlos said, calmly lowering the great knife, "it's what's customary. What we're looking for, you understand, is a good effect. We've always tried to picture that look on somebody's face when they open an envelope and see a finger inside. We figured, 'That's a good reaction; now they know we mean business.' I mean, think about it. Ross opens an envelope and sees your finger, it blows his mind."

"Oh, he'd be shocked, no question," Bibby agreed. "See, my problem is that I think it would really hurt my ability to hold a racket."

"Really? The fifth finger's that important?"

"Oh, extremely so."

"Well," Carlos said, "if it means that much to you . . ."

"Oh, it does, it does."

"All right," Carlos said, "we'll take a piece of your ear instead."

"What?" Bibby yelled as the rebels reapplied their grips.

"Ha, ha, ha, funny comeback," Carlos said. "Don't worry, we're not going to take the hearing part, just something from the tip. Don't worry, it'll hurt even less than the finger." He raised the machete above his head again. But whether he saw the fear in Brent Bibby's eyes and took pity, or whether he himself grew suddenly afraid that he might slip and slice the top of Bibby's head off like a ripe melon, the rebel leader stopped and lowered his knife. "Ah, forget it," he said. "I've got the wrong tools. You really need shears for this sort of thing. A machete is for chopping. We'll have to think of something else to cut off."

"No!" Bibby yelled, but even before the sound had left his mouth, he saw that the rebel leader was already exiting the hut.

Nineteen

Back in the Sit, Ross was in a bad mood as he settled into his chair at the head of the meeting table. This was the downside of taking advice from Lucinda: more meetings with doughnuts. More properly, more meetings with doughnuts and the men who eat them. He should probably make a point of it to inform Wooten and Banks that it was he who had personally ordered Ms. Meara to increase the number of chocolate-covereds. Hang the expense, he told her, just try to keep these dimwits content. Try to make it a little more bearable to be with these people. Which, again, was the downside of taking advice from Lucinda. She, after all, didn't have to sit here. She got to stay in bed and have a nice breakfast—unless she felt like getting up and putting her Jane Fonda workout tape in the VCR, and putting on a leotard and doing some of those butt-tightening exercises he liked to watch her do. Liked to watch her bend over, watch her bounce, bounce, feel himself get hot, and then jump all over her and have this just incredibly hot sex.

"Mr. President," he heard Crane calling him gently. "Mr. Pres-i-dent."

"Crane, please, don't treat me like an imbecile," he said sharply. "I happen to have a lot on my mind. Does it bother you if I contemplate the consequences of these important matters before trying to undertake a course of action?"

"No, sir," Crane said, pretending to be scolded.

"All right," Ross at last began, "as many of you know, we have received a reply from the Hondanistas. They have sent what appears to be"—he accepted a piece of paper from Ms. Meara and scanned it—"and what I am now informed the FBI laboratory in Quantico has verified *is*—a lock of Vice President Bibby's hair. As well as a dead iguana."

"Why the hell are they sending us lizards?" Wooten boomed as the rest of them mumbled.

"Well, General," Ross said evenly, "we don't know why. The CIA's working on it, the Library of Congress is working on it, some army intelligence boys even got in touch with a Wendell Smith, a professor of Central American literature at the University of Texas, and no one is quite sure what this means at all. For the time being, we are treating it as a confrontational response, although it's possible that the iguana died en route, and that it was meant as a peace offering or gift of some sort. Our terrorism experts are mulling that one over."

"No message?" Ingram of the CIA asked.

"Oh, yes, indeed, there was a message. Sorry I forgot to mention it, because it's pretty important. It further confuses matters. 'Dear Gangster Ross' it says—I dismiss that, they're just trying to rile me when they say stuff like that—'Dear Gangster Ross, send us seventy-five million dollars, or you'll never see Bibby alive.'"

"So they lowered their demands," Ingram observed.

"Yes, so you see my dilemma. A ransom demand, obviously, is unfriendly, but now they're offering us a very nice discount. I'm sure many people would look at this and say 'The price is right—dealing days are here.'"

The phone rang. "Pardon me, Mr. President," Turnbridge of the NSC said. "It's Horace Bibby on the line."

Oh, I guess I have to do this, Ross thought. Talking to Horace Bibby had never been easy under any circumstances. He always wanted you to know that he had earned his reputation as the meanest son of a bitch in the world fair and square, and had no intention of resting on his laurels. But ever since Ross had cho-

sen Brent, well, things had become additionally strained. Ross
remembered how Horace had practically broken his hand greeting him on Inauguration Day. "Congratulations," Horace had
snarled, and grasped Ross's hand so tight that Ross thought he
would need to call in the Secret Service to pull the old tycoon
off. "Tell me, Ross," he'd said in his gravelly, nearly menacing
voice, "I've always contributed to your campaigns. Why do you
want to turn me into the laughingstock of the nation?" Well,
what could Ross say? That, no, Horace wasn't the laughingstock
of the nation, that his son was? Or, no, Horace was just the
laughingstock of the Century Club, which as far as Horace was
concerned was about as much of the nation that he cared about?
"Oh, don't be silly," was about all that Ross had managed to
utter before wrenching his hand away.

  "Excuse me, everyone," Ross said. Should I make Friedman
talk to him? I made Friedman inform him when the Hondanistas grabbed Brent. It would make for continuity. Nah, can't
avoid it. "Sorry, I have to take this. Horace and I have been miss-
ing one another. You people just talk among yourselves and
come up with some—I don't know—options." He grabbed the
receiver. "Hey there, Horace. Sorry about this game of phone
tag we've been playing. Where'd we finally catch up with you?"

  "Just so you know, Mr. President, after fourteen calls, I've
caught up with *you*. I'm in Bibbyville, if you must know."

  "One of my favorite towns. How's your beautiful wife, Gwendoline, holding up?"

  "She's fine. They just upped her dosage. I tell you, Valium is
a blessing. I wish I had invested in it when I had the chance. But
enough of this bullshit. When are you going to get my boy out?"

  Here he goes, typical Horace, going straight for the throat.
"Well, it's just not that simple, is it, Horace? I have our nation's
interests to think about, our image in the world. We don't want
to look like a toothless old tiger that can be led around by any
bunch of banana pickers who can get their mitts on some surplus
uniforms, now, do we?" Well, so far he's bought this National
Image line without a peep. Let's try finances. "Besides, there's

some question about where we get the money. Some of the budget fellows are saying we spend too much on the vice president already. They'd just bust if we shelled out any more—"

"Who's the president there, Ross, you or them?"

Ah, the familiar boorishness. Now that's more like the Horace we know. "Well, that's a silly question, Horace. *I'm* the president, of course."

"Well, are we ever going to see you act like one?"

"Whoa, there, Horace, remember who you're talking to."

"I remember exceptionally well. Why don't you just pay those Hondanista bastards and get on with it? It's only a business matter, Ross. Sometimes you got people by the balls, sometimes they got you. When they got you, give in fast, 'cause you get nothing by giving in slow."

"Well, thank you for that lesson, Horace, but let me ask you: If it's so easy to give away seventy-five million—"

"Seventy-five?"

"Yes, that's the good news. Brent has been marked down. Now, if it's so easy to part with seventy-five million, why don't you come up with the dough? You could probably get that much from selling off Bibby Publishing or Bibby Paper Products or Bibby Resorts or any of your divisions."

"Well, uh, well, uh, well—," Horace Bibby said, and Ross was delighted to have reduced the old bastard to a stammering bluster. "How am I supposed to get fair market value under these circumstances?" he finally got out. "What about my tax consequences? The sharks would eat me alive."

"Exactly, Horace, you're absolutely right. You should worry about fair market value and taxes and everything else. And so should I, Horace, I should worry, too. I'm in the same kind of boat. I have to worry about the country."

"You know that I'd pay the money if I could," the old man said, and Ross thought there was some kind of softening in his voice, which momentarily confused Ross, since he knew that Horace Bibby was a heartless cutthroat and would have enough cash to ransom twenty vice presidents and still have piles of money left over. Perhaps when Horace said "if I could," he meant it in some metaphysical or psychological way. "Yes, it's funny," said Ross, trying to keep pace with that turn of the conversation, if that was indeed what was happening, "but when you stop and think about it, once you start to evaluate the mitigating factors, one individual's life—even if it's someone we love and respect the way we obviously love and respect the vice president—well, one little individual's life just isn't all that damned important."

"It's important to Gwendoline," Horace said. "You want to hear something funny? She says she would just pay it. Any amount, from anybody's pocket—yours, mine, the mailman's, it makes no difference to her. I mean, it's lucky I never put very much property in her name, or it would have been gone the first day Brent was captured."

"That's a mother's love for you, bless her heart," Ross said. Feeling he'd done pretty well in this talk with the old man, he wanted to quit while he was ahead. "Look, Horace, we're trying awfully hard here. We're doing all we can, and we're looking for ways to do more. As soon as I think we can strike a deal, we'll jump on it like fleas on a dog. Try to have a little confidence."

"I'll have confidence a little while longer, Ross. After that, somebody's head will roll."

"Okay," Ross said, escaping. "Nice talking to you. Love to Gwendoline." *You mendacious old bastard.*

Ross hung up the receiver and thought for a moment. He felt cheerful at having avoided complete humiliation from the old tycoon. "You know," he finally said, feeling very daring, "if the Hondanistas went from a hundred down to seventy-five, they might go lower yet. Let's see if we can't sweat a better price out of them. Alcozar's men will surely come up with something soon. And maybe it's just a hunch, but I don't think they're ready to kill Brent just quite yet."

Twenty

"Okay, put the chairs over there, in front of the trees," Carlos was yelling. "Raul, you did remember to charge your battery, didn't you? Bien. You bought a new videotape, didn't you? Okay. Come on, everybody, hurry up. We have about an hour of light left, and I want to get this shot."

Esteban came up with Bibby. "I made sure he had a clean shirt."

"Good," said Carlos. "How you feel, Bibby? Good? Loose? Ready to reach millions?"

"I guess so," Brent said. "Listen, I'm not going to be called a traitor for doing this, am I? I'm not going to go home and get spit on and run into people who want to shave my head, am I? I mean, if I am, I'd just as soon pass."

"I don't think anything will happen to you," Carlos said.

"But isn't there a rule? Aren't I supposed to just give you my name, rank, and serial number?"

"Okay, what is your serial number?" Carlos asked. "See? You don't know it. You know why? Because you don't have one. Now, just relax. I'll make it clear on the tape that you objected to participating in this." He heard Raul calling out, telling him everything was ready. "Now, let's go do this. By the way, your hair looks very nice."

Bibby and Carlos were sitting in chairs that had been set up in front of the trees. Raul stood about eight feet in front of them with a Panasonic camcorder. "Okay," Carlos asked, "are we rolling? . . . Good afternoon, I am General Carlos Amaro, head of the Hondanista Freedom Fighters, and my guest today is that international criminal and crypto-fascist, Brent Bibby, the vice president of the United States of America. By the way, let me mention at the outset that Mr. Bibby had very strong reservations about participating in this program, but that he overcame them. How are you feeling today, Mr. Vice President?"

Smile. Remember to smile. "I'm doing pretty good, thanks."

"Vice President Bibby arrived just the other day in San Rico and got to spend a day with that despot, Alcozar; the rest of his time he has been in hiding with us. Are you enjoying your visit to San Rico de Humidor so far?"

"Well, in many respects I am." He was vaguely aware of Raul moving the camera in closer. "The weather is beautiful. I thought it would be a lot hotter, but in fact it's quite pleasant. And the scenery is lovely, the people are friendly, and the food is magnificent. Esteban, the cook here, is just a magician."

"Bugs?"

"No, there are surprisingly few. No, the whole thing, has been—in its own way—quite relaxing."

"But of course you miss your homeland," Carlos said sympathetically. "The baseball, the rock music, the Kentucky Fried Chicken . . ."

"Sure I do," said Brent. "Who wouldn't?"

"Well, we'd like nothing better than to send you back. Let me ask you, Mr. Vice President, did you know we lowered our monetary demands?"

Smile again. "Yes. Or so you've told me."

"Now, did you know that your government is attempting to drive the price even lower?"

"I thought I'd heard something like that on the news, yes."

"So you've kept up with the latest developments in this crisis pretty studiously, haven't you?"

"I'd like to think so, yes."

"Well," Carlos said with a Bob Barkerish grin, "here's a

brand-new one. What I bet you don't know, and what I bet the mighty President Ross in Washington, D.C., doesn't know either, is that another party has made a bid for you."

Bibby was completely shocked by the news. "Wh-who?" was all he could manage to ask.

"Hold onto your hat, because, ladies and gentlemen, the exciting new bidder is Emir Faisel Ibn al-Yabani, the mad oil sheikh of South Djibouti. He has offered us eighty million dollars for you."

"Really?"

"Yes. And he says that if he gets his hands on you, he's going to put you in the center of town and make you empty your bladder on the American flag."

"No!" Brent said. He sat open-mouthed in fear and horror. "Well, he couldn't make me. I'd hold it in."

"Face it, Mr. Vice President, you couldn't hold it in forever."

"Well, you just tell him to forget it," Brent said, the pitch of his voice rising, his eyebrows flung up in desperation and confusion. "I'd bust before I did anything like that."

"Well, you might," Carlos agreed. "But if you don't pee, he'll behead you. I guess he might behead you in any event, he's unpredictable that way. But here's the thing for everybody to remember: The Hondanistas are not unreasonable people. We don't really want to sell you to a lunatic pump jockey." Then, in a masterstroke of communication that was praised by media analysts on all three network morning news shows the next day, he looked right into the camera and said, "Mr. President Ross, we'll lower our price to sixty million. You can afford that. If you come up with sixty million dollars, then there's no sheikh, no humiliation, no beheading. That's not such a bad bargain, is it?"

He smiled his big, friendly smile, and held it for five full seconds. "Okay, that's a wrap," he then said. "Let's make a copy and get it Fed Ex'ed up to New York in time for the nightly news. He then turned to Bibby. "Hey, nice job," he said. "You were very natural."

"You thought so? You know, they never let me go on TV."

"You're joking!" said Carlos. "But you're so telegenic. I think they're making a big mistake. I'd put you on all the time."

"Listen, I don't know if this is a good time, but about this sheikh—"

"Bibby, baby," Carlos laughed, "would I let you get beheaded?" He put his arm around Bibby's shoulder. "There's no offer," he said. "We just needed something to force your people to get off their butts and send us some money."

He saw the tape the same time everyone else did, when it led the evening news broadcasts of all three networks as well as CNN. He felt himself awash in disbelief—at their audacity, at poor Brent's peril, at the terrible possibility that the vice president of the United States would somehow be transported to Djibouti and humiliated. And he felt anxious, a feeling no doubt aggravated by the fact that he had just shelled out $172 of his own money for pizza for everyone in the Sit, none of whom seemed at all moved by Bibby's plight. Everyone watched the tape, of course. But as soon as it was over, it was business as usual: Wooten blowing smoke about how the Air Force could intercept everything between San Rico and Djibouti; Friedman on the horn, leaking to some favored journalist how Sheikh Yabani—the liar!—had immediately called to deny making any offer to the Hondanistas; Ms. Meara and Turnbridge of the NSC breathlessly agreeing about how crises have a magical propensity for bringing people together; three guys from the Pentagon playing Michael Jordan Nerf ball basketball with a hoop that they stuck on the Strategic Air Command Readiness Screen; everybody grabbing pizza and arguing about who ordered what beer. Finally Crane stood up and with bearish indignation shamed them into silence.

"What is wrong with you people?" he snarled. "Have none of you any sense of propriety? Have none of you any decency? This isn't a party. We're not having a good time. This is not a golden moment over which we'll wax nostalgic in the years to come. One of our country's leaders is being held by a gang of terrorists, and you're arguing about pepperoni and sausage and who gets the Heineken. Now I know it's just Brent Bibby they've captured. I know America's future does not rise or fall with his fate. I know that few of you think he's worth the time of day. But you are all wrong. Brent Bibby is somebody important. He is somebody worthwhile. And I say let's call an end to these little junk-food banquets we keep throwing ourselves and pay what we have to pay to get him back." With that he put on his coat. "Good night, Mr. President. I can't stand to be a party to this circle jerk anymore. Call me if you need me."

Over the next three hours, Ross thought, nothing happened to counter Crane's arguments. Since the start of the evening news, 23,000 calls had come in to the White House from people around the country; 97 percent of them favored paying the ransom. The press office reported that the *New York Times,* the *Los Angeles Times,* the *Chicago Tribune,* and the *Washington Post* all intended to urge Ross to pay the ransom in their lead editorials the next morning. The Reverand Jerry Don Taylor closed his Christian Broadcasting Network interview program, "Speaking with Jesus," with his personal prayer that God would give Ross the strength to pay the guerrillas and that God would then smite them before they got to spend any of the money. When Ross saw a copy of the front page of the next day's *New York Post* somebody had faxed from Manhattan—it featured a drawing of Bibby holding his crotch under the headline PAY OR BUST—Ross knew that he had no alternative. "Marv," he said to his secretary of state, "have some of your people make some discreet inquiries tonight. Figure out the best way to pay this ransom. This crisis is no damn fun anymore. I want it to go away."

Slowly he made his way out of the Sit and through the corridors of the White House toward his sleeping quarters. Not so busy now, he noticed as he passed through the hallways. Not so bright, not so sharp. Just a fancy old house where the shit had hit the fan.

He found his way to his bedroom. Lucinda was inside. She

had put on her nightclothes—an oversized gray-and-navy Georgetown T-shirt—and was in bed, watching "Nightline." Ross slumped back the pillows on his half of the bed, not bothering to remove his jacket or tie or even his shoes.

"God, can you believe this bastard Yabani?" she said heatedly. "He's just sitting there, swearing he's never even spoken to the Hondanistas. Look at him! Lying right in Koppel's face!"

"Doesn't matter," Ross said, not even bothering to look at the screen. "He's lying, he's not lying, it just doesn't matter. We've been overtaken by opinion. I don't see how we can avoid paying the ransom now."

"Really?" Lucinda said. It was just one word, but the level of skepticism that she so forcefully invested in it intimidated Ross, and he raised himself up on one elbow to hear her out. "Well, that's where our thinking is headed, anyway. Why?" he asked. "Do you have another point of view?"

"I don't know," she said, shifting on the bed to get behind Ross, where she began rubbing his shoulders. "You say you don't see how we can avoid paying the ransom now. I, on the other hand, just don't see how you *can* pay it now. You know, darling, I love Brent. I think we all do. None of us wants to see even the tiniest hair on his head get hurt, but—"

"A little to the left," Ross said. "But what?"

"But now, when it's the toughest, is the time we have to bite the bullet. Brent is a soldier, and if he dies, well, he dies in the service of his country. And I guess I'll shed a few tears, but I'll try to be strong as I accept that folded up flag by his casket, and I'll feel very proud."

Well, it's hard to argue with a brave woman, Ross thought. Brave and brilliant, he corrected himself, feeling the tension slough away from his neck as she massaged him, feeling also her perky breasts press against his shoulder blades. He could take a lot of strength from this woman, he realized. When all the world wanted him to cave in, maybe she could give him the fortitude he'd need to hold the line against these Hondanista terrorists. "You know, there would be a lot of problems if Brent was exe-

cuted," he said. "There'd be second-guessing, there'd be inves-
tigations, we'd probably have to convince Alcozar to station a
couple hundred thousand of our troops down there. . . ."

"Yes," she agreed, "there will be burdens to bear."

"Not to mention that we'd have to go through all the riga-
marole of finding a new vice president."

They were both quiet for a while. "Well," she finally said, "I
suppose you could appoint me."

"Appoint you?" he said. "I could do that?"

"Sure," she said, moving back around to sit close to him, face
to face. "Why couldn't you do it?" she asked with an excited
smile. "Wives of dead elected officials are forever getting picked
to fill out their husbands' terms. It's the American way."

"I suppose," he said suspiciously, thinking it was all too good
to be true.

"And then, darling," she said, "you and I could get married."

"We could?" he said, in excitement and amazement.

"Of course we could," she said, putting her arms around his
neck, leaning in so that their foreheads touched. "And then we
could run for reelection together."

This was getting better and better, he thought. "Okay," he
smiled. "We'll do that."

"And then," she said, "about a year before your term expires,
you could resign, and I would become president."

Suddenly the happy Ross faded, leaving room for the suspicious Ross to return. "I don't know if I'd want to give up the
presidency, Lucinda. I mean, it would be nice that you could
move up, but what would I do?"

"Silly!" she said. "Do you think I'd forget about you? I'd
appoint you to be *my* vice president. And then we'd run for
reelection, and we'd win; and then just before my term was up,
I'd resign, and *you'd* step up and become president again; and
then you could appoint me vice president again, and so on, and
so on, and so on . . ."

There was a long pause as Ross mulled the plan over, though
Lucinda never doubted the outcome and experienced not the
slightest surprise when Ross at long last stopped stroking his

chin and spoke. "I suppose we could go on for years," he observed.

"Yes! Like king and queen," she said sweetly.

"All we would need is for the Hondanistas to kill Brent," he said, nodding slowly.

"And think of it, darling," she said eagerly, "his life is in extreme peril already. Why, he may be dead, even as we speak."

"Well, that would be fine," he said, "but I do have responsibilities. I think it's wrong if I just sit here on my hands hoping they execute. I can't do nothing."

"Look, Roger," she said, her voice suddenly stern, "get it through your head: You're not doing nothing. You're engaging in a war of nerves with terrorists, and you're waiting them out. Maybe their price will drop through the floor, and we'll get a deal you won't be able to refuse. Brent will come home, and we'll have had our amusing little fantasy. On the other hand, their price might hold steady. If so, you threaten an invasion. Alcozar will probably forbid it. If that happens, what happens to Brent is no longer your responsibility."

"But suppose Alcozar permits an invasion," Ross said. "Then we'll have to go in and look for Brent."

"Yes, we'll have to look for him. And we'll probably find him. And I bet when that happens there will be a heated, chaotic battle, in which the crossfire will be unbelievably intense."

"He might get hit," Ross said, brightening.

"Right, he might get hit. But look, if worse comes to worst, he survives and we carry on the way we have. What else can we do?"

She then smiled at him so lovingly that he found himself boundless and burdenless, freed from the workaday concerns of his existence, buoyed by the knowledge that he had found a woman who seemed able to make his life richer in every way. "My God, Lucinda," he said, grabbing her and slipping his hands under the cotton Georgetown shirt to feel her breasts, "not only are you a beautiful woman, you're clearheaded as well. Oh, Lucinda!" he said as he stuck his head under the shirt, "I love the way you think!"

Twenty-one

Crane woke up the next morning feeling as good as he had in a long time, as good as he'd felt in months, as good maybe, *better* maybe, than he had ever felt in his entire life. He whistled as he watched himself shave in the mirror, he sang in the shower as the water gushed down on his head, he saw the sunlight shining through his kitchen window and was suffused with its power as if he'd never seen sunlight before. He heard the burble of pigeons on his fire escape and thought it was the exultation of larks. Crane was feeling very—oh, go ahead and say it—chipper.

And why not? The performance he had turned in during last night's meeting of the Sit Group was, he concluded after careful consideration, one of the finest of his career. All those eggheads and prima donnas and nut cases were overwhelming Ross, Crane thought, just poisoning his mind. Face it, Ross never had been a guy who did all that well when a barrage of opinions was banging into him all at once. Listening to a roomful of certified experts mouth off in succession could be confusing for anyone, and Ross wasn't a man who could handle confusion all that nimbly. Ross, Crane knew, liked to be liked, and when there were too many opinions in front of him, too many options, too much to choose from, too many people giving him advice, he just tightened up, until it dawned on him that some of the options were never going to get chosen, and that the people who were pushing those options were going to get angry, or insulted, or maybe just miffed, but even so, *somehow put out,* and they weren't going to like Ross quite as much as they had, and he just didn't want to contemplate that possibility. Ever.

So Crane had worked up his little speech and waited for three days for the most effective moment to deliver it. For a while he didn't think he'd ever get the chance. There were times when it appeared that the Wootens and the Banks and the Friedmans would never tire themselves out, or that the media would somehow fail to heat this thing up and get the public and Congress to demand some action. There were even times when the thinking seemed to be that the Hondanistas might let Bibby go. But as luck would have it, the situation kept getting worse and worse, and lo and behold, Crane got his chance, which made him very pleased. Pleased that he'd gotten his chance, pleased that he'd used that chance to put one out of the ballpark.

His little talk had stunned them well enough, Crane thought. But when he'd packed up his things and walked out, well, they'd been speechless. *Gaga.* Leave a meeting of the Sit Group? *Before* the president? Unheard of! *Without eating?* Shocking! Old Crane must be really serious. When he'd shut the door of the room behind him, it was all he could do to keep from dancing.

Not that he much cared all that deeply whether Brent Bibby lived or died. Oh, *now* it made a difference, of course. *Now* he wanted Bibby to live. But a week ago, had he been given a choice—morality-free, no sanctity-of-life stuff to think about, and all nice-guy bullshit aside—of whether he'd have preferred to hear that Brent Bibby had been shot dead by rebel assassins on the tennis court behind Our Lady of the Junta, or had been kidnapped and hauled off to who knows where—in turn instigating a tense international crisis and a test of Ross's presidency—well, he'd have picked dead Bibby. Anybody in his position would have. For one thing—understand, those nice-guy considerations still off to one side—Crane would probably have been in charge of the funeral, and that certainly would have been a feather in his cap. It was a small enough circle of operatives who'd run a presidential campaign, an even smaller one who'd run winning ones, but practically none of them had gotten to run a state funeral to boot. And a state funeral sort of on the cheap, too: It wouldn't be like *Ross* had died. Ross would still be alive and could still stand for reelection. Meanwhile, Crane would get to run things, and produce all those wonderfully telegenic images: casket in the Rotunda, the solemn Marine guards, the dignified honorary pallbearers for the martyred vice president, the catafalque, the caisson, the stately train ride back to Bibbyville; sending Lucinda back to Bibbyville, watching her image receding in the rear view mirror, reading in years to come about the Widow Bibby twisting the night away—or fruging, or whatever the hell dance people did these days—in Manhattan or Beverly Hills or Palm Beach or Cap d'Antibes or anywhere but where Crane was. The prospect cheered him immensely, and as he contemplated it a small smile crept onto his face.

But it was all just a pleasant fantasy now. Brent Bibby was no longer much good to him dead. Oh sure, there'd still be a state funeral, but nobody would be paying much attention to the pomp. People would be sitting in their overstuffed armchairs watching the funeral cortege, but they'd be thinking of when the news first broke, remembering the pictures of Bibby's bullet-ridden corpse. They'd be struck by the cuts the news directors would make, ones that would deftly fade pictures of Bibby, wearing that well-known deer-in-the-headlights expression of his, into shots of those same vacant little eyes lifelessly rolled back in his forehead. And they'd remember that it had been Roger Ross who had turned down the chance to bring Bibby home at the fart-in-the-wind price of sixty million.

The political cost would be incalculable. People liked to think their president was a good guy, Crane said to himself, repeating things he already knew well. They didn't like to think he was the sort of fish who'd remain cold and cheapskatish on hearing that a citizen—let alone someone he knew and seemingly thought highly of—was in danger of entering a state of rigor fucking mortis in some humid, overheated jungle. And that the endangered person would be the vice president (in national mythology, the friendly, somewhat-less-intelligent brother of the national father), particularly *this* vice president (in this administration, not just somewhat less intelligent, but the teeniest bit above functionally retarded)—well, it was all too much. It was unacceptable. It was explosive. Crane had to step in and put an end to it.

And he had. He *knew* he had, the minute he'd left the Sit. He'd felt so good that he'd treated himself. Left the White House and gone to Joe and Moe's, his favorite hangout. Had a sixteen-ounce steak and a rather generous amount of bourbon. Run into Gaston Castleberry and some of his pals from the Democratic National Committee, and passed an enjoyable evening talking about Michael Dukakis and his little tank driver's helmet and Fritz Mondale and his pledge to raise taxes and Jimmy Carter and his attack rabbit and his malaise speech and his hostages. Everything they talked about had made Crane laugh, and he'd kept on laughing, even after Gaston had stopped and gotten sort of cranky and snippy and tried to bring up Nixon and Reagan and Quayle. Go ahead, Crane had told him, bring 'em up all you want. There's only so much fun you can make of winners. They take it for a while, but then they get tired of listening and go inside and have fun at the party, and leave the losers to hang outside and play kick the can. Not even Castleberry's snide parting crack about Ross having his own hostage crisis nowadays had had any effect: By morning there would be no hostage crisis. Crane had gone home, put on his pajamas, put a stack of Sinatra albums on his hi-fi, and contentedly fallen asleep.

"Good morning, Car-*LOTTA!*" Crane boomed happily to his secretaries upon his arrival. "Good morning, La *VERNE!* Any messages?"

"Mr. Forrester called from San Rico City," he was told.

Ross rang Forrester up at once. "Can I come home yet?" Forrester asked him meekly.

"Oh, not just yet," Crane said. "The president isn't in a good enough mood. But I don't think you'll be out there too much longer. He hasn't mentioned you for three days, hasn't reminded me to get you off the payroll in four, hasn't asked me why your office hasn't been cleaned out yet in five. I think you'll be back in no time. I just hope it was worth it."

"Frankly, if by the first *it* you mean a memorable-for-a-life-time erotic encounter with two Humirican beauties, and if by the second *it* you mean the possible ruination of my career and the imperiling of the vice president's life, then I would have to say no, the first was not worth the second. But I would hasten to add that there is a whole range of trauma short of those described that would definitely, gladly be worth another few hours with those vixens."

"You know, I kind of miss you, Forrester," Crane said, "even if you are a perv. You must feel really out of place. I mean, apart from any new friends you may have made."

"Actually, I'm having a rather good time. People think I'm still with the White House—an accurate perception, I hope—and they accord me a rather wide berth. It has occurred to me to think that if I have to remain fired I'll stay down here, at least as long as my business cards hold out. I get to go anywhere and see pretty much anything I want."

"What do you see?" Crane, having reached his fill of small talk, wanted to know.

"Many, many things that would make you very, very amused, as only you can be amused."

"Like?"

"Like the Humirican Defense Forces hanging around San Rico City. They go out in the morning and rumble around the foothills—you can see the dust kicking up at about the same elevation every day—and then they come back around four o'clock and bivouac right outside of town. I also see the Humirican Air Force, such as it is, sitting on the landing strips and in the hangers of Estilo International Airport. I don't see troops going up into the mountains. I don't see planes in the air. And I don't see how they're going to find Vice President Bibby unless he pokes his head out of Colonel Caliente's pocket. And even then, I would give you odds."

Crane felt a little less happy after talking to Forrester, but he didn't get a chance to dwell on it, because just a few minutes later the president called to tell him he had decided to hold out for a better price.

The news couldn't have hit harder if Ross had delivered it with a two-by-four. "Forgive me, Mr. President," Crane sputtered, his head ringing with shock, "but I—, but you—, but he—, but that's—you're nuts! That's just a nutty thing to do!"

"I'm not surprised to hear you say that, Crane. I know you felt strongly the other way."

"You know, people aren't going to stand for it if that boy dies now," Crane nearly spat.

"Crane," Ross said sternly, "get ahold of yourself. He's not a boy, and if he dies, he dies, and people will stand for whatever we persuade them they have to stand for. And, bottom line, this is what I've decided."

"Well," Crane said, making little effort to hide his sarcasm, "you're the president."

"That's right, Crane, I am."

Crane sat at his desk twitching, his anger throbbing, roiling, growing hotter by the minute. Not once in twenty-five years had he and Ross disagreed on matters of fundamental importance. And now three times in the last six months—*three times! and twice in a week!*—Crane's strongest, shrewdest advice had not only been rejected, but it had been undermined at the very moment he thought he'd had the president's agreement sewed up.

It was embarrassing. And it was bad for the country. Ross was infinitely less capable of governing the country alone than he was with Crane doing most of his hard thinking for him. And that was just simply a fact, even if Ross would never admit it.

Of course, Crane realized, Ross wasn't governing the country *alone*. It was very clear to Crane that he was being replaced. Had been replaced. By somebody in a position to get the last word.

You've played a good game, Lucinda, Crane said to himself.
But now it's for keeps.

She sat on the floor of Ross's bedroom, stretching out, legs in
a V, performing her cool-down exercises. She watched herself in
the mirror as she extended herself, hair pulled back, skin rosy,
sweat crescents under the arms of her snug, gray-cotton, sleeve-
less jersey. Not bad, she thought as she contemplated her appearance. Better than the way I looked twenty years ago. Of course,
twenty years ago, she'd never exercised, and she'd worn discount
clothes and drug-store cosmetics. The natural bloom of youth
had served well enough—well enough, anyway, to attract college boys and the guys at the singles bars, and that was as much
of the world as she'd known. Later she'd gone to work at the savings and loan, and begun to realize how much a woman's
appearance meant. There were too many old leches around not
to realize. At first it had bothered her and made her angry,
because she was smart enough to get ahead and too smart not to
understand why she didn't. But it had soon become clear that
she could play it easy or play it hard—carry a banner for some
distant ideal about equality and merit, or just discreetly show a
little cleavage when discreetly showing a little cleavage made
strategic sense—and she had decided not to fight.

Besides, it all evened out. The men in the office could always
talk about football with Filson when they wanted his attention,
about football and baseball, about basketball and boxing, about
an endless supply of big plays and big games and great moments
for the highlight film. She could never do that, not well enough.
But she'd known when she stood at her desk and stretched, Filson craned his head to ogle her; and that he liked to look down
her blouse if presented the opportunity, and she'd been satisfied
to let that be her equalizer. Besides, it hadn't lasted long.

One day the bank had sent Filson to Bibbyville to talk about
underwriting Horace's new printing plant, and he'd insisted that
she come along. She had worried what horrors this trip with Filson might entail: an unseemly grope-athon she would have to

decide whether to endure; a tedious chase around the suite she wasn't sure she should win or not. But as it turned out, Horace had dragged Brent to all the meetings—this was when Horace still had hopes that Brent might have some head for business, before he'd given up and bought Brent his senate seat—and while Lucinda's boss had talked to Horace about investment credits and pay-out rates, she had talked to Brent.

It would, of course, be a lie to say that she had met him and fallen head over heels in love. It was enough to be honest, she thought, enough to say that she had met Brent and quickly realized that from her vantage point, as she scanned the world's great gamut of masculinity and realized what was out there— the abusives and the compulsives and the sadists; the cheats and the liars and the congenital losers; the vain and the ugly and the mean-by-nature; the poor, the weak, the worthless, the delusionary, the dull, and the dangerously idealistic—picking one who was good-looking and good-natured and heir to a billion-dollar fortune, however stupid he might be, was a reasonable if not hardheaded thing to do. It would have been nice if she had been in love with him, she'd thought at the time. It would be nice if she was in love with him now, she thought. But long ago she had concluded that it was not to be her lot in life to be loved like some heroine in a romance novel. As though it were anyone's.

Though now it did seem as though her lot in life was going to include becoming the first woman president of the United States. And if attaining that office seemed an accomplishment beyond the abilities of a person who had barely maintained a B average at UC Santa Barbara, and whose work experience, apart from a summer job in a boutique, had consisted of two years as a junior assistant to Filson, the admittedly criminal and now incarcerated vice president of a defunct savings and loan, well, these were days of miracles and wonders. And miracles had always been available to those willing to pay the price.

She was going to miss Brent, she thought, rolling on her back, aligning herself to perform her kagel repetitions. They had passed many pleasant moments together. She thought it would be like when her dog died when she was thirteen, a terribly sad moment that she would never entirely forget. Ah well.

Oh, this is just too morbid, she thought, suddenly sitting up. I'm going stir crazy. I need to get out.

"Mr. President, Mrs. Bibby's on the line."

"Lucinda?"

"Good morning, darling. Listen, I've been cooped up in this stuffy old mausoleum for a week now, and I feel like going out and doing a little window shopping. Tell me: As far as you know, is Brent still alive?"

Twenty-two

When Raul heard the whine and moan of the big motor coming up from the valley, his first thought was that at last the guests were arriving and he could call an end to his stint on guard duty and go get some lunch. Still, he reminded himself, you can't be too careful. Motioning to Esteban to stay low, he clicked the safety off his machine pistol and slid his finger onto the trigger. When after a minute or two the big vehicle he'd been hearing came into view around the last curve of the hidden road to the camp, Raul was modestly relieved to see that it was the large black Mercedes 600 SEL he had been expecting, and not some light-armored personnel vehicle belonging to one of the scout units of the Humirican Defense Forces.

Raul stepped out from behind a banyan tree and raised his hand, partly in greeting, partly as an instruction to stop. One, two, three, he counted the silhouettes beyond the windshield, though once the Mercedes had slowed and rolled up to him more gradually, he could make out faces behind the windshield glare: Ambassador Oakley at the wheel, President Alcozar with his big hat on in the passenger's seat, Colonel Caliente in the rear. Oakley rolled down his window and leaned his head out. "Where d'ya want me to park?" he asked.

"Over there, under the coconut trees," Raul directed.

"It's not going to get toucan shit all over it there, is it?"

"No, Mr. Ambassador," Raul said sarcastically. "We had a long talk with the toucans about that."

The passengers disembarked. "Hello, Raul," Alcozar said and nodded to the rest.

"How was the drive, Mr. President?" Raul asked, flicking the barrel of his weapon toward the campsite to indicate which way they should walk. They all turned and headed that way.

"Not bad," Alcozar said, shaking the stiffness out of his shoulders. "We made great time. Oakley's a wild man. Did I tell you that, Oakley? You're a wild man! Did ninety all the way up here. My back is all tight, though. I thought you guys were going to fix that chewed-up part of the road outside Adalapaño."

"No, sir," Esteban said, "Carlos told me the government was going to fix the road."

"No, no, no, no, no," Alcozar said. "That's not how I remember it."

"We fixed the road *up* to Adalapaño," Caliente pointed out.

"Well, somebody's got to fix the road," Alcozar said. "What do you think, Oakley? Is there some way we can get Washington to pay for it?"

The burly ambassador shrugged. "Maybe," he said.

Ten days now, Bibby thought as he reclined on the cot in his hut, ten days. And if you forgot about the parts when he was afraid that he was going to be killed or have one of his body parts amputated, and if you forgot about how much he missed Lucinda, well, the fact of the matter was he was having a very nice time. Kind of a rugged place, granted, he wouldn't mind seeing some indoor plumbing if the opportunity arose. But the weather was good and the guys were friendly, and let's face it: When you got right down to it, he'd been to a lot of thousand-dollar-a-day resorts where he hadn't had near as much fun.

No tennis, true, but he was going to fix that. Maybe. He'd been scouting around, and that morning, out jogging, about a quarter mile to the north, he'd spotted a pretty good-sized meadow—well, not a meadow, but something pretty flat and open—that could be cleared and tamped down and maybe turned into a pretty serviceable clay court. Maybe. He was going to surprise Carlos with the idea after lunch. Couldn't imagine why he wouldn't go for it. It seemed like a good project for the Hondanistas to undertake when they weren't training.

And speaking of speaking to Carlos after lunch—*lunchtime!* Wonder what's on the menu. Hey, there's somebody—what? No! This must be a hallucination. Raul, Esteban, their guns! Alcozar, Oakley, Caliente, walking in between! Toward Carlos's hut! And Alcozar clutching his back, looking like he's in pain! What's that—? Can't make out—why is Alcozar saying, "No, no, no, no, no"?

"My God!" an aghast Brent Bibby said to himself, "they've captured President Alcozar!" Then the stunning, shocking realization began to sink in. This is incredible, he thought. This is unbelievable, this is terrible, this is awful, this is a catastrophe, this is the worst. The rebels are going to win. The rebels *have* won.

But if they had won—why weren't they marching triumphantly into San Rico City? And why weren't they getting stinking drunk and firing their weapons into the sky in a dangerous celebratory frenzy? Maybe they hadn't won. Maybe there was still something he could do.

He watched Alcozar and the others enter Carlos's hut, then slumped to the floor. "Gotta think," he murmured to himself frantically. "Gotta think."

"He-ey, Julio!" Carlos greeted the president expansively. "Nice of you to come up."

"It was the least I could do," Alcozar said. "You always have to make the drive into town. I saw a little opening in my schedule, thought I'd take the opportunity to reciprocate. I've long wished to visit your pleasant little compound here in the country. Here," he said, shoving a large cardboard box across the table to the Hondanista leader, "I brought you some stuff."

"Thank you, Julio," Carlos said, stripping the masking tape

off the lid. "Once again you have shown yourself to be the living definition of thoughtfulness." He pulled open the flaps as eagerly as a child. "Let's see what we got here. Cigarettes, good. The new Stephen King, good. Oh, Tom Clancy, I *love* him."

"They were all out of Jackie Collins, I'm sorry."

"That's okay," Carlos said. "Nobody really likes her except Raul. Right, Raul?"

"Oh, man," he moaned, "one time I said I thought *Hollywood Wives* was a good read, one stinking time! And now I never hear the end of it."

"Now for the real question," Carlos said. "Not to seem like an ingrate, but did you bring any girls?"

Alcozar rolled his eyes. "I've told you and I've told you, we can't bring any outsiders up here. I thought you agreed. Besides, you like the girls at that bordello in Las Cruces, don't you?"

"Yes, I like the girls," Carlos said. "I like the girls quite a bit. It's the jukebox I can't stand. It's like all K.C. and the Sunshine Band. 'That's the way, uh-huh, uh-huh, I like it, uh-huh, uh-huh.' I mean, it's an okay song, but over and over?"

"And it's twenty years old," Raul said.

"That's right," Carlos said. "It would be nice to hear Madonna. It would be nice to listen to some Guns N' Roses, some C+C Music Factory."

"Well, all you have to do is say something," Alcozar said. "Make a list. We'll get one of the arts agencies to appropriate some funds to invigorate musical awareness in Las Cruces. Hey, Oakley, what do you think? Would Washington pay for it?"

The ambassador shrugged. "Maybe," he said.

Bibby peered over the bottom edge of his window and tried to figure out what was happening inside Carlos's hut. He could just make out the shapes of figures moving past the windows. Well, it all seems calm, he thought. Not intense. Not heated. No screams of pain. Wait, there's Carlos. Oh, he's just tossing a cigarette butt outside. Seems cheerful enough. Of course, why wouldn't he be cheerful? He's just won the damn war.

Won the war. And dealt the Ross administration a major defeat. Which means, probably . . .

Probably we might be in more danger than ever.

Gotta do something.

"Some pâté, Julio?"

"No, thanks. I'm trying to watch my waistline."

"Eat more gravel," Carlos suggested with a smirk.

"He told you about that, did he?"

"Oh, man, like eighteen times a day. It made a bigger impression on him than sex."

Alcozar chuckled. "I hope he didn't enjoy it more," he said. "But you tell me, what's wrong with those people? Fifteen years we've been pulling that gravel bit on them, and it always works. I still get letters from Oliver North asking for recipes. What's their problem? It's *corn!*"

"Man, I wish we could feed Bibby gravel," Carlos said. "He eats like a horse. Esteban had to go halfway to Las Cruces before he caught an iguana yesterday. He thinks Bibby's eaten all the ones around here. I mean, the guy's in captivity and he's gained weight. We've got to get him out of here."

"Mmmh," Alcozar said. "Unfortunately, I don't think anybody wants him."

Oakley cleared his throat. "I've had exploratory discussions with Secretary of State Friedman, and frankly, Carlos, there doesn't seem to be any number at which Washington says yes."

"Oh, come on."

"Carlos, I've gone down to one million dollars, and all they say is that it's our policy not to negotiate with terrorists."

"Bullshit artists!" Carlos sneered.

"I know," Oakley agreed. "Think of all the times they've chucked that principle aside when it's suited them. I can't believe that they're sticking to it now."

"Such lousy, stinking hypocrites!"

"In point of fact," Alcozar said, "they're closer to invading than paying."

The news hit Carlos hard. "How can they invade?" he asked, his voice soaring in exasperation. "I mean, I saw Bob Novak say that on 'Capitol Gang' last week, but he's always wrong. I figured some pal in the White House fed that to him just to keep us on edge. They can't really be considering that, can they? They'd send in troops just to chase after one shitty little guerrilla? Isn't that illegal?"

"I think so," Alcozar said, "but I'm not sure. I was trying to find where I put our copy of the OAS agreement last night, to see if there was some little clause buried in it that gave the U.S. the right to invade, but it wasn't where I thought I kept it. We'll check it out, though. But just on the face of it, you'd think they couldn't come in here unless we invited them. Wouldn't they get pissed if we invaded their country just to catch some outlaw?"

"Damn straight!"

"But let's not be naive," Alcozar said quite seriously. "It's just as obvious that if they decide to invade, nobody's going to stop them. I mean, I'll kick and scream, but face it: How much can you complain about something your chief benefactor wants to do before he decides your opinion is a luxury he can no longer afford?"

"Dear Lucinda," he wrote, lacking paper, on the back of his tennis shorts, "if I go to my final reward today, please know that I was thinking about how much I love you. I will see you face and think of our song, and how our life was as much a 'Thriller' as anything Michael Jackson could think of. And please tell President Ross that I regret that I have but one life to give for my country. Love, Brent"

He read it over. Upon consideration, he added 'Bibby' to his signature, just to make sure that whoever found it would know it was from him. Then he climbed out the window, snuck over to the brush by the side of the compound, and began to creep along the edge of the jungle towards Carlos's hut.

"Hey, Bibby!" he heard someone call his name. He turned

and saw a bearded guerrilla brandishing two rackets and a shut-
tlecock. "You want to play badminton?"

"Shh!" he said, waving him off. "Not now, Che. In a little
while."

The guerrilla shrugged and wandered away.

"You know what I'm thinking?" Alcozar said.

"I bet you're thinking what we're all thinking," Carlos said. "I
bet you're thinking that we ought to give him back."

"I'm afraid so," Alcozar said, shrugging as he watched all present shake their heads in disappointment.

"Oh, man, so frustrating," Carlos sighed. "So, how exactly do
you propose we accomplish this?"

"Well . . ." Alcozar hesitated.

"Well, what?"

"You're not going to like to hear this."

"So I'm not going to like to hear it. So say it anyway."

"Well . . . we could raid your camp."

"And what?" Carlos countered. "And pretend that my gal-
lant, field-hardened troops were routed? That we turned tail and
ran?"

"I knew you weren't going to like it," Alcozar said. "I wish you
weren't always so selfish."

"Now, come on, boys," Oakley broke in, "squabbling among
ourselves isn't going to solve anything. Carlos, you know, this is
something that can benefit all of us. Frankly, I think I could just
about guarantee that a successful resolution of this crisis, one in
which the vice president is returned and the rebels get a spank-
ing, would be viewed in Washington with heart-warming gratitude and a munificent outpouring of generosity."

"Forget about it! It's too hard. We'd have to move all this
stuff."

"Well," Alcozar said, "in actuality, you'd have to leave a lot
of it, to make the capture look convincing."

"Leave a lot! Like what? Not—*not my dish!* Forget about it,

Julio, get it out of your head. Wait'll you try living a few years in the bush, you'll never make fun of television again. And remember—your turn is coming. We agreed that the Hondanistas would win this revolution. Then you'd come up to the hills and be a counterrevolutionary while I got to live in the palace."

"Actually," Alcozar said calmly, "we wanted to talk to you about that. We were thinking the oth—"

"We, *who?*" Carlos interrupted.

"We three—Caliente, Oakley, and me."

"Oh, making decisions behind my back now, are we?"

"Are you going to get paranoid on us?" Alcozar asked. "Nobody's making any decisions without you. Listen to what I say. What did I say? 'We wanted to talk to you.' And what are we doing? We're here talking, aren't we?"

Carlos looked from one to the next. "I guess so," he said, hanging his head. "I'm sorry."

"It's okay. Now, as I was saying: We were talking the other night, and we thought we ought to see if there might not be more money all around if, after your revolution succeeded, Caliente came up to the hills and became a counterrevolutionary, and I became a president-in-exile in Miami."

"I see," Carlos said with a grin. "I know what you're doing. Caliente has to sit out here in the jungle, while you live in Miami. You go to big dinners in Washington, you do the talk shows, you go to college campuses to make speeches and end up in a dormitory trying to get some pretty coed to drop her panties for the great noble defender of freedom and human rights. You know what, dude? You're getting soft."

Now they were all laughing again. "My belly's getting soft," Alcozar said when the hooting finally stopped, "but my mind's still sharp. Look, if we go with the new plan, Caliente gets the aid from Washington, and I get to go on the lecture circuit and raise money from wealthy Americans who think it's awful that the rebels have stolen my country."

"And what's in it for me?" Carlos asked.

"You'll get a lot of money from those rich liberals in Holly-wood and New York," Alcozar said brightly.

"Maybe," Carlos grunted dubiously. "I'll think it over."

They're in there, Bibby thought as he duckwalked along the edge of the little porch that surrounded Carlos's hut. I can hear them talking. That's Carlos. Carlos laughing. Laughing the happy, full-throated laugh of the seemingly victorious. Well, laugh on, Carlos. This time, the har-di-har-har's on you.

"Okay," Carlos said, "try this instead. Tomorrow we'll raid the city. We'll take Bibby along and dump him somewhere. Then you can say you recaptured him or that he escaped or something."

"Not bad," Alcozar said, mulling it over. He took out a long cigar, clipped its end. He thought for a long time. "What are you going to do when you raid the city?" he asked.

"I don't know," Carlos said grumpily. "Do I have to think of everything?"

"Are you going to blow anything up?" Alcozar asked, lighting the cigar.

"I guess so," Carlos said. "That's what we usually do."

"Blow up what?" Alcozar

"Do we have to decide that right now?"

"Yes, absolutely, we must decide that now," Alcozar said sharply. "It's very important."

"Oh, come on, we'll just pick something out when we get there. What are you trying to pin me down for?"

"Because it's important!"

"Dios mio!" Carlos cried. "You're such a control freak since you took this job. I told you you were going to turn out just like your father, and man, have you ever!"

"Just decide!"

"Okay, fine," Carlos said. "We haven't hit the post office in a couple years, maybe we'll do the post office."

"No," said Alcozar curtly. "See? This is why I'm glad I brought this up. You'd have gone down there tomorrow and blown the post office to smithereens."

"And what if I had?"

"Look, compadre, after you blew it up last time, Washington built us a brand-new one with all this great new sorting equipment, and it's just wonderful. For the first time in the history of San Rico de Humidor, you can shop by catalog and be reasonably confident you'll get your package."

Carlos rolled his eyes. "All right, Julio, then why don't you just tell me what you would like us to blow up? I really don't care."

"Why don't you blow up the baggage room at the airport?" Alcozar suggested. "We need a new one. Plus it'll be Saturday night, nobody will be there."

"What do you think, Oakley?" Carlos asked. "Would Julio get something more out of Washington for a rescue than a new baggage room? Or would that be it?"

Oakley was about to answer when Brent Bibby kicked in the door and, in virtually the same motion, snatched Raul's machine pistol out of his grasp. "Don't anybody move!" he shouted, his voice shaking. The sight of the wild-eyed, highly agitated Bibby waving the barrel of the volatile, deadly weapon while fumbling for the trigger inspired immediate obedience, and there resulted a stillness among those present verging on petrifaction. "Esteban!" Bibby shouted. "Put down your guns!" The guerrilla cook shifted his eyes toward Carlos to see if a countercommand might be forthcoming, but it was a pro forma consultation: Even as he was looking, Esteban lowered his assault rifle and began unbuckling his shoulder holster. His easy compliance left Brent both encouraged and astonished. He seemed unsure about what to do next, until it occurred to him that now he'd better get Esteban's weapons off the floor. "Caliente!" he barked. "Get the guns!" Caliente, too, seemed surprised to be taking orders from Bibby. He shot a glance at Alcozar, who puffed out his lower lip and shrugged. "So do as he says," he said.

The colonel swiftly scooped up the weapons and, keeping the pistol, turned the rifle over to Oakley. "All right, we're getting out of here," Bibby said. Suddenly he was aware that he had begun to imitate John Wayne, which made him feel very relieved, for now he had a role model and some idea about how to behave. "Carlos," he said, "you're a nice fellow, but somewhere along the line, you were led astray. Democracy is the way to go, my friend, not violent revolution. It's too bad. I think you have a lot to offer your country."

The guerrilla leader could not stop himself from snorting. "Watch yourself, mister," Bibby said. "You're the one who's put himself on the wrong side of history." Then, still waving his gun around, he began to direct the escape. "Okay, Mr. President," he said to Alcozar, "out the door behind me, I'll cover you." As the portly president slipped out the door behind Bibby, he gave Carlos a look and an exaggerated palms-in-the-air shrug. *Who coulda figured?*

"Now Caliente," Brent commanded, and the army chief slipped past. "Okay, Oakley, now you." Like the others, the stealthy ambassador slipped behind the vice president. He, however, paused, raised his gun above his head, and brought it down onto Bibby's head *hard.*

"Will he be all right?" Carlos asked, bending over to peer at the unconscious Bibby.

"Maybe," the ambassador shrugged. "Probably. Of course, if I did any real damage, how could we tell?"

Twenty-three

"Wake up, Mr. Vice President," he heard a man calling. "Come on, Mr. Vice President, wake up." There were sounds, things moving, then jostling. "Madre de Díos, Oakley, how hard did you hit him?" he heard the man ask again. President Alcozar? Could be. "Mr. Vice President?" the man asked again. Yes, that was the voice: Alcozar's.

He tried to open his eyes. Did. How weird—just a lot of feet around him. Shut them again. Another voice: "Here—he's coming around now." Was that Carlos? Open. Yes, certainly looked like him. Why were all these people looming over him?

"Bibby, baby, are you feeling better?" Carlos asked again, his face drifting close.

"Am I on the floor?" Bibby asked. The crowd of faces hanging above his head nodded. "Wh—why? What happened?"

"A rebel hit you," Alcozar said, lying with great facility. The only thing that tended to undermine his credibility was that at exactly the same moment, Carlos was matter-of-factly saying, "Oakley hit you."

At first, Bibby thought his senses had gone cuckoo. But even with his still somewhat blurry vision, he could see that Carlos and Alcozar were glaring at one another and that Alcozar seemed particularly mad. "Oakley hit me?" he asked, and Alcozar said, "Car-r-*los,* don't even think about it—"

"Oh, what's the point?" Carlos responded, throwing his hands in the air. "Come on, man, we can't maintain this charade forever."

Bibby pulled himself to his feet. It still wasn't very clear to him what was happening. "What charade?" he asked. "Come on, what's going on?"

"You don't think we could have maintained this charade forever?" Alcozar asked dryly. "I think we could have kept it up for decades. But then, you never could keep a secret. It's just like when you told Father Sweeney about the beer."

Carlos grabbed his head, then threw his hands in the air in exasperation. "There you go again," he said. "I didn't tell anybody about any beer ever." He turned and faced Bibby. "Here's what happened. The priest is in charge of the dormitory. He comes into our room. He sees a keg of beer in the closet. He says, 'What is this?' A rhetorical question, obviously, he can see it's a keg of beer, it's not like he hasn't seen ten thousand kegs of beer in his life. But still, I answer. I say, 'It's a keg.' Now I ask you—" And with this Carlos turned back to Alcozar and, emphasizing each word, shouted, "How does that mean I'm telling him about the beer?"

"You guys know each other?" Bibby asked.

Alcozar shook his head, a small disdainful, I-told-you-so smile on his lips. "We were college roommates," he finally said. "Notre Dame '69."

"Wow," Bibby said, his eyes growing large in astonishment. "Imagine that—college buddies ending up as bitter enemies! What are the odds against that?"

"Madre de Díos, Bibby!" Carlos said, rolling his eyes. "Man, you've got to learn to put two and two together. We're not sworn enemies, Bibby."

"You're not?"

"No, we're best friends."

"We just pretend to be enemies," Alcozar said. "It's our way of doing what's best for our country."

"What's best?" This was all too fast for Bibby, dented skull or not.

"Yes," Carlos said, "what's best. You know, it is not so easy to be a little country in this world, unless you're sitting on a lake of oil or something. You have to have friends."

"Or be a little crafty," Alcozar said.

"That's right. And guess what? We're a little crafty."

"You see," Alcozar proceeded, "when Carlos and I returned from college, San Rico was a peaceful little country, but very, very poor. We asked the United States for help. And we got help."

"A little," said Carlos.

"Some seeds."

"Some tractors."

"A couple of Peace Corps volunteers. Nice people. Lorraine Cademartori, from Hoboken, New Jersey. I'll never forget her. Very pleasant personality."

"And we were grateful for your government's help," Carlos continued, "but much more than that was required. So we asked for more. The man in the State Department said, 'You got any insurgencies? Any Communist guerrillas? Can't help you unless you got some Communist guerrillas.'"

"Well, we didn't. And he said 'too bad.' He told us all the rest of your aid was going to places where there was a military conflict."

"Oh, that couldn't be true," Bibby said. "Could it?"

"Examine the evidence," Carlos said.

"Look who was getting aid, Mr. Vice President," said Alcozar. "Vietnam. South Korea. The Shah. Angola. The Philippines. Jonas Savimbi. El Salvador. The wants and desires of the United States seemed perfectly clear to us."

"So we made a plan," Carlos explained. "Julio became president, and I became a guerrilla leader. I got some guys together, we moved up to the hills, we put out some pamphlets full of some revolutionary bullshit, and then we launched a few offensives."

"And bingo!" Alcozar said, a measure of disdain in his voice. "Washington just started pumping in the aid."

"Be fair, Julio, Moscow did, too," Carlos said. "I got stuff from Russia, China, Nicaragua, Cuba, Albania, you name it. I got stuff from Reds in places I'd never even heard of."

Could this be true? Bibby wondered. Could it possibly be true? Cause if it was true, wouldn't he have heard about it on TV? Or heard people talking about it at the club? Wouldn't his staff have mentioned it? Or Lucinda? She was always talking about stuff that happened. Carlos and Julio couldn't have kept it a secret, could they? And another thing: If it was all a big con job, well, that was bad enough . . . but . . . "But you were killing people!" he blurted.

"Oh, we never killed anybody," Carlos said. "I had to teach myself to kill mosquitoes."

"It was all staged, Bibby," Alcozar said. "They'd let us know when they were coming, we'd clear the area, they'd set off the bomb, and Caliente would pull out some corpses he'd dragged over from the morgue that morning. Then we'd let the reporters in."

"And you got away with that?" Bibby asked.

"Who's going to talk?" Carlos replied. "Dead is dead. Who's a reporter going to interview? Caliente, who could explain from which direction the rebels attacked, and how many rounds were fired, and how much damage was done? Or a corpse, who no longer can quite muster the oomph it requires to help a writer meet a deadline?"

This can't be true, Bibby told himself, this just can't be true. And yet, open your eyes and see what's right in front of you: Alcozar and Carlos lounging around, friendly as you please, knowing all the ins and outs of this big deception; guns lying all over, nobody lunging for a weapon, nobody guarding anybody; Caliente mixing drinks, Raul nibbling off the cheese plate, everybody acting like they're the oldest friends in the world, *everybody acting like this is one big Central American Dockers commercial.* And of course this explains how the rebels avoided capture for so many years, Bibby realized, and why all the citizens of this war-torn land seem so jolly and laid-back. And it explains why Oakley—why Oakley what? Why Oakley's here, Bibby finally concluded. And why was Oakley here? "You were in on this—this—this *fraud*, weren't you, Mr. Ambassador?"

The closed-mouthed Oakley answered Bibby with a flinty grin. "I take the Fifth," he said.

"Of course, Mr. Vice President," Alcozar responded, "he had to be. Somebody had to take care of the visiting congressmen and generals. Somebody had to report to Washington. Oakley had a real knack for making the Hondanistas seem just frightening enough so that nobody was tempted to stop the flow of aid, and yet not so frightening that the crazy right-wingers in your country felt obliged to agitate for military intervention. Oakley was very important. We needed him."

Oakley shrugged modestly. "You have to know which way the wind is blowing, Mr. Vice President."

Yeah, I'm beginning to see that, Bibby said to himself. A thought occurred to him: "Now with all the military aid we've given you," he said, "you must have weapons coming out your wazoo."

"We have a lot," Alcozar acknowledged.

"But, hey," Carlos protested, "it's not like we're gun nuts. We've sold most of our weapons. After all, our people need food more than rifles."

This just gets deeper and deeper. "You sold the guns we gave you?" Bibby asked. He wondered for a moment whether he was still groggy from being clubbed.

"Oh, sure, lots of them," Carlos said. "Qaddafi bought some. Saddam. Sheikh Yabani. The IRA. Noriega. The Romanian police were steady customers until Ceausescu was executed."

"But they were all pretty small customers," Alcozar said. "We sold most of our stuff to gun collectors in the United States."

"Be careful when you go to California, Bibby," Carlos cautioned. "There's a shitload of assault rifles in Orange County."

"Well, now you know our story," Alcozar said glumly, bringing the mood in the room right down. "It was fun while it lasted. But now the Cold War is over, and the pipeline from Washington is nearly dry. With Moscow out of the picture, it's hard to believe any of you Yanquis would give a damn about our little squabbles here."

"Which is why we went for the big strike," Carlos explained.

"Kidnapping me, you mean."

"Sure," Carlos said. "Grab you, get the cash, put it into some nice safe bonds."

"Build up a little annuity for our people. Have some dough around to put into economic development."

The realization of what had happened to him suddenly weighed on Bibby like an anvil. Being kidnapped by guerrillas? That's one thing. Being kidnapped by an ally? *Way* unfair. No point in ignoring these hurt feelings. No point in not being frank. "Well, Mr. President—Julio—," he said, pursing his lips, "I'm not going to sit here and pretend that everything is okay between us. I'm just sick about this whole thing, and really just *p.o.'ed* by the way you lied to me. Your country and my country were supposed to be friends."

"Oh, Bibby," Alcozar said, "don't get yourself bent out of shape. We are friends. You're the rich friend. We're the poor friend. But without this fraud, we wouldn't have much in common to base our friendship upon." Then he said something that made Bibby's cheeks burn with embarrassment. "It's just business, Mr. Vice President. You should learn to play this game."

"Yeah," Carlos said, "but unfortunately the game is starting to come apart. We made one mistake. We never figured that nobody would want you back."

Understanding all at once that the length of his capture wasn't entirely, or maybe even mostly, the fault of the Humiricans hit Brent hard. "Nobody?" he asked in a small voice.

"No," Alcozar said, "not at any price."

Seeing Bibby's sad little face, Carlos tried to console him. "Aw, come on, don't jump to conclusions, Bibby, man. It's not like they'd mind if you came back. It's just that they don't want to pay for you. Don't take it personally, dude. It's just politics."

Twenty-four

Work, work, work, work, work, he thought to himself, fingering through the pile of manila folders in his in basket. Geez, you spend a few days holed up down in the Sit and the decisions really pile up. Does the House really expect us to have a budget over there by the first of the month? I understand they have their deadlines, their precious little rules, but doesn't any of them realize we're having a crisis here? Don't they watch the news?

Obviously, not everything was supposed to grind to a halt, he knew that, but *still* . . . And stuff like this: deciding whether to go ahead with the Red Dog Gulch Dam project in Idaho if it meant destroying one of the last four habitats of the rosy-nub-bined toad. As if he gave a rat's ass. Dam, no dam, toad, no toad, what did he care? Why couldn't Interior Secretary Belknap decide these things? Really, if he couldn't decide things like this, what the hell were they paying him for? Get him out of there, get somebody else in there who could chew through some of this crapola. Better yet, get Ms. Meara to run the Department of the Interior during her lunch hour.

Not such a bad idea, that Ms. Meara notion. Just make her deal with all the budget people and the Interior people and all the rest of those guys. Have her force them to figure out their own problems and stop relying on him to make all the damn decisions. Of course, he reminded himself to tell her, they would have to let him know what they decided. Didn't want them

174

going off half-cocked. And didn't want to take the heat for some idea he'd never heard of.

Write that down: *Make sure they tell me.* Insist on it. Don't want anybody to forget who's the president here.

Someone behind him clearing his throat. "Oh, Crane."

"Sorry to disturb you, sir. Horace Bibby is here to see you."

Punctual old bastard, Ross thought. "Well, show him in."

Crane returned a moment later with the news magnate. There was an exchange of the usual pleasantries—perfunctory ones, of course, and quite insincere—then Ross offered Horace a seat.

"Thank you, Mr. President," he said, then, tilting his head back toward Crane, added, "I'd prefer if we spoke alone."

"Horace," Ross demurred, "Mr. Crane is my most trusted advisor. I have no secrets from him."

"President Ross," Horace said, sounding suddenly a trace more intense, "Mr. Crane enjoys my full respect. There's no one better at cleaning up the little piles of shit your administration has left behind as it has wandered through time. But this discussion is just between us. If you want to tell him what we've said when we've finished, be my guest. I'm not sure you'll want to, but it's up to you."

Well, Ross thought, he wants this to be grim, doesn't he? Yet, if a private citizen wants a private discussion with his president, well, who am I to say no? "Mr. Crane," Ross said, "would you please excuse us?"

"I'll come to the point, Ross," Horace said once the door had clicked closed behind Crane. "I want my boy back. I never much cared for the kid, I think he's sort of a dunderhead, but he is a Bibby. And besides, his mother's all worked up. Doesn't want to go to any of her charity functions, doesn't want to play bridge, doesn't want to fool around, just wants to sit and mope about Brent. I can't stand to watch it anymore. So here's the bottom line: Either you pay the ransom or you send in some troops. If those tortilla-munchers can't find my son, maybe some Marines can."

Ah, the terrible tragedy of Alzheimer's, Ross thought. We've had this discussion, old man, don't you remember? Well, at least I know what to say to shut him up. "Horace," he said gently, "I'm afraid it's not that simple. A great nation has many responsibilities, and a president must prudently weigh . . ."

Weigh many factors before making a decision, he was about to say, ready to place a special emphasis on the word *many,* but the old tycoon broke in. "Save the palaver, Ross. You want something simple, here it is. Right now, bivouaced near an airstrip outside Brownsville, Texas, three hundred ex-Green Beret mercenaries under the command of former Brigadier General "Crazy Bull" Catwalader sit ready to fly, at my command, to San Rico de Humidor and to take that country apart branch by branch until my son is located."

Fine by me, Ross thought cheerfully. In fact, yippee. You want to take matters into your own hands, *be my guest.* Can't let him see me being too agreeable to the idea, though. Have to maintain an air of responsibility in the face of this vigilante yahoo-ism. "Well, Horace," he said, trying to sound weighted down with wisdom, "I'm sure there's some law against that, but if that's a risk you're willing to assume—"

"Risk, Ross, is something to which I've never been adverse. But I ought to tell you there's something else involved."

"Oh?"

"Yes. The moment Catwalader's men enter Humirican air space, I intend to stop the presses of the *Bibbyville Gazette* and publish an extra edition, which will describe in detail the story of the president's affair with the vice president's wife."

Steady, Ross told himself, give nothing away. Just sit there, don't move, don't not move, just act natural and relaxed. He's bluffing, just bluffing his butt off, and he knows it.

"With pictures, Mr. President." And with that, Horace reached into his briefcase and pulled out a dozen eight-by-ten glossies, which he tossed across the desk. Ross did not have to so much as incline his head to see the snapshots. They showed him making love to Lucinda, in a variety of positions, in the most graphic detail.

"I think the likenesses are quite good, don't you, Mr. President?" Horace asked calmly. "And here, even though your face is all contorted in what must have been a moment of particularly exquisite pleasure, your identity is quite clear. And it's obviously Lucinda as well. Her face doesn't look contorted by anything. If I didn't know better, I'd say she was examining her nails. I'm sure she really wasn't."

Ross sat for a long time without responding. He wasn't even really thinking. Wondering was more like it. Wondering who. Wondering how. Wondering what was going to happen next.

"Don't get me wrong, Ross," old Bibby said softly. "I don't particularly care if two consenting adults decide to play a little touchy-pokey under the covers. Certainly I've never felt bound by traditional morals. For that matter, neither has Gwendoline. And I never knew what a bright girl like Lucinda saw in my son, except his money. But I don't think the public is as—sophisticated—as I am. I think a great many of the American people would be shocked to hear that the president was refusing to pay ransom for the vice president at the very moment he was carrying on with the poor heroic bastard's wife." There was some sarcasm in his voice, but he was surprisingly gentle. There was no reason to be any other way: He held all the cards.

"How—how did you get the pictures?" Ross finally managed to ask.

Horace leaned back in his chair and smiled. For the first time, he allowed himself to seem smug. "I don't know firsthand how a man gets to be president of the United States," he finally replied. "But I know you don't get to be as rich as I am unless you know what's going on with the people who affect your life."

He'd let that sink into Ross's head for a moment, Horace decided. He'd let Ross stare at the pictures a while, and realize a little more thoroughly that he had no way out, and arrive a little more firmly at the conclusion that he owned his balls. Okay, that was time enough. "So what's it going to be?" Horace gently pushed. "Do you want to look like a hero, or do you want to be impeached and have people spit on you wherever you go for the rest of your life?"

Slowly, Ross offered a slight nod of submission. "I believe I'll be paying the ransom."

"I thought you would. It's the smart move, and you're not that stupid a fellow. Now, there's just one more element."

"What's that?"

"I want the Marines to deliver it."

"What?"

"I want the Marines to deliver it. I'd send my mercenaries, but frankly, that Catwalader's a lunatic. No, you send some Marines down there with the money. If the Hondanistas cut the deal, fine, bring the boys back home. But, if they don't, the guerrillas will have to deal with more than those useless conscripts the Humiricans call an army.

"Well, hell," Ross exploded, "why the fuck not? Eh, Horace? You're calling the shots now. Who am I to get in your way? Any special regiment you want? But as long as we're on the subject, I have just one more element of my own: I will be getting all the copies of these pictures, won't I?"

Horace let Ross have his little moment of pique. "Certainly, Mr. President," he said. "And all the negatives, too. And I give you my word that these are the only copies. Unfortunately for you, I have an awful reputation for breaking my word. It's only partly deserved, but still, you'll never really believe that I'm telling you the truth, and so you'll sort of always think that I'm holding out on you, and you will therefore feel constrained to accommodate any little whim I may have from time to time. And that'll probably last for the rest of your presidency. Am I right?"

It was at that moment Ross realized with thudding finality that he had become a slave. "Don't be silly, Horace," he said blankly, "why would I ever think of not accommodating you?"

"Good answer, Ross. Now, you'll let me know where the Marines'll be leaving from. I'll be wanting to go with them."

"You'll want what?"

"It's a big story, Mr. President," said the old newspaper magnate, snapping shut his briefcase. "Imagine the headlines: BIBBY

RESCUES BIBBY FROM RUTHLESS QUERRILLAS. I think it's Pulitzer material. Best-seller material. With a seven-figure paperback sale. Not to mention movie rights. I'd like that. I see Paul Newman playing me. So: You'll call?"

"I'll call," Ross said. "I'm picking up the phone as we speak. Look—I'm dialing—" But Horace had already left the room.

I wonder who'll play me, Ross thought.

When the door closed behind him, the tycoon found a dour Crane sitting outside the door at an empty desk, staring straight ahead. Crane glanced back at him, then resumed his gaze, his expression, if possible, even more sour than before.

"The ransom," Horace Bibby said steadily, "with the Marines in reserve, just as you advised." Crane nodded without changing expression, and Horace did not know quite what else to say. "I want to thank you for your help," he finally said. "How to get the cameras in and so on. I know it was difficult for you."

Crane shifted, maybe shrugged, pinched his nose and blinked. "He was letting his dick do his thinking," Crane said in a scratchy voice, blinking some more. "It happens to everybody. The thing is, when it happens to most of us, people don't die."

Suddenly the door knob turned and Ross came out of his office. His appearance surprised Horace, who burbled an excuse that perhaps at another time would have seemed too obvious: "I was just giving Mr. Crane my phone number so that I can be reached." Had Ross bothered to think about it, he would have realized that Crane probably had Horace's number in a hundred different places. But Ross was beyond being suspicious: He was too busy accommodating himself to the role of wholly owned subsidiary. "No need for that, Horace, I can give you the news right now. The mission will depart Parris Island at 1300 hours. You'll be there just before nightfall. A General Garrison's in charge; he's expecting you. And you, too, Crane. I want to make sure there's somebody down there I can trust to look after my best interests."

"A good choice, Mr. President," Horace Bibby said. "Mr. Crane does that, perhaps more than you'll ever know."

Twenty-five

Whenever he thought about it—which wasn't all that much, actually, he had been pretty busy—but whenever he did think about it, the news that he was to be released confused him. He was relieved, obviously, happy to hear that he was going to be heading home, seeing Lucinda, being in his own house, sleeping in his own bed, resuming the old routine—boy, would he have some stories to tell at the next cabinet meeting!—and just getting back to normal. Play some tennis again. Phone Mother and Dad once a week. Mow the lawn.

And, of course, on the other hand, sadness. Of course, sadness. Say what you will about Carlos and Julio and the other guys—frauds, hoaxers, liars, probably thieves and, no two ways about it, kidnappers—they were fun to be with. They laughed, they told jokes, they razzed one another, and—and they liked him. They seemed to enjoy having him around. That wasn't the case with oh, say, the cabinet. The fellows in the cabinet were nice to him, sure, but—well, back up there a minute. Carlos and Julio had told him he ought to be more frank about things, express his true feelings more frequently, so fine, he'd be frank. The fellows in the cabinet weren't nice. There. He'd said it. They weren't nice. Sure, they said hello. Sure, they smiled at him. But did Marv Friedman ever ask him if he wanted to play badminton? Did Marv Friedman ever say, Hey, Bibby, man, come on over and watch the ballgame? Did Marv Friedman ever ask him if he wanted a beer? The answer—answers—if you couldn't guess, were no, no, and no.

On the other hand, he couldn't see Marv Friedman being part of the gang last night. Or Secretary Carrera, either. Or Secretary Belknap, or Joint Chiefs Chairman Wooten, or Attorney General Bigert, for that matter. It was all too—fun. Esteban barbecued a big side of beef Alcozar had brought up and afterwards they all sat around the camp fire and drank beer and took turns singing songs in Spanish. And when it got to be Bibby's turn, he said he didn't know any songs in Spanish, so they told him to sing in English. And so he sang one of his favorite songs, and was astonished when Raul and Caliente began harmonizing on backup. "Oh, you know 'My Girl?'" Brent asked, and of course, the answer was yes, and so they sang other songs, songs like "The Tracks of My Tears" and "Standing in the Shadows of Love," and "Baby Love." Then Alcozar said, "Hey, if you're going to do Miss Diana Ross, then do her right." Then he sang Diana's part and the rest of them played the Supremes, and they sang "Stop! In the Name of Love" and "You Can't Hurry Love," and a pretty nearly dead-on version of "Love Child." Then Carlos said, "Enough Motown," and led everybody in "Help Me, Rhonda." Face it, Bibby thought: Marv Friedman couldn't sing "Help Me, Rhonda" to save the lives of his wife and children. And probably wouldn't want to learn.

After that, unfortunately, Oakley had to play the responsible one and remind everybody that he and Alcozar and Caliente had to drive all the way back to San Rico City that evening, and that it was just about time to hit the road. That the night ended so abruptly kind of brought Bibby down. After saying good night and doing his part to clean up, he found himself back in his hut, unable to sleep, thinking about all the things Carlos and Julio had told him. *Wise up. Play the game. It's just business.* Why had no one ever spoken to him that way before? Why had he never learned to put two and two together on his own? Why had no one ever explained to him what that clever two-and-two expression meant? And though he didn't specifically blame him-

self for not catching on to the Humiricans' massive fraud—
heck, nobody had—he wondered how he had allowed himself to
be fooled by that ridiculous gravel business, and by who knows
what else besides? Not just here, but always, and everywhere. By
things his father did. Things Crane did. Even things President
Ross did. How did he get to be a senator? Why had he been chosen? What did his dad mean when he said Ross was turning him
into a laughingstock?

Am I that dumb? he asked himself.

Am I really that stupid?

These thoughts provided him a fitful sleep and stayed with
him the next morning as he put on the clean fatigues Raul had
given him, and later, as he watched Carlos's men load up their
vehicles in preparation for the long drive down from the Santa
Euphoria Mountains, across the Rio del Bundegas, and into San
Rico City. "What is it, Bibby?" Carlos finally asked him. "I see
you staring out into space. Why so down in the dumps?"

"I don't know," Bibby sighed. "Carlos, tell me something.
And don't spare my feelings. For the last twenty-four hours or
so you've been honest with me. Do you think I'm stupid?"

Carlos grinned wickedly, as though he were going to be unable
to resist giving a flip response. But he saw something in Bibby's
face that caused him to pull back, and he answered more carefully. "No," he said, "but I think you're extremely and sometimes pathetically innocent. And innocence, in a man in your
position, is almost a crime. Look, if something happens to Roger
Ross—a vain and corrupt man, in my estimation, that was one
opinion I never pretended about holding—you would become
the leader of the world's most important nation. Now, even if
we agree that you aren't stupid, what have you ever done to qualify you for that position?"

Bibby thought for a moment. "Nothing?" he finally answered.

"Precisely," Carlos agreed. "And that is why people think
you're stupid. Partly because you've never done anything, but
mostly because you accepted the job despite that."

Bibby thought for a moment about what Carlos had said. It

Twenty-six

n't be long now, Crane thought, checking his watch for about
twenty-seventh time since takeoff. Touchdown, he con-
ed, would be less than an hour away. The trip had been
oth: With military precision, the three C-5's that carried
e hundred Marines and their equipment and vehicles had
n off from Parris Island at exactly 1:00 P.M. They'd hit some
ulence over the Gulf of Mexico, a storm, maybe a big one,
Crane reckoned: From inside the dark, windowless fuselage
uldn't see much of anything, but he could feel it, could see
eps and other matériel trying to shimmy under their canvas
rings. Nobody seemed much concerned. On the other side
e plane, the lean, rough-edged Marines dozed in their nylon
s, taking on the slightest aspect of gentleness as their lower
uffed out like babies' in their sleep, an appearance imme-
ly undercut by the rifles they cradled against their thighs.
e himself had several times tried to doze off, something he'd
had trouble doing during his hitch in the army. But his
ad gotten a little too wide over the years to fit comfortably
hese narrow damn seats, and besides, every time he got
to dropping off, Horace Bibby—*his new best friend,* as the
coon had started to put it, his way of describing the guy
ad helped Horace out when Horace was in a jam—would
im on the thigh and shout something like, "Ain't this

all made sense, however painfully. "But how do
he asked.

"Ah," said Carlos, "you need to do somethin
"Grand? Like what?"
"A deed. A gesture. An exit. Something mag
It was not long after they had finished talking
to head down to San Rico City and play out th
Bibby's escape. All the way down from the m
through the mist, ducking under low tree
thought about what Carlos had said, and what
would qualify as grand. After a few hours, ab
mist cleared and they could see down to the c
roofed houses of San Rico City, Bibby decided
got back to Washington, he would ask Lucin
about what to do. He could always count on l

W
the
clu
sm
thr
tak
tur
too
he c
the
moc
of tl
chai
lips
diat
Cra
neve
butt
into
close
old
who
slap

livin'?" Let's see, Crane counted, so far we've had *Ain't this livin'?*, *Ain't this the life?*, *This is the life!*, and *Isn't this exciting?*

"Getting laid on my sixteenth birthday was exciting," Crane dryly replied on that occasion. "Seeing Maris break Ruth's record was exciting. Managing Ross's campaign was exciting. Parts of it were, anyway. This? This is somewhere between nerve-wracking and just plain frightening."

"You think so?" Horace laughed explosively. "Not to me." No, obviously not, Crane thought, *you're into it.* Horace had had a team of tailors custom-fit him six pairs of fatigues for this mission, and he was the only man on the plane who'd felt like wearing his helmet, with the big branch of camouflage (he called it) that he had personally cut from a palmetto tree near the runway in South Carolina, into the fifth hour (so far) of the flight. No, he was into this as only an old, bloodthirsty adventurer could be. At the last minute before leaving Washington, he'd even insisted that Ross commission him an officer, a brigadier general in fact, arguing that he needed a rank in case he was taken prisoner-of-war. Crane had done his best to point out that they weren't actually fighting a war with anyone to be taken prisoner of, that there was little chance that a real war would be declared by Congress anytime soon, and that everyone still harbored sincere hopes of not actually having to open fire on anybody. "Oh, who cares?" Ross had said, signing the orders. "Let him get taken prisoner. And if he could guarantee he'd get shot, I'd put him on the Joint Chiefs of Staff."

Aw, here he was back again. Every time Horace got tired of bothering Crane—*his new best friend*—he got up and went and bothered the pilot. "Guess what, Crane?" Horace boomed, his ruddy face glowing. "Major Cosgrove let me fly!" Great, thought Crane, just what I wanted, to have my life put in the hands of a seventy-five-year-old, thrill-seeking amateur. The old tycoon plopped back into his seat, the palmetto branch on his helmet scraping past Crane's face for a second. "Guess what else the major says?" he roared above the drone of the engines. "Says we caught a terrific tail wind. Says we'll be in San Rico City more than a half hour early."

"Goody," Crane said. Mostly he said it for effect, but he meant it, too. He could get out of this damn airplane: *goody.* He wouldn't have this damn palmetto branch in his face: *goody.* See? Crane told himself, there was an upside to everything.

"Here, Crane," Bibby said, pulling out a silver flask from his special-cut Eisenhower jacket. "Want a drink?"

At long last, Crane thought, accepting the flask with gratitude, this new-best-friend business has proven good for something.

Alcozar, Oakley, and Caliente got to Estilo International Airport late and in a highly agitated state, slamming their car doors and striding with fierce determination up to the men waiting for them on the tarmac. It certainly didn't help their mood that they found Brent and Carlos and the half dozen Hondanistas who'd made the trip with them lounging in the back of their truck, listening to Radio Mexico's broadcast of the Dodger game. "What the hell are you morons doing just sitting there?" Alcozar boomed.

The intensity of his anger took everyone by surprise. "What do you mean, What the hell are we doing just sitting here?" Carlos bristled. "We're waiting for your late ass to show up so we can work out this escape."

Alcozar ignored him. "Is anybody here?" he demanded, scanning the landscape, his agitation still pronounced.

"No," Carlos said, "nobody. Some planes landed up at the north end about twenty minutes ago, but they didn't come down this way."

"None of them?"

"No. I think it's just smugglers or somebody. Look, man, what's going on? What crawled up your ass and died?"

"Haven't you heard the news?" Alcozar asked.

"What news? Man, we've been driving all day."

"Don't you have a radio?"

"Hey, excuse me, we were listening to tapes."

"Well, here's a bulletin. The Americans are coming. Ross has agreed to pay a million dollars for Bibby. He's sending Lionel Crane with the money. But there's a detachment of Marines making the trip, too, and if you don't make the deal pronto, the Marines are going to come looking for him. And for you, too. And I don't think they're the sort of troops who'll pull up at the foothills of the Santa Euphorias and spend the afternoon skinny-dipping."

"Well, then," Carlos said, rubbing his palms together, "I guess dealing days are here. I say we make the swap before those Yanquis get excitable and restless." His fellow Hondanistas murmered their approval.

"Excuse me," Brent interrupted, "but that's it? A million? That's all?"

The Humiricans seemed sorry that Brent was unhappy with the offer. "I think a million is an okay number," Alcozar said, trying to sound encouraging. "Given the circumstances."

"Hey, dude, nobody would pay a million for me," Carlos argued.

"I'm sorry," Brent said, shaking his head, "I just think I'm worth more. I mean, this wasn't something I wanted to bring up while you were in the middle of your negotiations, but I have more than a million I could give you to save my own life. And my dad—my dad routinely keeps a hundred thousand in his sock drawer. Frankly, I'm insulted."

"Look, man," Carlos said, "what can I say? Nobody wishes they would pay more for you than I do. I would love to get more for you. But it's just not realistic. Yesterday, we were ready to give you back for nothing. Right now a million looks good. Besides, they've brought themselves a pretty big hammer this time. I, for one, am not particularly excited at the prospect of having elements of the United States Marine Corps taking a deeply personal interest in my whereabouts. I'm a pretty contented cowboy staying on their B list."

"Aw, come on, Carlos," said Bibby, his voice taking on an earnest, pleading quality. "Where's that old guerrilla spirit? We

don't have to be afraid of the Marines. We could go on the run—
hide in the jungle, live off the land, survive by our wits. We'll use
ambush tactics. Hit 'em when they don't expect it, slash and
burn, fade back into the brush without leaving a trace. They'll
never find us, they'll never defeat us, and one day they'll give up
and drag their sorry butts back to where they came from."

No one quite knew how to respond to Bibby's emotional per-
oration, and it was a long time before any of them could even
begin to make sense of what he was suggesting. "Ah, Bibby,
man," Carlos at last softly said, as he draped a friendly arm
around his shoulders, "you gotta come back to earth. They're
your people, man. They've come here for *you.* Try to remember:
We're the guerrillas, you're the Yanqui vice president. If you
like, we could all do something together later on. Have a nice
ceremony, make you an honorary Hondanista, whatever you'd
like. Nothing would make me happier. But now is not the time."

"He's right, you know," Alcozar reassured the downcast
Bibby. "We've got to keep our eye on the ball. Do we want gun-
fire? No. Bloodshed? No. The million? Sure. And if you still feel
undervalued when you get home, no problem, send us a check
when you get a chance. But now, we've got to maintain our
focus. Here's what we need to do: Carlos, why don't you and
Bibby and the rest of the boys go into town and kill a couple of
hours? Go to the movies, maybe."

"What's playing?" Carlos asked.

"Ah, *Bonfire of the Vanities,* I think."

"Oh, no. That got terrible reviews."

"Please, Carlos, the point is not to see a movie," Alcozar said,
straining to keep his temper. "The point is to have somewhere
to make the exchange, and the movie theater is really an excellent location. In a couple of hours, Lionel Crane and I will come
by with the dough. I'll tell him to leave it behind the candy
counter. Then I'll send Caliente in to find you. When you see
him, you go out the emergency exit and come around for the
money. Once Caliente tells me you've left, I'll send Crane in to
get Bibby. They can have a nice little reunion, and tomorrow

everybody goes home." Alcozar looked up, quite pleased to see everyone nodding in agreement.

"Hey, Julio, do you still want to blow up the baggage room?" Raul asked.

"Mmmmmh, good question," Alcozar said, stroking his chin. "Oakley, what do you think? Could we still get Washington to pay for a new one?"

"If Bibby gets rescued?" Oakley nodded firmly. "I'd say that's a sure thing."

"Then let's do it," said Alcozar with a mischievous grin.

"Um, excuse me," Bibby said. "I don't know if this is proper etiquette or not, but if I'm not going to get my way about the money . . . may I please blow up the baggage room? I've never done anything like that before. And it is kind of like a bridge opening in reverse, isn't it?"

Raul passed Bibby the plunger. "Do it, man," he said. It was hard to tell which was brighter: the fireball that rocketed toward the sky or Bibby's excited, beaming face.

"We landed up at this end so that we'd have room to unload," said the press officer, a captain named Cleary, to Celestine van den Hurdle as they stood amid the hubbub of the Marines' disembarkation. "We're due to have an official greeting from President Alcozar in about twenty-five minutes."

Van den Hurdle was on hand in San Rico after managing to persuade a reluctant Pentagon to make room on one of the transports for herself and her crew. This she was able to do in exchange for her solemn promise not to reveal the particulars of their mission on the evening news. Her inexplicable and unauthorized possession of all the pertinent details alarmed the Pentagon, and before they gave in, the security division blustered about, banging on tables and threatening to launch a full-scale investigation to find the source of the leak. Celestine sat through all that, an infuriatingly tolerant expression on her face, and waited for the security officers to finish. It was all nonsense. They knew perfectly well that van den Hurdle would never give up her source, and she knew perfectly well they would never investigate. More to the point, they didn't really want to investigate, because if they investigated, they just might find the source; and that would just embarrass somebody at the White House, whoever it was there who blabbed the secrets away.

All of which made Crane very happy. He was nearly positive that Christine wouldn't surrender his name, but you never knew about people until things were on the line. It was just as well she didn't have to be put to the test. Still, it had been worth the risk. Crane wanted the cameras to be there, wanted them there badly. It was his feeling that on most occasions when things started to get weird, the reminder that about a billion people were watching tended to help keep matters from blowing off the scale.

"Okay, Captain," van den Hurdle directed, "while you guys unload, we'll set up our link with New York. Then we'll go live. I'll do my stand-up, get some words from Horace Bibby and General Garrison, then sum up."

Ross hadn't seen much of Lucinda since Horace Bibby had sprung his little trap: just a brief, quiet conversation in the Oval Office during which he informed her first of the ransom plan and then of the Marine Corps option. Only then did he break the news that they had been observed by a third party or parties during at least one, but more likely several, of their moments of intimacy; and that it might be a good idea if they agreed temporarily to place their ardor for one another in a personal repression mode. Lucinda had barely had time to agree to this instruction before he was ushering her out by the elbow. She tried to ask questions, but he'd abruptly shushed her, then opened a manila envelope and flashed one of the photographs. That was enough to give her the gist. She was a bright girl, and she quickly realized that her husband's possible release, coupled with the news that someone in the world knew she was an adulteress, significantly lessened her chances to be president. For the moment, anyway. But she was resilient. It was never a good idea to live in the past, she told herself before she was out of sight of Ms. Meara's desk. Now it was time to think about tomorrow.

Of course, Ross now thought, he probably *could* see Lucinda. There was no real impediment. Almost as soon as Horace Bibby had left, Ross had had Connolly from the FBI come over and remove the damn cameras. He didn't ask the Secret Service to do it, that's for damn sure, it was probably one of them who'd planted the damn things! Connolly took care of the removal double time, but he didn't find any prints on the equipment, or any other clue. Not that Ross needed prints or clues, he knew perfectly well who was behind it—Horace Bibby, obviously—but he did want to know how he did it and who helped him. Of course, he wasn't likely to find out, since he quite specifically didn't want Connolly to know *what* had happened, which left Connolly's chances of figuring out all the whos and hows sort of on the slim side.

But Connolly had assured him that there weren't any cameras left—absolutely, Mr. President, positively—so that, really, he and Lucinda could probably do whatever they wanted to. It didn't really matter all that much anyway, even if there were cameras still around. Horace Bibby already had pictures of them doing just about the worst thing they shouldn't be doing; it wasn't like he and Lucinda had been working their way up to cannibalism or anything. But even if they'd wanted to do something, as he kept reminding himself, even if they'd been going to get into, like, threesomes, there weren't any cameras anymore. Which meant it would probably be okay if they watched some TV together. Just watched. Not even entertainment programming. If they just watched the news. "Would you like to watch the news?" he asked her. "They're covering the landing. Don't worry, we're just going to watch the news. Down in the Sit. Where there never were any cameras, anyway. And where I'm pretty sure there aren't any now."

Van den Hurdle stuck a microphone in Horace's face. "Your observations so far, Mr. Bibby?" she asked.

"We made tremendous time," Horace said. "I think we got here a half hour early. But that's not what impressed me most, Celestine. What impressed me most was the courage of the fighting men I met on the plane. One young man—I'll never forget—told me that he wasn't nervous. 'No, sir,' he said, 'I just want to kill some guerrillas.' We should all be very proud."

Van den Hurdle had about concluded that she had gotten enough clichés out of the old blowhard when down at the terminal, about a mile and a half away, a tremendous explosion sent a fireball high into the sky.

For the briefest part of a second she stood transfixed, watching chunks of debris sail through the air. Then she came around. "Jesus Christ, there's just been an explosion!" she shouted into her microphone. "Jimmy, for Chrissake, put your camera on that thing. There's stuff fifty feet in the air—is that a piece of luggage?—and it hasn't stopped going up yet." All around her there was an eruption of movement as hundreds of men broke into frantic activity, running to and fro, barking commands, wheeling jeeps into position, shouldering and mounting weapons. "Peter," she said, "there's just been a tremendous explosion, we don't know the source of it or the location, but I want to remind our viewers that the president's chief of staff is on hand, as is the vice president's father, and it's possible this was some sort of attack directed at them. Again, we're live—"

In front of her, six or seven jeeps, each with fifty-caliber machine guns mounted on the rear, each holding four or five Marines, wheeled to the front of the landing area and positioned themselves to advance on the terminal. She saw Horace Bibby in his ridiculous palmettoed helmet drag Crane past General Garrison and into the back of the command jeep, which, activated by a great roar of authority—the general and Horace gave the command to advance together—began to lead the approach to the site of the explosion. Suddenly there was Captain Cleary, the information officer, pulling up in a jeep and beckoning her to get in. "Go, Jimmy, go go go," she hollered as she clambered aboard. "Don't lose me, New York, don't lose me."

"My God, Roger," Lucinda asked, hearing van den Hurdle's excited report, "what is going on?" Instinctively, she reached for Ross's hand.

In front of the terminal, bits of debris were drifting out of the sky, but the imminent danger of being clunked by a rapidly descending American Tourister traveling case didn't prevent the Humiricans from celebrating the explosion. They yipped and hooted and slapped Bibby on the back. "Un-fucking-believably good," Carlos said, high-fiving Bibby. "You sure got all of that one!"

"Aw, give the credit to Raul," Brent said modestly. "He made the bomb."

"Now, now, that's very diplomatic of you," Alcozar said, "but Raul would be the first to tell you, you've got to give credit to the thumb that's on the plunger. And that was some blast! I'm still hearing the rumbling."

"Me, too," said Carlos.

"Me, too," said everyone.

"Wait," said Oakley, "that rumbling's not from the blast! Those are—jeeps! It's the Marines!"

The vehicles raced down the landing strip, made a wide, ninety-degree turn at the edge of the terminal building, and halted. Immediately, Crane and van den Hurdle and Horace Bibby and General Garrison and everyone else saw the same thing: Eleven men, two in civilian garb, one in the uniform of the Humirican Internal Police, nine in fatigues. It was impossible to see their faces, but from the totality of their reactions—freezing in place, pointing at the jeeps, throwing hands into the air, scurrying around as chaotically as roaches caught under kitchen light—it seemed clear that they were all surprised to see the jeeps, and that most of them seemed highly alarmed as well. "Stop!" General Garrison boomed into a battery-operated megaphone. "Stop in the name of—" He pulled the megaphone down. "Excuse me, sir," he asked Crane, "in the name of what? Not the United States, huh? We don't have jurisdiction, do we?"

"How about in the name of Bibby International Holdings Incorporated?" Horace suggested.

"Just say the United States, General," Crane snapped. "We'll sort out the legal niceties later."

In front of the terminal, some of the Humiricans obeyed the general's command. Caliente, for one. The head of the internal police calmly raised his hands into the air and slowly began to back out of what he gauged, based on the officer's training program he had attended in San Antonio, Texas, to be the field of fire. Several of the Hondanistas put up their hands as well, though Raul and Esteban broke into a dead run and sprinted for the tree line. Nobody paid much attention to them. Most of the Americans seemed to be caught up in the activities of the mustachioed guerrilla and the tall, blond guerrilla, and the dark, dumpy civilian in the white suit; activities which, in fact, consisted of Carlos shoving Alcozar and Bibby into Alcozar's Mercedes, then frantically trying to start the engine. "Man, I told you to buy a Volvo," he hollered.

"Carlos," Alcozar yelled, "give it up!"

"No way! They'll kill me now!" he shouted as the engine sprang to life. "Did you see those machine guns? I'm getting the hell out of here. We can sort it all out later."

"He's getting away!" Oakley called to General Garrison as the jeeps pulled up and the Mercedes sped away. "The kidnapper! Carlos the Puma! He's got Alcozar and Bibby! And he's getting away!" Hey, you have to know which way the wind is blowing, Oakley ruefully said to himself.

"Blow the tires off that car!" Garrison ordered, and several dutiful subordinate responded by sending long streams of bullets after the swerving Mercedes.

"Goddammit, I'm getting out," Alcozar shouted, starting to climb through the sun roof. He didn't get very far. Bullets tore through the crown of his fedora. "Díos mio, Carlos, they're shooting at me," he exclaimed. "Yoo hoo, don't shoot, it's me— friendly President Alcozar," he tried telling them, waving what was now not even a very effective sun visor. Then there was another volley of bullets. "Jesus Maria, Carlos," Alcozar shouted, "step on it!"

Two long bursts of fire had been directed at the departing Mercedes, two long bursts that got off before Crane was standing in the back of the jeep, holding General Garrison in a headlock. "No more shooting, shithead," he spat. "'Cause if the wrong person in that car dies, you'll be licking latrines clean for the rest of your career. Now, let's just chase 'em down and surround 'em."

And so a somewhat sulky Garrison gave the orders, and off they all went in a madcap chase through the streets of San Rico City, the Mercedes roaring into town, the jeeps tearing right after, van den Hurdle's cameras sending it all back to New York; New York, in turn, advising the local affiliates to delay their broadcasts of "Wheel of Fortune" and "Jeopardy" in order to bring to that sizable post-dinnertime, pre-prime time audience this exclusive live video of this incredibly dramatic and tension-packed real-life chase, one complete with as many squealing tires, clouds of dust, panicked passersby, and as vast a swath of destruction cut by quarry and pack, as ever showed up on any season's worth of "The Dukes of Hazzard" episodes combined. Plus there was the real threat of death.

"Amazing video," Ross said, tightly clutching Lucinda's hand. "Oh, ouch. Poor chicken."

Bibby was enjoying the chase terrifically, and he thought there was an excellent chance that his team was going to get away. The Mercedes was gaining ground against the jeeps, and having a hometown driver was a tremendous advantage. Bibby sincerely hoped they'd get away, and that wasn't only his competitive instincts talking. He didn't feel good saying it, but frankly he felt safer in the company of his friends the kidnappers than with the soldiers of his own government, the ones who, in hot pursuit, had so recently been firing live ammo not two feet above his head. Still, you couldn't always get what you wanted. Carlos swerved suddenly to avoid hitting a Coca-Cola delivery truck, and the Mercedes slithered off the road, banging into the front of a—well, Bibby wasn't sure what this El Trocadero place was, but from the outside it looked an awful lot like a topless lounge.

Alcozar and Bibby climbed out of the tilted sedan and ran to help Carlos, who had banged his head on the steering wheel and had blood trickling from his forehead. Into the bar they fled, scattering the patrons and inspiring the dancing girls to scream and cover their breasts. Straight to the back the men ran, and up onto the stage. "Come on," Carlos said, grabbing Bibby's arm, "out the side!"

"No, Carlos," Alcozar said, grabbing Bibby's other arm, "let them capture you! We'll let you escape next week!"

"Bullshit!" Carlos yelled, tugging on Brent's arm. "They'll kill me now! I'm taking Bibby out as a hostage!"

"No! Let's do it my way!"

"No! We always do it your way! Doing it your way is how we got here!"

"Come on!"

"With me!"

Just as Brent was concluding that he could not be pulled apart any more widely without splitting, a Marine Corps jeep with a battering ram affixed to the front broke down the front door, taking much of the front wall as well. Suddenly the room was filled with Americans: Marines with their weapons pointed at the three men on the stage, van den Hurdle with her cameraman and sound man, crouched front and center pointing their lens and microphone stageward as well. All Brent could hear was an ominous concert of noise: the clatter of ammo cases being attached and safeties being switched off, the nearly inaudible whir of the film, the snapping, spinning sound of the motordrive of a 35-millimeter camera running in fifth gear. There were lights in his face, and guns and cameras in his face, and he didn't know quite what to do—how to explain what he was doing there, why these men were clutching his arms. At the rear of the room he saw his father climbing over the rubble of the front wall, his face streaked with dirt, the palmetto branch pretty wind whipped, followed closely by Crane, who was clutching a suitcase. Then there was silence. His father stood and looked at him. Crane stood and looked at him. It seemed that everyone was waiting for him to speak.

Something grand, he remembered Carlos saying.

He cleared his throat. "I'd like to thank you all for coming today," he began, haltingly at first. "I have a brief announcement, after which I'll take your questions.

"I'd like to begin by explaining that a rather large fraud has been perpetrated against the people of the United States," he said, and at that he heard Carlos and Alcozar groan in dismay, and he felt their hold on his arms slacken. But he grabbed them more tightly and went on. "For that, you have our apologies. But I'm quite sure that if we hadn't maintained this charade of a kidnapping, I doubt that we'd have achieved all that we have. Which is a lot."

He caught Crane watching him with a strange, bemused expression on his face. He took it to be an encouraging sign. "Last week," he went on, "President Ross, out of his deep concern for conditions in this region, sent me on a secret mission to this poor, violence-plagued nation to attempt to negotiate a peace treaty to end the fighting here. We're sorry about concocting this kidnapping tale, but talks had to be undertaken in the strictest secrecy. I'm pleased to say that our mission has been successful, due in large measure to the statesmanlike vision of these two men." With that he pulled Carlos and Alcozar close to him, and pushed their hands together. "I can't tell you how much they have taught me during these last few days."

Carlos and Julio smiled humbly at the cameras, while shooting him nervous glances out of the corners of their eyes. "Here is what we have agreed," Brent announced. "The Hondanista guerrillas will end their insurgency as of this moment, and a cease-fire is now in effect. President Alcozar has declared a general amnesty for all who were involved in the fighting. He has further agreed to name Carlos Amaro to his cabinet. Señor Amaro will hold the newly created post of Minister for Tourism and Commerce."

In what had been the back corner of the lounge, Crane began punching numbers into a cellular phone. "Patch me through to the president immediately," he whispered.

Play the game, Brent told himself, just keep playing the game. "I am further authorized to announce that contingent upon the signing of a treaty—a mere formality at this stage—Bibby Resorts International will develop a resort complex in San Rico de Humidor," he announced. He saw Horace's jaw drop. "I know my father will personally want to reveal the details of the project after consulting with his people, but what's being considered is something on the order of an eight hundred-room hotel, with a pool, golf course, tennis courts, sauna, whirlpool, weight room, game room, massage room, sailboating, windsurfing, and casino gambling. Oh yes, and for the children, bus rides into the Santa Euphoria Mountains for tubing on the Rio del Bundegas. There will also be Guerrillaland, a theme park that will consist of a replica of an actual Hondanista camp. There they can sample such traditional rebel favorites as stewed iguana, learn bomb-making and other crafts, and otherwise be educated and entertained. The resort will of course create jobs and stimulate the local economy.

"Oh yes, one more thing. As part of this agreement, the United States will terminate all military assistance to this country, but will now offer an economic development grant—the first installment of which I believe has been brought by Mr. Crane personally—that will pay for the construction of new highways and a new airport, to make the resort economically feasible. In fact, demolition of the old airport has begun. That blast you heard as you arrived was merely the ceremonial first explosion, which my friends graciously allowed me to set off."

"Have you been watching this?" Crane asked Ross over the phone. "If you want a share of the credit, you'd better grab it now."

"I guess it's the thing to do," Ross observed.

"Mr. Vice President!" Crane shouted as he slowly began picking his way to the stage. "A call from the White House!" he shouted, and passed Brent the phone.

"Congratulations, Mr. Vice President!" Brent heard Ross say. "What a remarkable job you've done! You've succeeded far beyond our wildest dreams!"

"Thank you, sir. I'm glad you had enough confidence to send me," he said, offering a quick wink into Celestine van den Hurdle's camera.

"I've got somebody here who I know would like to say hello," Ross said. "And Brent—sincerely—congratulations."

"Brent!" Lucinda said, her voice a mixture of warmth and excitement. "I've missed you so! When are you coming home?"

"Just as soon as I can, darling, just as soon as I can. I love you. I can't wait to see you."

"Oh," she sighed, escalating her flattery to a new dimension. "My *hero.*"

Brent handed the phone back to Crane, who grinned at him and slapped him on the back. "You really showed me something there—sir," he said. Then another face came into view—Horace Bibby's. Brent had never seen him smiling more widely.

"Brent," Horace said proudly. "My son! *Mister* Vice President!" His father spread out his arms and cloaked his son in an embrace. It was as happy a moment as Brent Bibby had ever enjoyed in his entire life.

Back at the White House, Ross and Lucinda rose from their chairs in front of the television set. They stretched, shuffled, expressed admiration, amazement, relief, and tried bravely but inevitably unsuccessfully to avoid what had to be said. It was Ross who caved in first.

"Well, I guess you'll be going now," he said.

She nodded glumly. "Yes, I think that would be wise."

"Lucinda," he began, "I . . . ah . . ."

"It's all right, Mr. President. I think I know what you're thinking. And I think you're right. We probably shouldn't see one another for a while."

He sighed, as much with relief as sadness. "I'm sorry it had to end like this," he said. "I think we had some very special, very marvelous plans in the works."

"I know," she said, smiling and gently putting a finger to his lips, "but let's not dwell on that. We had some very happy moments, and I will always, always remember them."

"As will I," he said, "as will I. Meanwhile—" he slipped his arms round her waist, cocked his head, and grinned "—what do you say? Once more for the road?"

"Well," she said, putting her hands on his chest, laughing a cool, throaty laugh, "*Why not?*"

FREEPORT MEMORIAL LIBRARY

3 1486

FREEPORT MEMORIAL LIBRARY

FIC   Malanowski, Jamie.
Malanows
ki   Mr. Stupid goes to
              Washington.

DATE

DISCARDED BY
FREEPORT
MEMORIAL LIBRARY

FREEPORT MEMORIAL LIBRARY
FREEPORT, NEW YORK
PHONE: FR 9-3274

BAKER & TAYLOR BOOKS